D0119807

# LOOKING DOWN

Richard Beaumont hoped to see the rarest species of crow on the white cliffs of Dover. Instead, he saw a young woman jump to her death, so that is the scene he painted.

Back in the London flat where he lives with his wife Lilian, Richard obsessively paints the scene of the woman's broken body. Two floors below lives lawyer Sarah Fortune; uneasy because she and Richard were lovers many years ago, and because her brother, a cat-burglar who 'liberates' beautiful paintings from their owners, has his eye on Richard and Lilian's flat. Even so she finds herself inexorably involved in a mystery that extends back to the coast: to the strange Edwin, keeper of the coastline; and to Medical Examiner John Armstrong, a man who becomes part of Richard's life and—intimately—Sarah's.

The dead girl, too becomes a part of their lives. For in the penthouse at the top of the block of flats, lies the clue that binds these people together: the clue to the mystery of the missing girl—and to a trade that is both breathtakingly lucrative and chillingly cruel.

# LOOKING DOWN

## Frances Fyfield

**WINDSOR**
**PARAGON**

First published 2004
by
Little Brown
This Large Print edition published 2004
by
BBC Audiobooks Ltd by arrangement with
Time Warner Books Ltd

ISBN 1 4056 1022 0   (Windsor Hardcover)
ISBN 1 4056 2017 X   (Paragon Softcover)

British Library Cataloguing in Publication Data available

Printed and bound in Great Britain by
Antony Rowe Ltd., Chippenham, Wiltshire

For Jennifer Davies, nee Curtis,
with love and admiration.

# ACKNOWLEDGEMENTS

To Dr Richard Meyer, artist first, and zoologist second, who introduced me to the chough and the raven, and informed me throughout, as well as commenting on Tiepolo and the subject of *zing*.

He is entirely the wrong shape for the Richard in this book, whom he is not supposed to resemble. And, as he would be the first to point out, all ornithological/art-appreciation/spelling/ semantic/ factual mistakes are entirely mine.

With many thanks.

# PROLOGUE

It was, in its own way, a beautiful day. By which he meant that the light was fine, and the sky provided a background, and if all else failed he could sketch the sky, because it was always there. Light permitting, he could put an angel on clouds if there was nothing else to do, although, perversely, he always preferred to look down rather than up, into and over the ground rather than turning his eyes towards the sky. There was a notice to his left: *Do not walk*, which had drawn him to the edge and from there to here, via the slippery path he had seen used by the botanists, to be where he sat now on a white clay shelf, twenty feet below the overhang, looking to his left at a bunch of pinks and wishing he was remotely interested in wild flowers. He had been panting *running* towards the edge, panting before he reached it, but now he could not remember why. The anxiety was gone, the view breathtaking and the loneliness blissful.

There was a strong breeze, typical of the days he had spent up here sitting to the side of the scant supply of scrubby bushes in the hope of other people who might sit long enough to be watched and sketched, only they never sat, they plodded past without pausing or seeing, hell bent on reaching the other end of the trek, too tired to stop. For some it was the beginning, for others the end. The breeze caught his hair, making the still unfamiliar length of it whip across his face. He was short, broad yeoman stock, not easily mistaken for the artist he hoped he was and more easily defined

1

as the amateur and out-of-date birdwatcher he also was. He did not care what he looked like: it was enough that he did not look like a man who ever wore a suit. Two days' growth of beard itched, pleasantly. *The middle of nowhere*, he wrote on his pad, ignoring the fact that his ears were suddenly filled with the dull, resonant drone of a hovercraft coming from across the English channel into port. On a rare, still afternoon the sound of it filled the whole horizon, and on a gusty day like this the hummm of it was interrupted, with the effect of a broken signal, always surprising when it resumed.

He was not a brave man, or immune from vertigo. It amazed him to have found this vantage point where he could see how the chalk cliff sprawled outwards and downwards, spilling its guts below in a tumbling process full of interesting forms, until the last of the tilting land reached the angry sea which gnawed and growled. He could discern crevices, and landings with more of those pink flowers. He was wondering if the hovercraft sound was actually musical or irritating, because when it became silent he found himself holding his breath. The cliff path had been almost deserted today: he had definitely not wanted people for sketching or anything else, thought he would look out for the birds. It was the birds that were the second love of his life. He was no longer a boy, but when he had been he had lived near cliffs like these, two hundred miles away, and adored the birds. He had once played with a chough. He was sentimental about birds, revered them for their grace and dignity.

And then the girl appeared, sailing over his head. Not a girl, but the body of a girl so near to death

2

she may already have greeted it, appearing from over the top of his skull without a sound at the moment he expelled his breath as the hovercraft noise came back and he was looking skywards and thinking, I am doing nothing here, except looking for the birds, probably at the wrong time of day; I shall go in a minute. A body with arms outflung, spreadeagled against the sky, reminding him of a parachutist before the cord was pulled.

She seemed to have been projected from a point above the cliff, hung there, level with his face, for a fraction of a second, and then moved into an awkward, flapping freefall, as if her body could not decide which direction to take, whether to pirouette, somersault, glide, or go back from where she came. Then It (it was already It) bent into a V and fell, quietly and certainly, an item of clothing detaching itself and floating alongside like a ghostly companion. She landed suddenly, before she had even begun, far below, on the penultimate outcrop before the cliff splintered into the rounded rubble which met the churning white of the sea. Lay there, peacefully, so near and yet so far, as if it was exactly as she had intended, turned in her sleep, to avoid the sudden, impertinent shaft of sunshine.

He could see the outline of her, graceful and abandoned, arm outflung, face turned to the view, the breasts and hips which had weighted the fall, one leg bent beneath her, the other straight, the shape of her defined by triangles of black knickers and bra, and the gauzy material of whatever else she had worn drifting down to the water, which captured it, wrestled it and began to bear it away. There was the mass of hair he had noticed as she flew past, paler than the pale, sharp rock which had

3

broken her back. Somewhere near her extended hand there was a flush of pink and green from those same flowers. He sat transfixed by the sight, terrified and enchanted, the sketchbook gripped tightly in one hand, the pen clutched in the other fist, shook his head slowly, then adjusted his hands and began to draw. Live models were hard to find.

*Woman at one with nature/Woman returns to nature*. Everything had a title. She was exquisitely beautiful. He was fascinated by the lines of black created by the bra, drew slowly, wished he could sketch with the insouciant speed he imagined of a master, but his own way was always painfully slow and deliberate. As he drew, the light began to change, altering the contours of her body, so that he etched the shadows she made, was tempted to start again. It seemed to take a long time, and after a while, as he grew colder and colder, as he wrestled with the form of her with increasing frustration, he saw that she had company. Black company, curious, lascivious, hungry, winged ghosts, swooping in to land and hover around her. He grabbed his forgotten binoculars, looked closely and blinked back tears. He had so wanted to see these creatures, but not like this. He wanted to love them. They strutted and hopped, flapped, busily, *Quork, quork*. They moved in.

*Oh, you bastards.*

His fingers were numb. He watched and watched.

Then one rose, level to his height, glossy and black, with bright red beak and red feet. He held his breath. A chough: oh Lord, how he had longed to see the chough. He had dreamt of seeing the chough; it made him hold his breath again. Quick, quick, before the light went, and before the sounds

4

intervened. It was becoming dark. His hands were paralysed; he pushed his finger and thumb to draw what he had seen. The hovercraft noise came back in a rough symphony with other sounds; a rope skimmed by his face over the cliff, engine noises intervened, and still he could not tear his gaze away to look towards evening clouds, went on staring, down, watching her, imprinting her and the solid ghosts on his memory, watching his pen on the paper, until the shadows were way too long and she was surrounded. Someone appeared beside him. Bigger, stronger, younger.

'What the fuck do you think you're doing?'

He had no response. Tried to stand and found it difficult. Suddenly afraid of scrambling back up that dangerous path, wondering why he had ever come down, what he had been hiding from. The other man, peculiarly dressed, his belt loaded with accoutrements, and big, raw fists, was unaccountably furious.

'I said what do you think you're doing, you sick bastard?'

He found himself hauled up by the neck, his sturdy body easily moved, and because his limbs had become numb, he was grateful. At the top of the steep path, near the notice which said *Do not walk* and nothing else, after a muttered conversation, he was punched in the head, and found he did not mind. He had seen and drawn the beautiful body and watched the chough fly. A man could only be so lucky in a single day.

There was a crowd at the roadside where the cliff path started and ended; some of them seemed to be baying for his blood.

Blood. He would close his eyes to whatever else

he had seen.

All was as wicked as it was beautiful.

Somebody hit him again. He felt sure he had somehow deserved it, and all he could do was sigh.

In a moment he would have to remember the other man he was, when he did not have a sketchbook in his pocket and visions in his mind.

'What's your name?'

He paused. 'Richard. I think. What have I done?'

# CHAPTER ONE

## *Trespassers will be prosecuted*

Lilian Beaumont looked down into the street below, wondered if she would be better off outside than in, saw the rain and decided not. The apartment was huge, with big, slightly dark rooms, panelled doors, moulded ceilings, a kitchen rarely used for cooking, two bathrooms, a porter downstairs with a uniform, and carpet like cushioned velvet. Silence indoors was assured. It was home sweet home, and yet a million miles from home, especially when it came to the silence. She had a childish dislike of silence. It made her want to stamp her feet.

The kitchen, like everything else, was a showpiece. In here her husband, or 'they' as legend had it, kept an impressive collection of antique glass, arranged against a mirrored wall and carefully backlit. He loved glass: he had once treasured it. Lilian was standing on an elegant library ladder, reaching for the top shelf, from which she plucked an ancient and fragile decanter of pink crystal and let it fall from between her varnished fingernails to the marbled floor beneath. It imploded, neatly, with a satisfying crunch. Good. The mirrored glass caught her reflection, slender, agile, tense. Still well groomed, even when slightly drunk at home, alone. No leisure track suits and slobbing out for Lilian, although her hair required attention. She had always been like that, even as a little girl, and she was scarcely more than a girl, now. She swept up neatly. There were now several holes in the display.

Then she replaced the library steps (old mahogany, beautifully carved and valuable in their own right) where they belonged as an adornment to the room at the front, where they stood against another shelved wall full of colour-coordinated books, rising to an impossibly high ceiling. The remainder of the walls were furnished with large, decorative paintings of flowers, older than the furniture, a *pleasing* room, capable of holding fifty for drinks and still leave gaps in between. Definitely the best room in the block, apart from the lighter penthouse, perhaps. The traffic hummed beyond the magnificent curtains. The boiler, hidden somewhere, made soothing, efficient noises to ward off spring. The place was as luxurious as a colossal suite in a luxury liner and made her feel as if she was on a ship going nowhere.

*Bastard. Absolute bastard. What about little me? I'm too young to be left alone.*

She could have telephoned her sister. Emailed even. Also her brother, her other sister and all those she had left behind when she married *him*. And been despised for it, even while they approved. She certainly wasn't going to phone them now and say, how are you all, I'm feeling like shit in W1, not after she had virtually disowned them for something better. Or inform them how the rich, much older man, so upper class, so blessedly respectable, who looked so good and provided a passport to another land, had turned out so badly. There was no way she was going to say anything of the kind. Although they might quite like it if she told them that the man they had liked, despite themselves and because of his relentless consideration of their preferences when it came to the wedding, had just been arrested in some part of the coast nobody acknowledged, probably for pissing downwind, somewhere a hundred miles from here, and that aside, only came home when he needed a wash, the way he did these days. Had enough money to sink this ship and several others, and what did he do?

Went weird. Decided at sixty years of age that what he wanted was the great open spaces, dirt, cold and feathered friends. Had a thing about birds, ha ha, which was not a preoccupation that could be cured by getting a parrot for the kitchen.

Nothing she did could keep him from his *hobbies*. Or nothing she did could keep him as sweet as he was. And she did not know what to *do*.

The wide corridor bisecting the apartment was precisely fifty feet long. She should know: she had paced it enough times. It was dark and artfully lit to show more of the decorative paintings, themed with pale green walls. She walked on angrily, trying to make a noise by stamping, but the carpet merely yielded to her feet. *She* had arranged all this, the pictures, the plants in silver containers, the gleaming candlesticks, the clever lighting effects, the impression of comfort and harmony, and he had been delighted with the result. Then she turned left, where the corridor led to the two commodious bedrooms, both ensuite, and then the third room, which was study, library, the darkest room of all, where she kicked open the door decorated only with the sign *Do not disturb* in blood-red lettering. She itched to scrub that door.

9

Here the harmony ended. The sweet proportions of the room were not enough to neutralise the contents, namely, an easel with the latest, virulent daub mounted on it, and a set of once beautiful freestanding bookshelves lugged nearby to be used for paints and palettes, brushes and whatnots, the surface of it scarred and stained beyond recognition. The polished wooden floor, similar, the walls half covered with sketches, roughly pinned, ruining the plaster, and everywhere at eye level abandoned paintings on wood or canvas to augment those stacked messily to the left. The light was an eerie daylight, brighter and less forgiving than any other. On top of the bookshelves was a stuffed bird with bright, glass eyes turned malevolently on her. Richard's mascot. Defying its gaze, she opened the window a crack wider to get rid of the pervasive smell of turpentine. Stood by it, looking into the dark well of the building with its ugly array of drainpipes.

You *pig*. What have you done?

What had he done? Plucked her, Lilian, from the back room of the Interior Design Company where she was earmarked for failure to create an apartment reflecting a man of exquisite taste, loved it, loved her, married her. Showed her off to his world and his forgiving children for three glorious years until she was as confident as to the manor born, and then gradually and insidiously created this hell-hole of a room, retreated into it with his new passions and all but locked the door. All that hard work for nothing. Never marry a man on the brink of retirement. They change. Never give a man time to think, more like, in case he discovers what he is. There is no such thing as a free lunch.

10

Why that cliché should come back to her as she stood on the threshold of his ghastly lair, she could not imagine. Only that when she met him she was running out of options, and thought otherwise. Her mind went back to the phone call earlier in the evening.

'We have a genullman 'ere, says his name is Rick Beaumont. And he lives at Cramner Mansions, W1, on this number. I'm Sergeant Rice, by the way. Am I speaking to Mrs B, by any chance?'

'This is Mrs Beaumont, yes. And it's *Richard* . . .'

'Yeah, right. Just trying to establish ID, that's all. And what is it your husband does, Mrs Beaumont?'

That had thrown her. What did he do? What had he done? Something in the City.

'Finance. Formerly. Now retired.'

'Was you expecting him home this evening, Mrs B?'

'I never know what to expect,' she said, sharply.

'Oh, it's like that, is it? Just wondered if you knew what he was doing today.'

'Depending on where he was,' she said, controlling the bitterness of her voice, 'he was probably watching birds. All varieties.'

The chuckle was insulting.

'That figures, Mrs B. Shall we let him drive home, or do you want us to keep him? Wasn't sure if he was quite well, at first, but he's had a long chat with Dr Armstrong and he seems fine, now.'

'What's he done?'

The friendly voice hardened. 'Fiddled while Rome burned, Mrs B. That's all.'

Yes, he would come home. Unrepentant, probably whistling as he went into his awful back room to turn his sketches into frightful, garish

11

paint. Smiling his sweet and vacant smile, telling her, unfailingly, how lovely she looked, asking what she had done, and then scarcely pausing to hear her speak. That was Richard. Lilian closed the door on the room full of daylight and went towards bed, hoping she would be soundly asleep before he arrived home.

The bed was sumptuous; it always did something for her spirit. Only, when she woke three hours later to hear the door to their room click open and then click shut as someone tiptoed away, only the bleary eye of valium-induced slumber made her fail to notice that it was not Richard Beaumont, but somebody else. Sleep saved her the trouble of screaming.

'Sarah … shhhhh. Don't scream, please, dear, don't …'

'Hmmmm … mmmm, geroff. Get your hand away from my mouth … Oh for Christ's sake … what the hell do you think you're doing?'

'Sarah, darling, wake up properly and come and have a drink. I've just made the most terrible mistake.'

'What time is it?'

'Early, by any civilised standards. Why does it matter what time it is?'

'Because I was asleep. Why can't you ring the doorbell like anyone else?'

She was pulling the duvet over her head and the sound of her voice was mumbled beneath it. A thatch of dark auburn hair protruded onto a white pillow and the sight of it enchanted him. He pulled at it and sat back on the edge of the bed, listening to her grumble, watched her finally unearth herself and sit up in her broiderie anglaise nightie which made her look quite angelic. Such a sweet little girl she must have been, snub nose and everything. She was supposed to have had a talent for turning cartwheels. She looked cross, ran a hand through her hair which obeyed the gesture and stood on end in a halo round her face. The other hand fumbled on her bedside table for her spectacles and stuck them, lopsidedly, on her nose. Apart from the treacherous hair, she could have been his primary-school teacher, Miss Prymm, who also wore clothes buttoned up to the neck, even in sleep. In fine cotton, too, and always white. Conspicuously clean. Hers had been the first house he had ever burgled.

'What mistake?' she said.

'I went to the wrong flat.'

She groaned, flopped back against the pillows, the hair still in a rage but the half-glasses over which she peered still in place.

'You look like a virgin madonna, by Titian. But it's hardly cool, is it, Sarah, to keep your specs on a piece of string?'

'Oh, shuttup. It's a silver string. And this was an early night. Did you lose your key?'

'You know I lost it last week. I just needed the practice and—'

'Don't even tell me. I don't want to know. Go away. *Far* away.'

'And I've just seen the head of a Sleeping Beauty.'

Sarah gave up. The time of day was never relevant anyway, not in this room which looked into the well of the building and was dusky dark twenty-four hours a day, seven days a week, winter

13

and summer, ideal for sleep. The view from it was only that of white brick, thick black drainpipes, metallic service impedimenta and other windows looking on to the four-sided centre leading down to a solitary basement quadrangle out of sight from the second floor. At a set time of day, the Romany wife of the Indian, lighter-skinned porter harangued him so loudly that echoes sounded and birds flew from distant chimneys. Then doors were slammed and they went inside. The quarrels might have been the result of living in a dark basement so near the rubbish room, from which Fritz, the porter, emerged sleek and helpful each morning in a clean pressed uniform. He had a vested interest in remaining deaf.

Without a hint, Steven left the room, out of respect for Sarah's modesty and out of respect for her house, and shed his bodysuit and belt inside the bathroom before she noticed how filthy he was, as if she hadn't noticed already. Black Lycra, like cyclists wore. Pliable, slipper-like shoes, a size too small, for grip. He removed the tape and washed the chalk from his hands, created a tidy, movable pile of his belongings. Day was night and night was day: there was a uniform for each. Back in her living room, swathed in towels, he sat down in an armchair and stroked the arm, disliking the embossed texture and wishing his domestic habits were better. It was irksome to find himself stroking things and noticing the quality of the fabric. People did not like it.

Sarah was in the silk dressing gown he had bought her last birthday, a scarlet clash with her auburn hair if it had not been interlined with soft black on the inverted collar; quite a find, that. She carried a tarnished silver tray with two glasses and a bottle of red wine, settled herself into the sofa opposite, waited for him to pour, curling her feet beneath her, spectacles still on nose. The dressing gown was more claret than sheer red. He decided she was right, and that wearing black and white really did suit her best, provided it was enlivened with a dash of the right kind of red.

Day was night and night was day.

'So,' she said, peering at him over the half glasses held on the silver chain, giving her the look of a judge, 'you came in by the alternative route to give yourself practice and got into the wrong flat. Tell me it isn't true. Tell me I'm dreaming.'

He poured the wine, handed hers over, took his own and put it back, willing his hand not to shake, because it did, slightly. He always felt slightly nauseous after a climb.

'You didn't answer the door so I went round the back. Need practice, as I said, but got so enthused I was up a floor further before I knew. These drainpipes are a cinch. Any old drunk could do it, what with all the other stuff and the windowsills. And then, led by an open window, I was in a room, full of painting clutter, wondered where I was, knew I was in the wrong place, so I thought I'd have a quick look round before I left. Until I looked in this room next door and saw this woman asleep, well, I only saw the back of her head, really, so I thought I'd better go out the way I came in. Same drainpipe. It's good of you to sleep at the back with the window open. I didn't wake her, promise.'

'You absolute sod,' she said, in a voice of icy calm which went with her luminous eyes, lamplights

15

from the depths of her chair. 'You complete bastard.'

He hung his head, and looked at his feet. He had long, prehensile toes, which he wriggled, restoring circulation to his cramped feet.

'Explain to me,' she said, 'why you abuse the woman who knows you best? Why you torment me, envy me, disturb me, ruin my sleep and make my life unbearable? What have I ever done to you to deserve this? For the first time in my life I'm feeling safe, and then you come along and wreck it. You come and go as you want, whenever you're sick of your own miserable places, though you won't make the effort to find anything better. All talk, you. You litter the place with your stuff and let me wash it. I don't mind that. But this is my *home*. I live *here* and what do you do? You crawl up the sodding drainpipe and burgle my sodding neighbours' flat, and then mine. Are we expecting the police to share this wine? Did anyone see? I wouldn't mind so much if there was any *need*.'

'I said, I needed the practice.'

'You were late and drunk. You still are. You could have fallen.'

'I don't fall,' he said with dignity.

'You will. Then you'll be a corpse or a casualty, and although I might be mightily relieved, how would I explain it? I'm quite sure there's something forbidding *that* in the lease. You wouldn't shit on your own doorstep, but you've done it on mine, you selfish swine. I live here.'

'Well, so do I sometimes. When I'm allowed to share your precious luck. And you always leave windows open.'

'Oh, come on, Steven. Am I hearing that hint of

16

self-pity again? You haven't done so badly for luck. You turn your back on it. You spit on it.'

'*I* haven't been given a flat, free gratis and for nothing.'

Definitely a jibe. She sighed in exasperation.

'It wasn't for *nothing*. It was a gesture of affection, thoroughly reciprocated over several years.'

'A very big thank you, from a man you slept with. He dies and leaves it to you. You're a tart, Sarah.'

She swiped the hair upwards from her face again, took off the glasses. He was sure she could turn that into a devastating gesture.

'Yes, surely, my dear, I'm practically an old lady and I've slept with a lot of men—what's wrong with that? Although it's a bit dramatic to give my particular form of therapy such a common and over-romantic description. Nothing wrong with it anyway. Don't be so pompous. I'm ten years older than you. Too old for criticism and too shocked to be angry. I want a *peaceful* life.'

'And still quite lovely in your dotage.'

'It's in the eye of the beholder, dear. And you, on the other hand, are a thief. I don't approve of that either.'

'Now who's being pompous? What moral high ground do you live on? Don't you dare criticise *me*.'

She shoved the glasses back. She should have been a teacher with that low, smooth, persuasive voice.

'I've been gainfully and respectably employed for most of my life, Steven, and I've always given *value*, given *something*, in whatever I have done, while all you do is *take*. I don't go where I'm not wanted. I

17

specialise in improving lives, in my own particular way, while you wreck them. There's that malice in you I don't understand.'

He moved to sit on the floor, with his skinny spine resting against her legs. She put down her wine and began to knead the back of his powerful shoulders. It was strange how, even in the midst of a quarrel, they were content to touch one another, and how even with the undertones of envy and occasional dislike the protective affection endured. In appearance he was a most insignificant-looking man, small, pale and sandy-haired, looking as if he never saw daylight, which was more or less true. Nobody ever remembered Steven, except to recall a harmless and reliable face, and perhaps his handshake, from which they recoiled. Sarah had often wondered if his insignificance was cultivated in response to the handshake, or purely a natural result of his overall appearance and the sort of muddy colouring which melded with brick walls.

'I'm sorry you think of it like that. What if I told you I thought that my kind of occasional, discriminating thieving is an honourable profession, or at least no more dishonourable than working for a bank, where we play around with people's money and take more than our fair share.'

'Bollocks.'

'What if I were to say that thieves like myself have the greatest respect for property? Far greater respect than those who own it. I *liberate* beautiful paintings from owners who have no idea of their value or importance, and then I pass them on, in due course, to a truly appreciative owner at a bargain price. For small, humbler items, the owner might be myself. Haven't got the right home for anything else.

And I don't believe I have wrecked a single life for longer than five minutes. That's the advantage in stealing from the vulgarly rich, because they don't know what they've got and it's all eminently replaceable. I just want stuff to be appreciated.'

'Rubbish. You don't know how your victims feel, any more than you know where what you sell on finally goes, unless you keep it. The rich have feelings as well as needs. They aren't any different and the world needs them. Would you steal from a rich philanthropist who was nurturing his possessions to give to charity? Of course you would. Perhaps I now count as rich, therefore a non-person in your eyes. Existing to be stolen from. Knocked down to size.'

'No,' he said, 'absolutely not. I love you, even when you criticise and trivialise my passions and talents, even when you share some of them. At least it's work. I'm not taking the easy way out. No simple, clean-hands, risk-free computer crime. I have to plan and scheme and climb and keep fit, accept challenges, and take risks, quite apart from mastering new technology. It's tough, and it's highly discriminating.'

'There's nothing new about being a cat burglar. It's ridiculously old fashioned.'

'My point exactly. Old-fashioned, sweated labour.'

'To add to a perfectly respectable salary.'

'Well, so was yours.'

'I suppose so.'

He looked at the large oil painting on her wall, fondly.

'You've got a good eye, Sarah. I love that painting. It still gives me *zing*. I love it. You react to paintings like I do.'

19

'Yes, but I don't steal them. You live by *zing*. You've never fallen in love. You get *zing* from paintings alone, you sad man. I get it from people.'

They sat, companionably. Night was day and day night in this household. The fury had died, but she felt heavy-hearted. There was a chronic difference between them which she could not cure, namely his loneliness, and her lack of it: his shunning of friends, her welcoming of them; her knowledge of loving and being loved, his denial that anyone ever did, would or could. He demanded a degree of total acceptance, even when he put himself beyond it, and he always had something to blame. If only he could secure the love of a good woman, it might mitigate the cancer within him, although the love of a bad woman might be better. If only he didn't put them on a pedestal and carry a torch for some hopeless, glamorous image, like a Gloria Swanson or a Marilyn Monroe, like the posters he once had on his walls. He shuffled up to sit beside her and put his hand on her knee.

'That colour does suit you.' He thumped his hand up and down, unromantically. 'Do you think I still blame *this*?'

It was a pale hand that reminded her of the colour of white fish, disfigured by scars.

'I know you do,' she said sadly. 'You have to have something to blame, give you reasons, excuses. You've got into the habit of it. Which flat was it exactly that you got into?'

He yawned. 'The one above this dark den of yours. Almost at the top. I just got carried away. I think that would make it number fourteen.'

*Oh no.* She counted on her fingers. There were two flats of different sizes on each floor, she was

12, so that sounded about right. She remembered the rain which had lulled her into that distant sleep, thought of the polished brick in the central well of the building, shuddered and then remembered that if it still rained as hard as it had there would be no trace of his progress, no footprints on walls. If it hadn't been raining, he might not have done it. Not enough of a challenge, but also a disguise: rain masked sound, delayed curiosity, washed away traces, but what a half-drunk idiot. The mere sound of breathing would become an echo in that well. Sarah tried to harden her heart because he was such a fool, but it was always the destructive, lonely fools who attracted her most.

'Get much business these days, do you?' he asked.

'Just a few regulars. I get referrals from a massage therapist, and old friends. The more liberated and nicer of my men might refer me to the next. There's a civilised network. Enough. Don't ruin my luck. If you should think of going back up there another night to burgle the Beaumonts—nice people by the way, I know them both—I shall phone the police, deny knowledge of you, and then, should you ever get bail, kill you, slowly. First by poison, then by neglect, and in your long sojourn in prison, never once bring you a food parcel. Nor will you ever darken my door again. Do you hear?'

'She has curtains of silk damask, the woman in that flat,' he murmured. 'She probably has everything. Some paintings in a room . . . And did I tell you I've seen the most wonderful drawing I've ever seen in my life? Seen it three times now, same zing. Oh, sis, I forgot . . . what happened about

21

Minty? The girl upstairs with the Chinese?'

'You don't care,' she said.

And then he was asleep.

Sarah put a cushion behind his head and walked down her long corridor for a blanket. Her brother could sleep on a board. She tucked the blanket round him and put the alarm clock next to his ear, considered the romanticised photographs of their parents on their wedding day that stood on a side table and wondered if a woman were ever more vulnerable to a man than to the one who was her baby brother. Or whether it was something in their genes that made them both essentially antisocial and ever so slightly corrupted by anyone else's standards of behaviour. She could spell violence, had suffered it and could never inflict it. He was different: there were no limits to what he might do.

She was anarchic, maybe, antisocial but sociable, and although she understood malice she had none of it in her. She had a definite if highly adaptable code of conduct and a fluid sense of moral values, while Steven had none, and no redeeming loyalties. There was always the horrible feeling with Steven that he was capable of the extreme, the knife in the back, the long, slow torture, pleasure in pain, laughter at suffering, potential perversions at odds with the rest. And to cap it all he was a naive romantic, terrified of women and hopelessly obsessed with art, which he used as a replacement for sex. She could not cure him.

It was 3 a.m. She made a decision and left him a note. 'Steven, you must leave. Find the home you talk about, leave the spare clothes, but don't come back for a month. I've told you I just don't want involvement in other people's pain, not even yours.'

22

At 8 a.m. Richard Beaumont let himself into No.
14, put his luggage into the room marked *Do not
disturb*, showered and shaved and got into bed
beside his wife. He held her face between his
hands, told her he had missed her and slowly,
luxuriously, made love to her, and she to him. Then
held her, as she held him, rolling softly together in
the sumptuous bed, talking of nothing. She dared
not and neither did he; this was enough, this was
heaven. And then he ruined it later, after mid-
morning coffee so good it stunned his palette, and
he remembered. Left her in the kitchen and went
to the daylight room and shut the door.

And she thought, Is that it? Was that really me
who was loved like that? Or is it what he thought I
needed, a good screw after three days' absence and
then I won't ask? Am I that easy? Does he think I
need nothing else? What am I good at? What am I
good for?

Then she remembered the click of the bedroom
door at around 2.25 in the morning. Ah, that
explained it. She had not been his priority at all. He
had come in, gone straight to his lair and remained
there until he imagined she might be receptive. She
was only another thoroughbred cow, mollified by
an activity associated with breeding. The ghastly
painting came first. And he had not noticed the
holes in the antique glass display, any more than he
had really noticed her.

He painted; she wept.

The body had been with her, but she was not sure
about the mind.

# CHAPTER TWO

## *Keep pets under control at all times*

Dr John Armstrong had found the reference that morning in his library at home by delving into the section that dealt with birds. He rarely looked at it now.

> The bird is about the weight of the jack-daw, but of a taller and longer shape. The bill is long, curved, sharp at the tip and of a bright red; the iris is composed of two circles, the outer red, the inner light blue; the eyelids are red, the plumage is altogether of a purplish violet black; legs brilliant red like the bill; claws large, hooked and red. It builds on high cliffs . . . in a wild state, it feeds chiefly on insects and berries. It is easily tamed, becomes extremely docile, and is very fond of being caressed by those to whom it shows attachment, but its shrill notes and mischievous qualities render it sometimes a troublesome inmate.

A two-century-old description of a bird, known as the chough, now almost extinct. There were other descriptions. *Acrobatic and overfriendly. Soothsayer. Omen of Hope.* He thought of all of these descriptions now. The wind blew and the sun shone. Good April weather, suitable for stilted conversation on the cliffs.

'Nobody knows who she is.'

'I think you mean "was".'

24

' "Was" then. But we still have a body, which is.'
He shivered.
'Getting cold, are you?'
'Not yet. You?'
'Never feel it, myself.'
Or much else, John thought, pulling the hood of his jacket closer round his ears, watching out of the corner of his eye the way his companion managed to keep alight the thin cigarette that looked damp against his stained fingers. It smouldered constantly, even in drizzle. The morning was bright with spring in evidence, but still that breeze, worrying away at his neck and making him regret the scarf he had left behind. Edwin, the expert, always wore a cotton scarf, winter or summer, which he used for innumerable other tasks than insulation; a multi-purpose item. Edwin could walk through a gale naked apart from the scarf, and always seemed to appear out of the blue, or the grey, to reimmerse himself within the landscape and take on its colours. He had good-quality, expensive outdoor clothes, however unwashed they were, which was surprising in a man with no visible means of support other than the dole he collected every fortnight. He did occasional odd jobs on the edge of town, fixing roof tiles and painting garden gates, always out of doors, to augment that income. Otherwise he was a moving fixture on the cliffs. A loner who watched out for the birds and shunned the people. He had always seemed ageless to John, although he was only a few years younger. They could have been children together, although on different sides of the tracks. His had been the luckier life.
'Nothing on her, I daresay,' Edwin volunteered.

'You saw. A stitch or two. Nothing to identify her, nothing at all.' He could not say why this bleak fact made him so sad, but it did. It afflicted him.

'Not one of the botanists, then.'

'C'mon, Edwin, you'd have told us first. You're everywhere on these cliffs. And they say not, and there's none of them missing. They've finished work now, and gone. I showed them the photo to remind them to be careful, and in case they might know her, although only a mother might recognise her from that. She was a bit of a mess. Head fell apart when they lifted her. It's the impersonality of her that's so haunting. I hate that. She's no one. What about her mother or her sister? Not to know . . . It's so rare to have no trace. No jewellery, no handbag, no shoes.'

The idea was choking him. Edwin was unmoved. Nothing moved Edwin but birds.

'And the fall killed her instantly?'

'It would, wouldn't it?'

'And no one else saw?'

'Unless you did.'

Edwin shook his head in that infinitesimal gesture which typified the economy he imposed on his movements as long as he was resting, sprawled on the chalk without ever moving or changing his position, his body supported easily on one elbow, while John sat, crossing and recrossing his ankles, hugging his knees, shifting his weight every minute to avoid the cold of the ground. It marked the difference between the visitor to the cliffs and the virtual inhabitant. John knew that Edwin lived in a tiny bedsit above a shop in the centre of town, but the cliffs were his real home. Old rumour had it that Edwin had escaped to the cliffs as soon as he

26

could walk, with good reason.

'Nope. I can't be everywhere. I was in Cable Bay, and a couple of the botanists saw me. Came over yonder after the others arrived. Lent a hand. You'd already got your bloke by then and there was quite a crowd. Don't ask me did she fall or was she pushed, I don't know any more than you do. Looks like someone stripped her first.'

'Took away her personality first. That's what bothers me. Someone trying to make her untraceable, forgettable. That's what so cruel. It's robbery of more than a life. I think she was thrown, Edwin. On account of what that bloke said. He said she seemed to have been projected out, "hovered", he said. She was only a little lightweight.'

Edwin grunted. 'And you'd heed what a bloke says when he's said he's seen the chough in flight? Here? More fool you. There hasn't been a chough here in over a hundred years. Some excuse, he has.'

'Some people live in hope, Edwin. Some have only read bird books from the last century. And miracles happen.'

'There's more of them plain ignorant liars. Why did they let him go?'

'Can't keep him, Edwin. No connection. I pinched a photocopy of his sketch. Rather good, I thought. Are you sure you'd never seen a girl like her before?'

'Did I say so? I might have done . . .'

John waited patiently until Edwin got to his feet, carefully, and stretched his arms above his head. 'I'll have to go over it in my mind,' he said. 'Things come slowly, you know. I'd seen *him*, of course. Trying to sketch from behind bushes, dirty bastard. He was always hiding. She might have been hiding,

27

too. I'll have to think about that.'

Edwin did not like to linger in this populated part of the cliff path, preferring the lonelier, more dangerous stretches of his favourite Cable Bay and beyond. Not such an invaluable source of information, then. His fierce shyness would have made him reluctant anyway. His whole manner of standing indicated that enough was enough and he was ready to move. Beginning at dawn he walked the coast path end to end every day, fourteen miles each way, varying where he paused and watched, sat and stared, acting as its very own policeman, although it was not the people he wished to protect. John wondered if every half-tamed, wild place like this had a similar, self-appointed custodian, an invaluable source of information—if he chose, and the choice was always his. He economised with his knowledge and information in the same way he did with his movements. Dr John Armstrong could not quite like Edwin, although he did admire anyone who could maintain such passions, and admiration was enough to sustain a close acquaintance of mutual respect, laced with a tinge of pity. He had treated Edwin for a broken leg years before, admired his bravery, and there existed between them a bond of ill-defined loyalty. It was slightly diminished by John's association with the police, which Edwin suspected, and John reckoned it was only because Edwin knew that he, too, dwelt on the cliffs as often as time allowed, walked the path at least once every month of the year and had some real knowledge of the flora, fauna and history, that he consented to talk to him at all. Plus the knowledge that John wasn't a policeman, merely a semi-retired, part-time medical examiner, hardly empowered to investigate, or arrest, a fly. The sort of harmless doctor at home in a police station, who made tea for the prisoner and held his hand rather than asking the questions, useful in welfare for his mildness of manner and a necessary presence when the health of a detainee was in doubt. They moved a few paces together, Edwin well aware that John did not like to walk all that close to the cliff edge and contemptuous of him for being so careful. He could not have known that John had liked the artist, the man Edwin referred to as 'bloke' or 'dirty bastard', because in their brief conversation he had admitted he felt the same fear. In a short time they had managed to discuss their vulnerability to vertigo and a number of other, surprising things. Yes, John had liked the artist a lot, thought about him and the girl ever since, to his own irritation. They were preoccupations that took him by surprise. He had become, to his own mind, a dry, dispassionate, emotionless man.

Edwin was suspicious of all authority in the manner of a loner who was always waiting for someone to take away what little he had. John remembered details of his background from those long-ago but plentiful medical notes. There had been a history of non-accidental broken bones. He had been taken into care as a teenager, abandoned by violent and abusive parents but only after the abuse occurred, and become apparently incapable of forming relationships, redeemed by his love of the birds and the cliffs. Maybe Edwin was not so impoverished after all, John thought. At least he had his passions and principles and lived with a kind of dignity, which was more than John felt he had achieved himself.

For all his irritating and cunning qualities, there was a harsh gentility about Edwin. He always extended his hand on parting and then wrung John's so hard that he felt his bones would break and the tender skin erupt in grazes. It was the only occasion of which John was aware that Edwin ever touched anyone, and it was as if he did not know how it was done. He had never felt skin like that, a series of knobs and calluses, like rusted iron roughly fashioned into the semblance of a hand and always cool on the warmest day. Edwin extended the hand, then withdrew it, remembering something.

'John, if you ever hear of any walkers wanting to go down to Cable Bay, tell them no, won't you? We've . . . we've rare visitors there. Oh, don't tell them that. Tell them it's dangerous.'

Rare visitors must mean blasted birds. Again.

'Surely no one but a fool would go there. The earth's still moving, isn't it, and the path's been diverted. What kind of birds?'

'The sort that nest early. Forget I said that.'

Bugger the birds, John thought, and waited.

'It's the pathways do it, you know. Always them.'

'Pardon?'

'Pathways. The thoroughfares that take people from one place to the next and open up the land. But what they also do is close it down. They give vantage points, all that, but what happens is that the land either side of them is never used, becomes less and less used, so that it becomes the wilderness, never used at all. Rank, unkempt, overgrown, full of hiding places, the new hidden zones that the pathway was supposed to open up,

30

while really it closed them down. Created a new habitat. Don't go off the path, John. Like she did. Like dogs do.'

Such a long speech. John was amused by it, and did not want to let the man go.

'Do all pathways go somewhere?'

'Yes and no. They make a matrix, like a cardiovascular system, going round and round on themselves but with connecting paths leading off. There's probably an interconnecting point on this path that leads straight to that man' s door, that so-called artist, all the way to London town. I could walk it in three days, I reckon. Without going on a path.'

Then he smiled and extended the hand again. The sun came out.

'You're a good enough man, John. Don't try so hard.'

John felt flattered that so many of the usually few words had been placed at his disposal, even if he did not understand them. No one knew more about Edwin's background than he did, and yet it was so little. He was a man with a certain insight, and that was all John needed to know. Perhaps it was all anyone wanted to know about Edwin.

'That artist,' he ventured, knowing that delaying Edwin could risk alienation, 'I don't know why, but I thought he was a good man, too. He was honest.'

Edwin was moving, from slow to fast, hands on hips to push himself forward and get his stride, talking back over his shoulder, not caring if he was heard and not raising his voice.

'I said you weren't a bad man. Doesn't mean you aren't also daft. No *good* man would sit still and sketch a body when she might still have been alive.'

31

'There was never a chance of that, Edwin.'

All they really had in common was surely their grizzled, grey heads. And one of those uncertain affections which arrives too late and has nowhere to go, making them pleased to see one another, and making Edwin ration information so that John would come back, as if he would not, anyway. Wily old sod. Patrolling the cliffs like the Lone Ranger, the only man he knew who actually loved seagulls and other winged scavengers. John shivered inside his jacket. Once he had loved and watched the birds. Now he preferred plants and flowers and it seemed a long time since he had felt anything at all. Until now.

He walked back the way he had come, back towards the car park, deserted apart from his Vauxhall, climbed into it. Pathways led out in the form of a road into the port; from there led others to every point of England and Europe. Trunk roads, ancient and modern routes connecting metropolis to metropolis. A route to his house. A route for refugees.

The photocopied sketch crackled inside his top pocket, where it had been for three days. Another example of unuseful, neurotic behaviour, since none of it was any of his business. His help had been solicited way beyond the limited scope of his usual role in this investigation simply because he knew the cliffs, was on nodding acquaintance with the botany team who had just finished work, and the beleaguered police service had got into the habit of taking help where they could get it, especially when they did not have to pay. Help us out here, John, and he did, willingly. But something had persisted, which might not have lingered in his

32

pragmatic mind if he had not had a daughter, had not felt, as probably every father would have felt on being told there was the body of a girl at the foot of the cliff, Oh God, is she mine? Followed by that sickening relief when it proved to be somebody else's. Why he should have thought the body was Maria when she, as far as he knew, was still at the other end of a pathway in London, tormenting him with silence, he did not know. Except that it would have been a fitting revenge on him, and Maria was good at that, although maybe not to the point of self-destruction. He would pay for his perceived neglect of her some other way, perhaps, until she was older and might begin to understand how it had been. Maria would always think that her father had let her mother die, rather than been powerless to prevent it.

Nor was the existence of a body without an identity sufficiently intriguing to warrant this attention, not in a town that was a conduit for immigrants, stateless persons of all ages, arriving in the dead of night, the uncontrollable trickle of those who did not want asylum or registration, separate from the constant flood who did. Immigrants like the container-load of Chinese youths who had paid to be smuggled direct to London, not trusting the sanctuary of officialdom, only to perish en route. Some of those who wanted entry and a hiding place simply died, were found in corners of this town and the country beyond, and were left unclaimed. But the sallow-skinned girl of the cliff with her dyed hair was well nourished, with a different profile.

His mind went back to the phrase 'well nourished', so commonly used in a post-mortem

33

report and frequently misunderstood. A young woman might find it an insulting description, meaning fat, but all it meant was adequate flesh on the bones, i.e. not actually starving. For the unidentified immigrants where he certified death, malnutrition and disease were obvious causes. What a cheerful occupation he had for three days a week: certifying death; identifying drug overdose, mental instability, drunkenness and bruises in the still living. It could explain a bleak outlook, but not entirely. It suited the needs of a man gone a little sour: he could be kind to them because he would probably never see them again and he preferred his contacts to be temporary. Like Edwin had always done, he supposed, afraid of the obligations of permanence.

But something had changed. He had been called to the scene to assess the mental and physical health of the artist, and his interest should have stopped there. The artist was a novelty because of his age, sobriety and ability to articulate, while most of the doctor's customers in the cells were young, speechless and brutal, spat rather than spoke and challenged his humanity as much as his ability to withstand halitosis at close quarters. He had only been called to the artist because of their doubts about his state of mind, and the bruise on his left cheek, which looked suspiciously like the familiar effect of a fist. About which the man made no complaint, although he winced when he was touched. A strong, able-bodied, older, but not old, man, definitely well nourished and obviously capable of shrugging off far worse.

Semi-retirement did not suit John. He had too much time on his hands, and enough money not to be hungry, leaving a vacuum for haunting. A dead wife and a daughter who blamed him for it, a mild case of depression. And if guilty curiosity about a single death out of the hundreds he had seen was a substitute for the intellectual challenges that no longer inspired him, he had better get back to his garden. Or live somewhere else, with less rough trade and fewer memories—if only he could bring himself to leave the cliffs, which would haunt him more than anything else, because he knew the temptation to jump. Go right to the edge and launch himself into delirious nothingness. Fall prey to that belief that a man could fly, like Icarus, away from his own loneliness, into a less sterile sky.

It was men who jumped. In his experience, female suicides preferred prettier, more controlled deaths, not in the presence of strangers. This one was surely pushed, and no one mourned her. He did not know why he took it upon himself to do so, or why it made him so angry.

Poor, well-nourished little stranger.

*     *     *

It was an area of strangers, and this was not, generally speaking, the sort of central London block where the occupiers of the different-sized flats associated with one another. Not much banging on the door opposite to borrow a cup of sugar, on account of the fact that half of the apartments were empty at any given time and only used by those in transit from the second house, or another country; there was the lack of a common language and circumstances. Some apartments were rented; of the other residents, half were rich, half not so rich, with at least one example of the league of distressed gentlefolk struggling to pay the service charges. No one knew who they all were, or on what terms they lived there—company let, money, inheritance, foreign money—except Fritz the porter and Sarah Fortune, who got much of her incomplete information from him and the rest from behaving as if this was not a remote, upmarket City abode where the very stairs looked discreet, but a small-town terraced street where the residents were related by common misfortune and it was perfectly OK to say hello and examine one another's washing on a line. Even in the absence of any children, which might have united them all a little, the disingenuous approach of friendly curiosity tended to work, but then Sarah had always found that breaches of commonly held codes of manners usually did. If the inhabitant of an apartment was rich and not riddled by suspicion, they welcomed neighbours and wanted to show off; if they were not, they wanted to moan. Midweek the place was virtually empty during the day. Few had been obdurate in the face of her knocking on the door, except for the Chinese, who rented the biggest flat, the penthouse flat, which straddled the whole of the top floor and was enviable for being light and bright. The Chinese paid the most, had the most power, trailed in and out with mobile phones, remained aloof and impervious to smiles, repelled any advances, and nobody knew what they did. Still, Sarah had reckoned, you couldn't win them all. Undeterred, and with the pretence of delivering a flyer, she had knocked on the Beaumonts' door and invited herself in the year before, just at a point when Lilian was dying to show someone what she was doing with the place, and in what colour. Sarah's charm was entirely natural and based on the fact that she liked everybody and assumed they were likeable themselves until they proved otherwise. Her manners were honed by long use; she was unfazed by rejection and more or less proof against shock or surprise, which was useful on that first occasion when she saw Richard come out of the kitchen with a glass in his hand.

Dear me, an old lover. An older, stouter Richard than the one she had comforted years before in the wake of his first wife's death; a jollier version of that grief-stricken, sex-starved man she had known for six months five years ago and parted from as amicably as she always did from any of them. She watched him standing in that long corridor, blinking, until she shook his hand firmly and said how pleased she was to meet him. Had they bought the place or was it rented, what a pretty lamp! A dim memory of the only lessons she had learned from her mother, viz: whenever you go into anyone else's house always say, What a lovely room! And mean it. And also forget that you had met the man of the house in an art gallery, staring at a picture with tears streaming down his face, and simply taken him home. Richard was no fool, returned the handshake, said yes, we're very pleased, let me get you a glass of wine, and she knew it might not be very exciting wine, but the glass would be marvellous. In that other flat he'd had there had been that terrific collection of glass, which had, she remembered irrelevantly, left her cold.

And then the wife ... shimmeringly lovely and adoring of him and delighted to have company.

Sarah was sincerely pleased for him. And he knew her well enough to understand that discretion about sexual relations in between marriages, or during marriages for that matter, was entirely assured. She had once told him she admired men who had the sense to find a sympathetic, semi-professional bed mate when recently bereaved or divorced because it certainly beat the shit out of the sort of baggage-laden, life-wrecking relationship which usually followed grief and foundered, messily, on the rocks of too much need and too many comparisons. I'm your interlude, she said; you'll move on when you're ready, and he had.

As for any suggestion that the presence of this overfriendly single woman on the floor below would cause a smidgeon of envy or suspicion in Mrs Beaumont's heart, nothing could have been further from reality. When Sarah had knocked on their door eighteen months ago, Lilian had been utterly confident in her own outstanding beauty, the patent love of her man and her own unlined immortality. To Lilian, stunning at twenty-eight, Miss Fortune, aged almost forty, with specs round her neck, could have been any old bag with awful red hair and the potential to be an agony aunt. Naturally, when visiting neighbours, Miss Fortune looked untidy and clean in her own favourite colours, but that was all. She had never been a sexy dresser, anyway, except when it came to her passion for belts. Big tan leather belts, cloth belts with tassels, tapestry belts cinching in the plainest black dress. Her aphrodisiacs were perfume and sympathy.

But, of course, her immediate acceptance chez

Beaumont created a bit of a problem in the long run. Because of the sympathy, and the availability, lovely Lilian Beaumont had taken to knocking on *her* door in the last months, and was sitting here, at the moment, on Sarah's shabby sofa, sniffing and tearful, and entirely unaware that her husband occasionally did the same, only without the tears. It was an awkward position, being confidante to both man and wife, but there it was, and Sarah had in a manner of speaking asked for it, so she would do the best she could and try to honour both, without betraying either. Provided they never coincided, which they never had (Richard either on his way out or on his way in, prefaced with a phone call; Lilian mid-morning and bored), and provided they didn't want counselling, only an ear, any old ear, and they were each entirely self-absorbed, it was not that much of an imposition, but she had the feeling everything was going to get worse.

Lilian sat where Sarah's brother had last sat. At the back of Sarah's mind was relief that Steven had gone so quietly, plus the nagging feeling that a lack of protest spelt trouble. Though why she should worry also nagged her. Steven had a perfectly adequate flat of his own; it was his fault that he dithered about getting anything more permanent. He had gone while she slept, leaving a note that stated, 'Darling sis, I completely understand.' That was ominous. Four days' silence might not have been ominous since he frequently disappeared for weeks, or, as he had once, for years, but it was.

'I don't understand,' Lilian was saying for the seventh time. 'I just don't . . .'

'Understand?' Sarah added.

'Exactly. *You* understand, don't you?'

39

'Well, no. Everyone's different, you see.'

'Exactly. But some are more different to others. And he's gone *very* different.'

This was hardly profound chat, and going nowhere, so Sarah kept quiet and waited.

'He's gone so different, it's as if he swanned off to another planet and came back an alien. I mean completely different. But I've stayed the same.'

Sarah thought that might be part of the problem. She was thinking this morning that Lilian was not exactly the sharpest knife in the box, although so easy on the eye one tended to forget that. It was obviously easier to listen to a musical voice speaking inanities through a perfect mouth than to listen to nonsense from someone less blessed. Lilian's voice had the knack of making everything sound intelligent, a very appealing voice, with a deep, rich chuckle when she was amused, so infectious Sarah found herself longing to hear it.

'What drew you to him in the first place?'

'He made me laugh.'

Ah yes, a man would turn somersaults to hear her laugh, invent jokes, make a fool of himself, simply to hear that sound. It had a powerful beauty, even to another woman, and if you added to that the potency of sex, no man would stand a chance with Lilian.

'And doesn't he still?'

'Oh yes,' Lilian said sadly. 'When he tries. When he notices me at all.'

She was not stupid, Sarah had long since decided. She had an intuitive intelligence which showed in her taste and her ability to create order out of chaos, but analysis was not her strong point. She could not hold to a subject for long, and did not

40

want to delve deep. Above all, she could not take blame, or have it pointed out to her that anything could ever be her fault, or even the result of something she had done. She wanted emotional massage, not suggestions. Concentration, even on her own preoccupations, was difficult. Sarah put it down to stress. And God, she was a beautiful girl. Not only classically lovely, but a male icon of beauty, with blonde hair, big boobs, tiny waist and endless legs. She had every excuse for imagining that was all she had to be, for dwelling in the cocoon of it and postponing for ever any consideration of what else she was. Beauty like that was a gift, with a curse attached.

'You never got those new curtains, did you, Sarah?'

'No, couldn't be bothered, and too expensive.'

That was where they had started, Lilian coming to her flat to offer advice, which fell on stony ground although Sarah had solicited it. This flat was half the size of the Beaumonts', and even if Lilian's ideas would have worked on a smaller scale, Sarah had never had any intention of doing more than listen to them. It was a neutral subject, was all. There were blinds at the window which worked well enough, minimal, comfortable second-hand furniture and the over-large painting which Lilian studiously ignored. As far as she was concerned, art in the form of paintings should go with the walls. The painting they faced was of a huge chestnut cow, predominating over a field of bluebells, entirely wrong for an urban reception room. Not the subject matter, necessarily, but certainly the scale. The animal practically lumbered into the room, salivating. Lilian imagined

41

she could hear it say *Moo,* glanced at it and glanced away.

'I don't know if it started with his getting interested in birds, or painting. First he went off birdwatching, made him feel a boy again, he said. Bless. Then he started to paint. Oh, he says he's always done it, you know, drawn things, but it's not as if he was trained or anything. Now he wants to do it all the time. He brings back sketches, goes into that hell-hole of a room and paints for ever. And he doesn't like towns any more. Always wants to be out and away. Doesn't always tell me where he's going. I have to ask Fritz; he tells Fritz, for God's sake. Doesn't notice anything. Especially me.'

Sarah knew all this and did not really want it to go on, not because she was unsympathetic, but because she also knew what the end result would be if Lilian told her too much. If she got to the point of tears, or specifying the last point Richard had made love to her and how, she would go away and feel ashamed of revealing so much, and the next time she saw Sarah she would smile brightly and scurry off, as if nothing intimate had ever been said. And that would go on for a week or three until she had forgotten her weakness and could convince herself it had not happened. Sarah would have dolloped out a few indiscretions of her own to even out the balance and make Lilian less ashamed of the gut-spilling but she could not think of anything that might fit that particular bill. It was better to let Lilian feel slightly sorry for her and tell herself she called on Sarah because it was Sarah who was lonely. A widow, poor thing, disregarding the fact that Sarah had been

42

widowed for fifteen years and was hardly mourning. Lilian's yawning gap of insecurity filled Sarah with pity, even if that was accompanied by irritation. Lilian at twenty-eight had no armour against disappointment, whereas Sarah with the benefit of years had long since developed the carapace from behind which she struck back, and she had no sense of shame whatsoever. Shame was alien stuff, worse than jealousy. It was useless to mention neighbourhood problems to Lilian, even by way of distraction. No good talking about Minty, the abused servant of the wretched Chinese in the penthouse, because she would not want to know. Unlike her husband, who was curious, courteous, liked gossip and always wanted to know. He knew about Minty. He had helped, and Sarah would have taken a bet that Lilian did not know about that, either.

'Well, it probably isn't so odd that he's taken up painting, you know. Not if he always wanted to and never had the time. It could have been so much worse. It could have been golf, or cricket, or gambling, or dangerous sports.'

'It is a dangerous sport,' Lilian interrupted. 'It gets him arrested on clifftops and stuck in mud. It makes him do things he isn't fit for and wear clothes he hasn't got, and it turns his mind inwards. And it's not so much the doing of it, but what he does with it, and the way he does it. Obsessionally.'

'Maybe he was always like that? Men don't actually change, do they?'

'I suppose he was. He was certainly obsessional about me. I think he was obsessional about his kids. He must have been obsessional about money in the days when he made it. Says he never felt safe, that's why he went on. He must have been obsessional about collecting things, too.'

'So maybe that's what happens. When he feels safe, it's like a gap in his life, and he doesn't quite know what to do with himself so he finds another obsession. You've made him feel too safe. It's a theory, anyway.'

'Hmmm.' Lilian was trying to work out if this was a criticism or a compliment. 'Maybe he does feel too safe. Safe life, ultra-safe block of flats. Nothing to alarm him. Plenty of lovely things to make him feel safe. All that comfort.'

'Perhaps it would help if you could share the interest?' Sarah hurried on. 'But I don't suppose you're much interested in art, are you? I suppose I mean paintings.'

'I like them when they look nice, yes.'

She was keeping her eyes away from the lumbering cow, obviously thinking hard. A delicious little frown line appeared above her huge green eyes. Appropriate that they should be green, Sarah thought. One day, my girl, if you aren't careful and find better things to do, you'll see that frown line in the mirror and have a fit. Lilian was suddenly cheerful and ready to go.

'Made him too safe, have I? Now that's an idea. I never thought of that. Must dash. Thanks ever so for the coffee.'

Which she had scarcely drunk. Sarah showed her to the door, only mildly curious about what she was going to do with the rest of her day, guessing she would do whatever kept wives did. Lilian's own total lack of curiosity about Sarah's daily life was faintly insulting but probably just as well.

'Do you ever sit for Richard?' she asked as she

opened the door into the empty and spacious corridor beyond.

'Sit?'

'I mean sit as in pose.'

'No. He knows I'd hate it. And I'd certainly hate the result.' She smiled, a smile as endearing as her chuckle. 'Does that sound selfish? I'm not that bad. Actually, he's never asked. And what worries me most about this painting lark is that it might break his heart.'

And that, Sarah thought, was genuine. Painting could certainly do that. Lilian went up in her estimation.

\*      \*      \*

Back inside the Beaumont apartment Lilian strode down the long corridor to fetch her coat and, sidetracking, flung open the door of the daylight room. Felt too safe, did he? She knew that the *Do not disturb* sign applied only when he was there, and she could never resist going in when he wasn't, simply to open the window on to the well and disturb the smell of spirits which seeped under the door. She'd show him *safe*.

He had been working hard the last three days, making a painting from the sketches he never showed her. She looked at the wet oil painting on the easel.

Screamed. Choked back the scream with a hand over her mouth and ran from the room, slamming the door behind her.

# CHAPTER THREE

## *Make no unnecessary noise*

Ten minutes later, unaware of the screams in this soundproof place, Sarah Fortune ran down the stairs to the foyer. She usually ran, not always because she was late, but for the hell of it, and she had the knack of running in heels, learned in childhood ballet class before she grew too tall and then, perversely, stopped growing at all and flung herself into any sport that did not require membership of a team. She ran whenever there was room. The last flight down was wide with a tarnished brass banister, and Fritz the porter could hear her footsteps over the carpet only as she reached the last three steps and appeared in the mirror opposite his desk. He straightened his tie and waited, pleasurably, his girth expanding in sheer relief that it was not anyone else. Her lightweight black coat flowed behind her revealing a broad, rusty red-coloured leather belt round her waist, knee-length skirt, sheer stockings and heeled pumps that matched the belt. The auburn hair glowed. It always amazed him how she could look so much like a ball of fire at one moment, and at another so desperately ordinary. She skidded to a halt, not even breathless.

'Hello, Fritz, what's the news today?'

His news was not always complete, but covered the essentials. Fritz did not sit at his over-grand porters' desk every hour of the day, but only when he felt like it or it was clearly expected of him, such as when there was a party, or in the mornings when the comings and goings were busiest, and he was intermittently observant. He could be summoned out of his basement by the front-door buzzer or the bell on the desk, the notes of which he answered with a sloth proportionate to the impatience of the summoner. Repeated hitting of the desk bell made him slower. He presided over the communal parts of the premises, which were cleaned, resentfully, by his wife, although it always fell to him to polish the mirror on the far side of the foyer, facing his desk, through which he watched Sarah Fortune emerge from the stairs, and everyone else who came via the lift, to his left. The mirror was useful, enabling him to watch the two internal exits simultaneously as well as the door. The lift was small and frequently non-functional. There was a carpet with geometric designs on the floor of the foyer, in keeping with the angular, deco moulding of the mirror. The disadvantage of the mirror was the fact that it repeated the irritating carpet design, which when he was bored or forced to wait drove him mad. He preferred puffing round the building with the post, pretending to be older than he was, and resented heavy deliveries.

'Haven't even been having time to read the paper, Sarah. Mr Beaumont collected his post, didn't even tell me where he was going like he usually does, so he must have been gone first thing, and since then I've been up and down, up and down to that sodding penthouse with a whole load of boxes, just got delivered . . .'

'Any messages for me?'

'Nope, although I did see your brother through the door. Thought he was coming in, but he went

47

away.'

'Oh. So tell me about the penthouse. You were going to get inside . . . has she really gone?'

'Yes,' he said, lowering his voice to a whisper. '*Yes!* She's gone, really gone. She went last week. I'm really sure of it now. Chinese woman wanted me to put stuff in the kitchen, so I got a good look. She's in a foul mood. No one's been cleaning in there, I tell you, and she wouldn't have let me in if Minty had been there to cart stuff, would she?'

'Well well, I suppose it's a relief. She got away at last. I only hope it wasn't going from the devil to the deep blue sea. And I wish she could have let you know where she'd gone.'

It was the wrong thing to say. It made him defensive.

'She couldn't, could she? Couldn't or wouldn't, same thing. But I think it was the money helped, Sarah. She let me save it up, see? And at least she wasn't starving. And I have to admit, although she was frightened of *them*, she still got plenty of gumption.'

He was still whispering. He always whispered when he talked about Minty. Minty was an abbreviation of a name he could not pronounce. Minty, who was the resident servant of the fluctuating Chinese tribe in the penthouse, although perhaps more aptly described as a slave, who never left the building. She had long been a source of anguish to Fritz and a shared concern with Sarah, who found the idea of anyone who was afraid to go out, because they had nowhere else to go, perfectly abominable.

'Remember when she used to come down here and just sit over there and look at the door?' He

48

pointed to the sofa and chairs arranged in front of the mirror, and then at the large plate-glass doors that led outside.

'Yes. Always fiddling with her necklace.'

'She was so thin.'

'Until you fed her . . .'

'It was my wife feeding her,' he continued to whisper, uncomfortably. 'She likes to cook. Said it was as easy to make stuff for three as two, and, anyway, Minty wouldn't talk to anyone else. Both Romany, see?'

'So, between you, you got the gist.'

'Only that she was illegal. Like my wife, 'fore we got married. Never found out how Minty landed up with the Chinese either, didn't come in on their passport, like some of them other slaves do. She was too frightened to say. She was stuck, anyway. They worked her to death, starved her and gave her no money. She'd no papers, anyway. Couldn't call the police, could I? Should I? She definitely didn't want that, and if the Chinese found out I'd caused that trouble, I'm out on my ears, like as not. I'd have risked it, mind, but she said no, no, no, and cried, and the wife wouldn't have had it.'

It was an often repeated conversation. Fritz always had to go back to the beginning, forgetting how Sarah had agreed with him, agreed still, that the choices about what to do about Minty were limited, so the plan they had formed was for the Fritzes to do the feeding, while Sarah and Richard Beaumont stuck money behind the desk regularly, followed by the gift of a prepaid mobile phone. Minty's stash, they called it. Minty could not take it upstairs into the penthouse; they would find it, she said, but she knew it was there. Minty stole out of

49

the top floor and left the penthouse door on the latch when they were out. She never went further than the foyer. No one ever spoke to the Chinese. A man, a woman and a selection of males seemed to live in the penthouse. They came in and out, always carrying something. Traders, Fritz said. None of them ever smiled.

'And then the stash was gone,' Fritz said mournfully. 'A week since. I don't like to think that was all she wanted.'

'Doesn't matter if it was, Fritz. It was choice she needed. You gave it her.'

'Did we? Me and the missus, and you and Mr Beaumont? Anyway, she isn't dead up there, she's gone. I'll miss her.'

'You can't help people more than they allow, Fritz. Never could, except for kids, and she wasn't one of those. What if you had reported her existence? She'd either be out on the street or sent home. If she had one.'

Fritz was often close to tears. He blew his nose and laughed nervously, staring at her through dark brown, permanently sad eyes. She always had the desire to make Fritz laugh and never managed it. He was the sort of man who gave her the desire to pull silly faces if only to raise a smile. He sighed, hesitated before he spoke.

'Home? Ah, I didn't say to you about that. That's the bit I never told you. See, the wife could never get her to believe what will be happening if she turn herself in. The worst and the best. She'd get sent *home*. And believe me, *that* was what she wanted most of all. To go home.'

Sarah buttoned her coat.

'I wish I'd known that. On the other hand,

50

perhaps I don't. We can only say good luck to her. She escaped on her own terms.'

She turned for the glass doors. They looked thick enough to withstand bullets, with large brass handles and lock. All the residents had keys, unless they were slaves. Then she turned on her heel.

'I suppose we'd better be on the lookout, Fritz.'

'Why's that?'

'For whoever the people in the penthouse get in next. There's plenty where Minty came from.'

Her own shoes silent on the pavement, she tried to remember the girl as she walked down the street, wondering when exactly she had gone, trying to picture the face she had seen behind the penthouse door putting her finger to her lips, shaking her head and shutting the door again. Doing the same thing on the second attempt. Three months before, the girl's elbows had been bigger than her knees, until the Fritzes fed her, and Sarah remembered the bare knees. Amazing what food did. Sarah's impression was that she was not as frail as Fritz thought; simply an ageless girl who had seen too much and was marked by desperation, but not helpless yet. A girl with a hardened heart, capable, therefore, of anything. Frightened but fierce, sinking but not drowning. Minty hung washing on the balcony; Sarah could just see from her window where the line had broken and hung down into the well, as if she had given up. Why hadn't she and Richard and Fritz joined forces and marched up to the door and demanded to know who she was? Because Minty chose not, and the Chinese paid the bulk of Fritz's wage, and that was not the way things were done. And because, to be honest, Sarah had not wanted to get more than

51

minimally involved. Her life was in control and that was how she wanted it to be. She did not want it riddled with pity.

Sarah turned back and looked at the frontage of the block. It was a confused design, Edwardian deco, originally experimental with lots of linear twiddles and red brick, built for luxury, descending to penury and shabbiness in the nineteen sixties, narrowly missing demolition fifteen years later and then restored to dignity at the beginning of the last decade. Now odd, but posh. A safe place for the conduct of private lives. The man who had left Sarah her flat in an astonishing piece of generosity may have thought it was still worth the pittance he had paid for it twenty years earlier. She was immensely grateful and yet it increased her debt to the world. She had not deserved it; no one did. And it was a flawed place, so solid and secure that it could contain with apparent impunity a slave, kept by people who could have afforded to hire an army to clear their stable.

None of these reflections were part of any firm moral agenda on the subject of asylum seekers, their criminal gangs, Albanian women with drugged babies wailing and begging in the Underground in a way which deadened pity. It made sense to Sarah that the deprived of the world should descend upon the relatively rich—who wouldn't? She didn't know what she thought about it as a global problem, but then she tried to avoid having opinions. She didn't envy politicians who had to have opinions without the luxury of being able to change their minds, and all she could really care about was individuals, one by one. There was no time to trouble the mind about what she could not change. Sarah Fortune was hell-bent on a quiet life, avoiding other people's pain.

Outside the block, beyond the glass doors and double-glazed windows, the noise of the traffic hit like a body blow, a reminder of how quiet it was within. Noise could never penetrate to the well of the building, and from where she stood the place looked impregnable, as safe as it felt inside. No one ever remembered that dark, interior well, or the tiny back door to the service area where Fritz kept rubbish. It looked as if it led to nowhere, unless you were Steven, always looking for a route.

Sarah could not run down this street because it was too crowded. There were shops: the florist's, the jeweller's, the wine shop, with tourists and people of all kinds en route to mysterious, urgent destinations. It would have been nice to run, because the thought of Steven made her not only want to run away from him, but also towards him. She was not going to feel guilty about him. She was not going to feel guilty about being a lady who lunched with men and went to bed with them in the afternoons if it suited them both. It wasn't as if it happened every day. She was not going to feel guilty about anything, except perhaps leisure. Leisure did not come naturally. Steven might be right: she had too much of it, although there never seemed enough. Perhaps she should get a job, but she had had a job for fifteen years, and the thought of ever doing anything responsible ever again filled her with horror. This was safer: a place to live, a coterie of generous male friends, the judge, the dentist, the stockbroker, the art dealer, all conveniently central. A little involvement in the lives of others, but not a lot. No missions to the rescue; she had done enough of that. And now she had the safety of the flat, she could give the money away. Money did not matter as long as you had a roof. Who needed more than a roof and a painting or two? She paused to check her appearance in the window of Penhaligon's. Delicious scents in there, and yes, they certainly counted as the necessities of life, but she also had plenty of those. What more did she need?

A small, expressive face grinned back. Notable for the peculiar colouring, sallow skin, auburn hair and brown eyes with crow's feet blurred in the glass. Nobody liked the onset of lines, but like the state of the wider world there was nothing you could do about it. Lilian Beaumont might imagine Sarah Fortune was beyond the pale when it came to luring the opposite sex at the advanced age of almost forty, but then Lilian Beaumont knew Jack Shit about men. Securing a man to keep on a permanent and official basis grew more difficult with the crow's feet and weight if a girl was competing for a commitment from a man who wanted babies, but Sarah was way beyond that. Marriage was a mug's game. And the sort of gentle, often timid and shy men she preferred would have run a mile from a Lilian Beaumont unless they were already married to her.

No, Sarah's chosen kind of men tended to be clever, kindly, successful in an understated way, and tending towards the socially inept. A teeny bit and not always fortunately eccentric. Such as George, with his passion for Russian icons and all things miniature, suitable for his own diminutive size and huge feet, alienating his customers with his myopic stare and contempt for their taste. Then there was William, six feet three inches high, with a permanent stoop from bending over his patients in the dental chair, whose practice made him ill-at-ease with most of humanity. At the moment she entered the restaurant he was absorbed in reading, and when she touched him on the shoulder he leapt to his feet in a confusion of angles, sending the water and cutlery crashing to the floor. Something he might do twice during a meal. It was never wise to drink soup near William, and yet in his surgery he was precise and soothing, as long as nobody tried to speak.

'Sarah,' he said, beaming and irritated at the same time, kissing her cheek and pulling at the tablecloth. 'You must stop sending me patients. I've too many already. And you never send me anyone straightforward.'

'I don't know anyone straightforward.'

'I forgot, of course you don't. What are we eating?'

He could never make up his mind and wanted someone to do it for him, although he loved food. Frightened of his own choices. She frowned over the menu while William unloaded the tragedies of the week. The waiter appeared and she told him what William would like. It was a quiet place, full of concentrated eaters who appreciated plain food served speedily.

'How many this week ... oh yes, I sent Steven,' she said, smiling at him, pleased to see him. 'It isn't as if he can't pay. I thought he might like the paintings in the waiting room.'

'You told me a little about your brother,' William said, mildly enough. 'And yes, he did like the paintings. Rather too much, I thought. Walked off

55

with the one in the lavatory. That nice little nude. Do you think you could ask him for it back?'

'How very rude of him,' Sarah said. 'But I'm afraid it's a bit compulsive, although he's usually more subtle than that. I think he's a bit out of practice. It'll come back, don't worry.'

'To tell the truth,' William said while chewing safely dry whitebait, 'he scared me to death. There's something about him . . .'

'I know, I know. I shouldn't have sent him, but he had toothache.'

'He had a simple cavity, and I don't want him back.'

'Oh, right.'

'He frightens me,' William announced in the clearly articulated tone he used with patients, 'because he looks like you and he doesn't at the same time. And because I know you're siblings and I think you might be like him.'

'Or he might be like me.'

'That would be fine. But you aren't being fair, are you, Sarah?'

'It was an emergency . . .'

'If you want me to get involved again, Sarah, not only with your friends but your family, will you remember what you said?' His voice was now distinctly loud and cheerful. The second course arrived. 'You said, my dearest, that I should desist, because I am, after all, *only your lover.*'

The words seemed to bounce off the walls. After a tiny pause, the eaters resumed eating.

'Ah, yes,' Sarah said. 'I did say that.'

They continued to eat, like old friends.

'Why didn't I know about this brother before? I've known you . . . how long?'

'He worked abroad for years. He works to finance an unfortunate hobby of climbing. Free climbing they call it, anything that stays still. He's clever and easily bored. Now he works here. In a bank.'

William dropped his fork.

'A bank? Good God, I don't believe you.'

'. . . And you'll get your picture back. It was probably it being in the lavatory that enraged him. He's like that, you see. Hates lovely things to be hidden away.'

They ate in easy silence. He sighed at the end of the efficient consumption of his food while she was halfway through.

'I did like that other chap you referred to me. Much more my type. Richard Beaumont, that's his name.'

'You might prefer the wife. She's a stunner.'

'Would I? Funny thing about him, though. He doesn't seem to feel pain.'

Sarah did not want involvement, but she did like a bit of gentle networking. Let the men help one another. It made her feel useful.

\*     \*     \*

Steven Fortune, bunking off from work, found himself, as he often did, staring into windows and never for the purpose of seeing his own reflection. This part of London was full of galleries (picture shops, he called them) and while the displays might fill him with rage, he could never resist. Art was the emperor's clothes. And then there were moments, faced with paintings or drawings in the vaulted hall of a museum or, as now, in the expensive, darkened interior of a discriminating private gallery, when the pleasure factor was so intense that it was almost painful, filling him with an aching warmth.

*Tiepolo, leading exponent of the Italian Rococo. Style characterised by airy frivolity, joyous sense of colour and playful effects.* It was the fourth time he had seen it. It haunted him.

A watercolour-and-ink drawing: *The Sermon on the Mount.* What would you call it? Sketch, watercolour using sepia inks, whatever. Why was it magic? Steven struggled to control the light-headed pleasure it gave him by making a strenuous effort to analyse why the painting should have such an effect, took a deep breath and tried.

Here goes: *The composition swoops up with fantastic triangular force (a pile of triangles within triangles), strengthened and dramatised by the uncanny use of light and shade within a limited range of sepia tones. The white-not-pale women at the very centre are droolingly beautiful (look at the bare shoulder and décolleté neckline). They form a triangle with the left arm of Jesus, approached by an equally white pathway through the bald old geezer in the foreground—youth, beauty and old age all in thrall to the wise one. And those ghostly white passages contrast powerfully with the dark backs of the foreground figures (another triangle) . . .*

Yes, that went some way to explaining it, about 2 per cent of the way, but it helped bring him down to earth and made him aware he was smiling so widely he must have looked an idiot. He turned away from the Tiepolo on its stand and walked to the other end of the room simply so that he could turn back and approach it again, get that feeling all over again. Enter the force field of the thing and get that unholy joy. No, it was a holy joy, but then he was used to thinking of all joy as suspicious.

It wasn't even as if he was usually drawn to this kind of thing; not his favourite century, but that made no difference. He loved it. He wanted it. If he never had anything else, he wanted that. Lusted after it. Measured it with his eye. Sizeable, but out of that frame it would roll up safely and insignificantly small. He would carry it away with the greatest of ease.

And yet what would he do with it? He would have to do as all those others did: hide it away and take what would be by then a definitely unholy pleasure in it. Like wanking in secret over a porn picture. But there would be a difference between himself and most of the others. He would love it. He would care for it, and he would know what it was. Quite different from *them*.

Steven lived for *zing*. That was what he had always called it.

Taking steps towards the Tiepolo, *style characterised by playful effects*, there was a repetition of the same joy of discovery, slightly diluted because it was not the first but intense all the same, and not disappointing for the dilution because he knew he could look at it for a lifetime of days and still see something else. Another angle, triangle, another fucking elbow, a gossip in the corner, a breathtakingly casual flick of ink. And then, as he walked towards it for the third time, still smiling, his view was blocked. Someone else was standing in front of it, nose to the glass, dusting it, fussily, hiding it. The urbane-looking gallery owner probably, fed up with Steven's visits and deliberately getting in the way. It was enough to remind Steven that the drawing was not his, would never be his and he might never be able to see it again. He retreated before he did something he might regret.

Outside in the street, smoking a cigarette, he thought he was going mad, shaking himself to death with his own fury. No one should be prevented from seeing fine art, even if it was for sale. No one should allow a rich buyer to buy for investment and put a Tiepolo behind bulletproof glass to rot in private. Steven wanted to scream. Instead he sat down in a café nearby, and then, after two cups of coffee, he took off his tie and stuffed it in his pocket, ruffled his hair and went back with his suit jacket over his arm, nonchalantly.

'Could you tell me if this is still for sale?'

The Tiepolo was still as it was, on the stand, the sight of it making his voice quiver convincingly for all the wrong reasons.

'No, 'fraid not.'

She lied. The girl who had replaced the man who had gone to lunch looked at him with a cool appraising eye, and for all his ordinariness, found him lacking. It was the hand, he decided, which made her so hesitant, rather than the rest of him, which, with a hasty rearrangement of his creased jacket over his arm, simply looked down on his luck. Not for sale to *him*. He liked to tease them.

'It should be in a museum. Going far, is it?'

She maintained her icy composure, eyes fixed on her computer screen.

'Something like this could end up anywhere. Probably the Emirates. Can I help you with anything?'

Oh God, that awful sing-song, eat-your-balls

voice. The tone of voice that defied him to ask, and how they infuriated him, those gallery girls with their casual superiority and get-lost voices. At least, long since, when his sister Sarah had part-timed as one of those, she smiled at people like the tart she was and gave them the benefit of her enormous enthusiasm. Not this brainless cold fish with the professionally tousled hair. He passed behind her seat and read the addresses on her screen, annoying her. Then, before she could ask him to stop, he went back to the Tiepolo, close to it this time, trying to memorise the detail he already knew. It felt horribly like saying goodbye. Next time he came in here, they would probably call the police.

'Nice meeting you,' he said. 'I'm sure we'll meet again.'

The girl turned in her chair and gave him her two-watt smile. The sort of smile to which he had become accustomed, the non-reactive, forced acknowledgement of his insignificant presence. Good, he wasn't losing his touch then.

His fingers tingled. Steven went back out into the street where the sun hit his eyes and made him stop. At least he had seen It, felt that *zing*, and that was all that mattered, wasn't it? No, it wasn't. You didn't fall in love with a thing (or a person, for that matter, although he confessed to ignorance of the latter experience) without *wanting* it. Or if not wanting it (her), since possessiveness was a terrible and destructive vice, at least wanting the best possible chance for it (her). A good life, no less. And he was sure that the single fact of appreciation applied equally to woman and painting, since without it they both seemed to wither and die. It was vital to the health. Shutting it (her) away made

61

it crumple and fade, as well as being an insult to the creator. But did the amount of the appreciation matter? Was it quality or quantity? Was the love of one person enough?

On the Underground, with his hands stuffed in his pockets, he began to think that such analogies could be as overstretched as canvas, and anyway comparisons of all kinds were odious. He was angry, in that non-obvious, understated way his sister would have denigrated by saying you're *cross*, and he knew his mind was as screwed as ever as soon as he started making comparisons between women and works of art, getting confused between the *its* and the *shes*, which was a really stupid kind of comparison to make, except for the fact that they were both alive and infinitely capable of *zing*. Although not that woman over there, on the other side of the train, a girl with a placid, made-up face, chewing to the hum of wheels over tracks in a half-empty carriage, which he disliked because it made it so much more obvious when you stared at people. She was just nothing, no hint of spirit or spirited artifice. When you looked at a woman like that, and he looked at them all the time, it was impossible to understand how anyone could feel possessive of her (it), and yet undoubtedly someone was. And when the train sped on past his destination and he remembered he had failed to get off, without caring either, and the anger was fading, it occurred to him that the shes and the its could be in terrible conflict anyway. You couldn't have *zing* for both. Whatever happened to lovers if they did not love the same things? Or one of them developed a competing passion for an *It*?

He alighted at the next stop and walked back to

the bank where he worked. It was a small, private bank, exclusively for the use of clients who had abandoned the high-street equivalent. The criterion for banking at Joseph's was the possession of a certain amount of money. The clients who banked here were not, in the main, the big high-rollers beloved of better-known private banks. There were no millionaires and only one faded pop star, but they did not have mundane things like mortgages and they did have money to invest. In the early days of burglary, when he was still perfecting the art of free climbing and taking exams, he had used the bank's client list for starters. It was a safe assumption that anyone who banked with Joseph's would have something worth stealing, although not the sort of conspicuous wealth which necessitated elaborate security systems, but a few forays into their empty houses were disappointing. If there was any art, it was not the kind bought for investment and not usually worth liberating. These people preferred bricks and mortar as an investment. Besides, the client list was of limited usefulness: if he confined himself to that, someone, somewhere would make the obvious connection that a series of not-so-fine-art burglary victims had a bank account in common. And some of them had taste. Steven thought it better to sell to them. He did not wish to disgrace the bank. There were nice people in there. They had given him a career and let him climb walls, literally and metaphorically, and they seemed to accept him as human, despite his churlish resistance and mocking of their culture. Remaining an outsider was entirely his choice. This was a grudging admission he made to himself

63

as he went through the doors.

There was not a single thing in this building which moved him, not a colour, an artifact, a water cooler, a door, a window or the flicker of a skirt which created a single impulse that was even a distant relative of *zing*. It was a deliberately faceless, featureless place, designed to provide no distraction from the task in hand. He nodded hello to others in the room and sat down as if weary from a tiresome lunch with a sober client distressed about market performance.

Tiepolo came up on the screen. Triangle upon triangle, *zing, zing, zing*, as if it were really there instead of imprinted on his mind. Then it faded, giving way to the usual jumble of figures. He thought of the journey home to the dark flat he disliked but was too lazy to leave. He thought of the Tiepolo again, sadly this time, and then, at one remove, he smarted with anger that his sister would no longer let him stay with her, for the sake of her rich neighbours, and his fingers began to itch with the desire to climb.

He tapped at the keys of his computer. He had always tried to say it was the hand that set him apart, but it was not. Scarred, ugly thing, minus the smallest finger. Never mind; the next finger did the work of two. That hand, crushed beneath the wardrobe he had tried to climb in a four-year-old's dare against himself, only to drag it down. And no one heard the screaming, because Mummy was too busy with ever-naughty Sarah. Oh God, that soulless little house of childhood, full of girls. No wonder he preferred *zing*. No wonder Sarah owed him something. Then he smiled, nodded to himself and smiled again.

# CHAPTER FOUR

## *Always use stiles and gates*

The sea always excited him, lifted his spirits, gave him a surge of energy. Richard Beaumont puffed up the path from the car park. There it was again, the seductive hum of the hovercraft with its effect of blotting the brain and then, in that odd moment of silence, unclogging it again. He felt odder by the second and did not care. Maybe coming back to the cliffs would encourage someone to hit him again and shock him into real life; maybe he was a masochist. Maybe he was simply drawn back to a place which had become familiar, with all the ingredients he needed. A bit of grandeur, a distinct lack of romance, ugliness mixed with beauty and sometimes hellish noisy, what with the wind and shipping and the crashing and bashing of the sea. There was also the allure of the human traffic, as long as it did not come too close. He had never wanted isolation for long, either in life or in art; he needed the human form as well as the landscape, and he felt ashamed for coming back. But he knew the way, and that counted for a lot. He knew the hotel, he knew the railway station and he knew the route, with or without his car. And he liked it. He felt like a determined child insisting on his own way in doing something unwise, but still, he was here, and he knew the way back.

Familiarity with routes was important because his memory had become so poor. His conscience was unaccountably heavy. There was something he had to remember, such as why, the other day when he had sat and sketched that girl, had he ever dared go down that path beneath the overhang. Whatever was it had provoked him to do that? He returned to the same spot, passing en route the place where he had sat behind bushes earlier in the spring, reaching the place where the path led beneath the overhang, near the *Do not walk* sign, which puzzled him, because half of it was missing and he had a vague curiosity about what the rest of it might say. What else could you do here than walk? He was feeling a little shaky, realising that he could not go down that path again, still puzzled as to why he had ever had the courage. And he would have to go there again, some time, and he was postponing everything by staring at the broken sign. He should have brought a hat. In the distance on this clear afternoon he could see France and it looked alluring. A voice spoke, unexpectedly close to his ear.

'It says "*Do not walk closer than twenty metres from the edge*". Or it used to say that once. None of these signposts last long in the wind.'

Richard turned to see the doctor. The name evaded him and the face swam into focus, slowly but surely. His own solid, almost ugly face split into a smile. The doctor had a narrow, canny face, not smiling yet but open to suggestion. He and this man, *What was his name?* had had a real conversation, all about bruises and vertigo but authentic communication nevertheless. The doctor and he had spent quality time together. Richard liked the doctor, knew it had been mutual.

'If I were you,' the doctor said, 'I would come away from here. If Edwin sees you, you might not like it. You're still under suspicion, you know. And

66

you're too close to the edge.'

Richard nodded. There was no point in arguing or asking who Edwin was, and feeling shaky meant he was also biddable. He followed the doctor back to the doctor's car, feeling generally but controllably unwell.

'Does your wife know you're here?' the doctor asked.

*John*, that was his name. John Armstrong.

It did not seem an odd question. Richard was trying to remember if he had told Lilian exactly where he was going, or if he had only mentioned for how long, or if he had told Fritz.

'I expect so. I hope so.'

They stood together in the car park, both with hands in pockets, curiously reluctant to part.

'They still don't know who the girl was, you know. The one you sketched. I wouldn't hang around here until they do, if I were you. You can't expect to be popular. Why did you come back? You're the first witness and therefore suspect . . . why did you think I took swabs of your hands and scrapes from your fingernails?'

'Did you? What a relief. That would prove I couldn't have touched her.'

'No, it wouldn't. Would you like a drink?'

'I think so.'

The feature of the old Vauxhall of which John was most proud was the miniature cocktail cabinet in the left-hand glove compartment. You still called it that if you walked on the cliffs because that was where you stuck gloves and hats, except in John's case they littered the back seat and the glove compartment contained a selection of miniature bottles of whisky, gin, etc., and two small glasses held stable in a homespun construction of wire. Richard registered the age and scruffiness of the car, sank into the passenger seat which looked as if it had been chewed to death by a dog, and let out a deep breath. Yes, a whisky, with the thought running through his head, *Why is this man being so nice to me?*

'I am kind and curious by nature,' John said, by way of explanation of the unarticulated question. 'And I dislike seeing suffering. I would rather try and head it off at the pass than witness the consequences. And you almost went over the edge of the cliff back there. I thought you were testing your vertigo. So why did you come back?'

Richard sipped, missing the hovercraft sound. The nausea passed, and the drink was heaven.

'Because the other day was one of the best days in my life,' he said slowly. 'I had a model. Models are hard to find, I tell you. She was beautiful. And I saw the chough. I've tried to paint it all and I think I've failed. So I had to come back.'

'You can't have seen the chough. The chough hasn't been here for decades.'

'Well, I saw it.' He swallowed. There were times when alcohol, in which he had never overindulged, tasted far more divine than any advertisement could describe. 'It was there. And now I've painted it. So it must have been there.'

'Ah. Imagination has its own reality.'

'It had red feet and a curved red beak. And there was a plan to reintroduce the chough to this coastline.'

A plan which had come to nothing yet. The doctor was silent for a moment. They both looked ahead at the vast expanse of sky through the windscreen. He noticed that Richard's colour had improved and thought how good the interior of a car was for encouraging conversation. Cars had an anonymous intimacy.

'So did you come back in the hope of seeing the chough again? Or to look for another body? They aren't that regular.'

'Neither, really. I've been here many times in the last few weeks, watching it change. Strange, isn't it, how a place you've chosen at random should become addictive. Perhaps because you've chosen it yourself and no one else has done it for you.'

'But why choose this? There are stretches of coast far more beautiful than this. Think of Wales or Cornwall ... You might actually see your red-beaked chough.'

'Too far away, and I was born there and I can't go back, but you've got the point about *this*.' He gestured towards the rising cliff path, visible to the left and marked by a litter bin. 'The point is that so much of it is bleak and ugly. And the town you can see isn't so lovely either. The cliffs have bald patches like an old head with alopecia. The wind stops it being lush. I couldn't do with it being completely beautiful. It would be too much for me.'

'I thought an artist might seek perfection?'

'No, and I don't much care for flowers. I don't know what I like until I see it. Bodies and shapes and something I can paint later.' He had balanced the whisky glass on the sketchbook on his knees. 'Do you think I'm odd for sketching her? There was nothing else I could do.'

'I've often found a certain beauty in a dead body,' John said. 'They sometimes look marvellous, especially the old. Streamlined and serene in a moment of perfection before the rot sets in. But not when the death is violent and untimely, and at her age it was definitely that. She was about twenty, that girl. I wish I could give her a name. Is this drawing and painting lark a recent hobby of yours?'

'The sketches are the ideas. The framework. I take them home and paint from them, and memory. I wish it was a hobby, but it isn't.'

John waited out the pause. Lord, they were sipping their whisky like little old ladies.

'It's an addiction. It simply has to be done. It's . . . like being blind and struggling to find sight. It must have grown on me over the years because suddenly it was there, a fully fledged disease.'

He held the whisky in his left hand, tapped the sketch pad with the fingers of his right.

'An overpowering desire to paint or die in the attempt. I've had an incredibly dull and boring life, making money, raising children. Second marriage, early retirement, and now all I want to do is learn how to paint.'

'Hmm. What does second wife think?'

'I don't know, which doesn't mean I don't care. We don't discuss it and she's waiting for it to pass. She also has to learn how to live by herself, anyway. It was high time she acquired a bit of self-sufficiency. She's much younger than I. She'd have to learn in time.'

'Not yet awhile, surely. You're a youth yet. Not even sixty, as I recall.'

Richard laughed, more relaxed and at ease than he had been in days.

'You're good at this, aren't you, Dr John? Good at asking questions. Well, as you know, John, we all have our individual span, which has nothing to do with the number of years. The body does quite well. It's the mind worries me. You assessed me for sanity, didn't you? As well as my general health, and taking scrapings from my nails.'

'So I did, but very superficially. I found you perfectly sane and lucid, but with certain gaps in the cognitive memory. I took a wild guess at a minor stroke, perhaps, with some residual memory loss.'

Richard looked at John and smiled. They were brilliant blue eyes, shockingly shrewd. Richard nodded.

'Which may also be worse than it seems,' John went on, 'or may improve.'

'Or not, as the case may be. I seem to have lost some of my senses and acquired others, or maybe it's painting does that. There are gaps. That's why I had to come back. Thank you so much for the whisky and your patience. You're indulging me, I don't know why, and I interrupted your walk.'

'Which I shall resume. Perhaps you'll accompany me. And I'm not indulging you. I've always wanted to know what makes an artist tick, and I've other reasons, too. Shall we go?'

'A pleasure. I'm all yours.' Richard hauled his bulky body out of the car, talking over his shoulder and gave a shout of laughter as the wind hit his face. 'You know one of the problems of married life? And retirement. One does so miss the company of men.'

They plodded back up the path, turning to bend into the wind, past the sign *Do not walk*, walking at the same speed like old friends who had often walked together. John thought that the single benefit of age was the gradual erosion of inhibition. When he had been a young and tongue-tied man

71

he would certainly have spoken to strangers—his profession left him no choice—but he would never have taken the risk of speaking openly for fear of being misunderstood. Then life delivered a series of whammies, you discovered the snakes and the ladders, or they discovered you, and you made a few dreadful mistakes, witnessed worse, and without coming to any particular conclusion about the whole damn thing decided there was no point pretending and certainly none in lying. Especially to a contemporary, who like as not had been through similar games. Contemporaries were a comfort, especially if linked by the language of experience, possibly the same kind of education, with the hint of similar standards imparted somewhere and an ability to use similar words. The artist was simply another middle-class professional. Perhaps that explained the liking and made him a snob, and if it did he did not care.

'Who's this Edwin you mentioned?' Richard Beaumont asked. Now fully in command of all his senses, puffing a little. Not as fit as he was himself, John thought, wondering if the competitiveness of men was so ingrained that the thought actually gave him pleasure. Well, it did give him pleasure all the same.

'Edwin is the keeper of the coastline for the next few miles,' he shouted back. 'Nobody knows it better. But he would regard it as sacrilegious for anyone to intrude. There was a team of botanists he'd almost tolerate, because they'd do what he said, and walkers and tourists he'll doff his hat to, but if anyone interferes with the birds at this time of year, he'd kill 'em. He's a harmless loner, always has been. Only man I know who loves crows.'

He felt defensive about Edwin, uncomfortable talking about him. He watched Richard pause, shake himself like a dog out of water, and then go on.

'What's strange about loving crows? I do, too. Think of the lovely chough. He's a crow. But then I was always sentimental about birds.'

They continued as the narrow path rose into a headland and then dipped sharply into a valley, clutching safely the side of the land with a shallower incline to their right, stretching down towards rocks and the mild sea, safer in a small steep bay and suddenly far away. The wind stilled as soon as they had turned the bend. John, who loved plants and flowers better than anything, always found he breathed deeper in the valleys, where the grass grew and the shrub trees were bent sideways, but there would always be dog roses and blackberries, and unexpected migrant growths of wheat and kale, plus the souvenir of some almost prehistoric crop inedible to rabbits. Or some token of the sheep that had grazed and created the bald patches beloved by clever scavengers like the chough, who needed grazed ground and had gone for the lack of it. Speaking for himself, John could not give a toss about the bloody birds. They had the knack of looking after themselves. They had no respect. A thought niggled. The light fell on the safely distant sea and he paused, suddenly, unexpectedly, profoundly moved and happy; the thought went, and a shout came out instead.

'Will you just look at that?'

The sea was calm, the pinks were pink, the vista huge. Richard had walked ahead a few steps and came back.

'At what in particular?'

'Just the bloody view. Can't you see anything without wanting to paint it?'

'No.'

That grin again, the eyes brilliant with self-mockery and mischief. If I were a queer, John thought, I'd fall in love with this almost ugly man, even though he might be a murderer, and I can quite see why the much younger wife would go for him. Then he wondered if this sweet eccentric had an unhealthy propensity for youth, and his bluff honesty hid perversion.

'No, I'm afraid I look at a view, waiting for a subject to select itself. And make me want to paint it. Then I get blind to the rest. It's a terrible affliction. Drives me mad.'

'Ah.'

Lately John had found himself saying 'Ah' a lot and nodding his head like a donkey, never sure whether this was an indication of wisdom, a necessary breathing space or a way of avoiding conversation. He had lost the knack of talking: too much time spent alone. The path was narrow, room only for single file, which might explain why the walkers were so uncommunicative, and the grass growing almost to waist height on either side. On the next headland it would be stunted. He found he wanted to show the artist more of the cliffs, make him look at the view as he did, make him talk more. And then he was put off by the sight of Edwin, striding into line in the distance, avoiding the path and walking in the grass. John turned back and beckoned Richard to follow. Edwin had said he did not like the artist; could not like anyone who had somehow brought disturbance to his territory.

74

And although Edwin was usually well mannered, it followed from his shyness and isolation that his manners were not always the same as those of other men. John did not want them to meet. Richard followed, cheerfully.

Back at the dismembered *Do not walk* sign, John led him to the overhang, close enough for them both to see the path that led beneath, beginning in stunted grass and only visible close to the edge where the wind blew fiercest. Richard began to tremble. John grabbed hold of his arm until he sat down, abruptly. John had been trying to avoid coinciding with Edwin, but Edwin was coming closer so he sat down himself, resigned to it.

'What did you actually see?'

'An angel, falling from the skies and merging with the landscape. That's what I saw.'

'Oh, for fuck's sake ... What happened before that?'

Edwin drew level and saw them sitting on the ground. He broke step, looked at Richard and spat on the ground near his feet. Then resumed the normal, abnormally long stride and went away, moving off the path into the long grass until he disappeared. Richard raised his blue eyes, which were no longer brilliant but misted with tears. He had not noticed the insult. John was shocked, ashamed of Edwin, but relieved that the artist had not seen.

'I don't *know*,' he said. 'I just don't *know*. I feel I led her here. But I just don't know.'

'We're getting cold. Need another warm whisky, I think.'

'Please ... Did I kill her to paint her? Did I?'

'I've absolutely no idea. Come on, there's a dear,

do.' They proceeded downhill, equally, with steps fairly brisk and uneven. This path was narrow, one person at a time, so that it was difficult to protect one another. Richard had recovered strength; John went on talking.

'So when you paint, does it matter if you're any good at it?'

'What?'

'Do you care if you're any good? Do you have to believe you have talent?'

'No. You have to believe you can find something. See something no one else sees.'

Oh Jesus, he was a nutcase after all, but an interesting one. They were back, standing by the car. By now there were several others: the late afternoon shift of strollers of the casual sort who would walk from here to the first high point, say oooh! and come back. The site where Richard had sat and the body been thrown, or jumped, was only a few hundred yards further than that. If it had been homicide, it was a lazy method to throw her where she would be seen so soon, but not too long a distance to persuade someone to walk from the car park, and a long enough distance for a row to develop, too. And, for a suicide, enough length of time to find the courage to say, Do it now.

'Why does that man Edwin dislike me so much?'

Ah, so he had seen.

'You must forgive him. He's a man with a history of rejection. Probably regards you as the bringer of trouble. He doesn't like strangers who keep coming back, and he'd rather push people away in case they do it to him first.'

'Was he there when the girl fell?'

76

It was a hopeful and frightened question.

'No, he was far away in Cable Bay with some botanists. Can I give you a lift somewhere?' John asked politely, interrupting his own thoughts and quite determined not to leave the man alone.

'That would be kind. I'm staying at the Trust House. Come and have dinner with me later. You've been kind to me, and I'd like to know you better.'

John was embarrassed, filled with doubt, then pleasure. Why not?

'Aren't you going home?'

'Not today. Tomorrow. Please come for dinner.'

'I . . . yes. Yes, I'd like that, a lot. But I must ask you something . . . You don't seriously think you had anything to do with her death, do you?'

Richard was tucking himself into the car, fussily, confused by his long coat. Not an ideal coat for a walker, better for someone who needed it for sitting on the ground. It was beige and grubby, uncomfortably reminiscent of a flasher's mac, John thought, and would not have added to his credibility in this town.

'The problem is,' Richard said slowly, 'is that I can't really remember how I arrived at that spot. Or why, on that particular day, I conquered the vertigo and went down that path. I'd never been that brave before. Could I have pushed her over and then gone down to look? Maybe I hired her to pose in the long grass, naked. Maybe . . .'

'I don't think so,' John said. 'You thought she was wearing some kind of dress.'

'Something that floated off her. And something shiny round her neck. At least I think there was.'

'Really? There was nothing found. Nothing on

77

your sketch.'

'Maybe when I painted her I adorned her then. Didn't want her so naked.'

'Have you finished the painting?'

'Yes, but it's awful, a nightmare.'

John started the car. 'Are they often like that?' he asked, genuinely curious as to why anyone would want to persist in an activity that gave pain. A far cry from the hobbyist watercolourists from the local club who brought tea and sandwiches and complained about wasps in late summer. Richard sighed. Even his sigh was full of life.

'Oh, yes, they're often like that. They fight you. Painting's like that. Would eight o'clock suit you? And I do like this car, by the way. Doesn't need any spit and polish.'

John signalled left, on to the road, and, ah yes, he remembered the best route to that hotel, the only place in town with a reasonable reputation for food. He was suddenly hungry.

'Yes, eight would be fine. What sort of car do you have?'

'An old Daimler and a Mercedes. Waste of money, don't use them much. Prefer the train.'

Oh dear, perhaps a mistake to let conversation reduce itself to simple, manly topics, like motor cars. John felt a clearly definable twinge of envy, accelerated so fast that the car lurched. Richard was entirely unmoved, sitting like a granny taken out for a rare treat, with his long coat tucked between his knees.

'They don't have glove compartments like this, though,' he said, stroking it. Honour was restored.

\*         \*         \*

78

To be fair to him, he had said he would only be gone overnight. And it would have been worse than this if she had thought he was having an affair, but at least Lilian knew it wasn't that. Such a thought was unthinkable. As for what she had done with herself all day when he had been at work (in retrospect, the halcyon days, when she worked on the flat and soaked in a bath before he came home), it was difficult to remember, but it was harder to remember what you had done when you had been happy than it was when you were miserable. She supposed, this time last year, she would have been doing something like this. The retail therapy which followed lunch, and really she shouldn't mind. Despite the shocks of the morning, lunch had been fun for at least the length of one and a half courses. She had almost forgotten that damn painting which had made her scream, but not quite. These meetings reminded her of one of the kindest things Richard had said when he had worried so much about the age difference between them in the very early days. When she was gobsmacked by him—a vulgar description of a neurotic state, someone had called it, and she didn't use that phrase any longer—and he was all starry-eyed about her, and said, in an intimate moment, that at least he would leave her with ready-made friends. Namely, his children. It was not something Lilian thought of as remotely important. She was not thinking of the long-distant future and he did not seem old to her, simply solid, good looking, such a far cry from the callow youth of spotty contemporaries, so much like the father she had always missed. She was bursting with pride in him. *Look what I've got! A real man!* It did not occur to her that his children would feature in her life any more than her own siblings would, and when she knew it was inevitable, she had dreaded the initial meeting so much she was sick.

There were three of them, and she need not have worried in the least. He described them as successful little brutes, although 'little' hardly came into the equation. They were all big and comfortingly on the stout side. A boy, Ben, thirty, a girl, Sally, married with baby, and a bit dull, to be honest, and Charles, known as Chump, the baby at twenty-six. Ben was in the City and more than comfortable, the sort of braying, good-humoured, always all right man Lilian had dated before. Sally was a physiotherapist, earnestly devoted to work and baby, the sort who would want to breastfeed in public, not naturally Lilian's soulmate, but endlessly, painfully *caring*, while Charlie was into infotec in a big way, and doing fine. Yes, there'd been problems with them all, Richard explained, such as Ben having his session with drugs and then being far too dedicated to money and cars, Sally getting God at college, but then giving Him up for sex and fecundity, and Charlie being promiscuous. Nothing life-threatening in any of that, Richard said: I'm incredibly lucky.

And so was Lilian. She liked them and they liked her. She did not think beyond that to imagine the mentality of the mother who had imbued these kids with such confidence, or the sleepless nights, devotion, expense and that element of luck that made them turn out the way they were. Sweet, pleasant, and united in their welcome of her. Nor did Lilian wonder why, when Sally told her in the ladies' loo that they were all so genuinely thrilled that Dad was getting married again. Losing Mum had been so hard, and he had been so lost and miserable, and they had all been so worried, you know? Lilian could have read between the lines that her future husband was presenting himself as a great big, lonely, overconcerned nuisance and a potentially awful future obligation to children who no longer needed him. She could have read between other lines and seen, not only their palpable relief, but also their fascination about the fact that good ole Dad had hit upon a bird of paradise, the old goat. Lilian might have seen that they were close enough to form a united front in the acceptance of the inevitable, and mightily relieved because she herself was a helluva lot better than they might have got. Or also seen, when she went out with Ben and Charlie, the nudges and winks behind her back when they told their mates she was their *stepmother*. None of that would have mattered, even if she had seen it.

Lilian met them regularly. She made them beautiful Christmas stockings. They joined in for holidays and behaved well. They came round in a posse on high days and occasional weekends, or she met them in various combinations of at least two. It had never occurred to her that they might, in some understated way, have been monitoring her. They were simply nice. They were mates from the very beginning.

'Do you know he hates cornflakes, or anything which makes a noise in the morning?'

A nudge and a slap, from Charlie to Sally.

'Did you know he snores? Only joking.' From Charlie.

'Do you how *critical* he is? Always criticising. Always gets the needle in. If you don't work, you go nowhere.'

And from Ben, who was always protective towards her, saying to her today, 'Is the old man behaving right, Lil?'

'Yeah, he's fine. Just a bit distracted, you know? Painting, you know. Goes at it madly.'

'Oh, Lil, he was always like that.'

It had a strange back-echo to what Sarah had said. *Maybe he was always like that—obsessional.* However protective Ben might seem, she knew she could not tell him that his father had become distinctly odd and had taken to painting obscenities. Nor that he appeared to have been arrested for something on a clifftop. That would have been an admission of failure, which she was not going to make to her own family, and even less to his. She had being going to tell Ben and Sally all about it, but in the end she had not because of the realisation that it might not be wise. Something about Ben's relentless cheerfulness forbade it and some latent instinct was telling her that yes, they might be mates, but they did not want her confiding in them on the subject of their father. *They* could criticise and tease; *she* could not, and if ever the chips were down and there was a division of loyalties, or she ceased to take care of their father, this friendship might be pretty short-lived. It was a lonely feeling, not assuaged by the lingerie department of Fortnum's. Ben and Sally had had to dash; they always had to dash towards the end of lunch, while Lilian did not have to dash anywhere. And she could not tell them *anything*.

Hanging from a padded silk hanger there was a

frothy concoction of a silk dressing gown of oyster white, edged at the neck and sleeves with similarly dyed ostrich feathers, matched with a nightdress of thin-strapped simplicity, adorned only with a single diamante button at the V of the cleavage. Definitely honeymoon stuff. In another mood, she would have laughed at its silliness, because those damn feathers would shed everywhere in a clinch, or get all over the bathroom when you washed your face, and the whole ensemble would spend most of its life in the dry cleaners. And besides all that, Richard detested feathers as much as frills and pastel colours, preferred her in red or black, slinky but unadorned, with a distinct preference for nothing at all. She stood by the side of it, not exactly wondering if she had a mind of her own, but peculiarly enraged by something she could not define, and because she knew he would loathe it, she bought the negligee anyway. It was wrapped with a great deal of tissue paper and fuss, which had her stamping her heels with an impatience she did not show. It might never be unwrapped, which made the wrapping a particular waste of time, for something bought as a gesture that already felt futile.

And then what? Home to a message from him, that he loved her and hoped she was having fun, would be back tomorrow. What had they ever done together? What did she know about him? He painted obscenities. He ignored her. She surrounded him with too many things, and made him too *safe*.

Later, she put on the ensemble. It had a certain old-fashioned, ridiculous glamour, making her imagine her name was Gina, or Gloria, or Bardot, or at least Juliet or Nicole. She wafted round the flat in it with a glass of champagne, swigging it carefully so as not to spill. In the bathroom, entirely according to her predictions, a couple of the feathers flew off while she set her blonde hair on heated rollers and played with the look of the unutterably seductive vamp with coiled locks, somewhere between Art Nouveau slenderness and a nineteen-fifties film star with a bosom and a breathy voice. She got well into the role, waltzing round to the right kind of music in the reception room, admiring her own work in all respects. Beautiful room, just as the bathroom was, in its own way, beautiful. An impressive row of invitations on the mantelpiece, including galleries, which she liked, and one to a Buckingham Palace garden party, which was very satisfying, even though she didn't much care for the Queen. Everything state of the art and everything on the walls *hers*. Except the glass in the kitchen, which he no longer wanted.

So, all right, then, why did he not want her any more? Oh, but he did. Surely he did. If only she didn't want him. There was a sudden panic. *What would she do on her own?*

*You make him too comfortable.*

Then she was angry. She went into the daylight room to make herself even angrier. Why did he hide in here when he had so much else from which to choose? A draught blew from the window. The painting on the easel was only a small thing, but it caught the eye and made her want to be sick. Lilian slammed the door behind her, went back to the kitchen and refuelled on champagne. This was no way for a girl to spend an evening, dressed like this.

She could go out; she didn't want to go out. She could find a girlfriend and sit in a bar, but she had never really liked doing that. Never gone for clubs and dancing, except in her teens, when it had quickly palled. She enjoyed turning heads but preferred the quieter environment where she could be noticed; she had always wanted exclusive attention. Perhaps this made her ideal for the older man. She had felt so safe as the younger woman. Her feelings for him might alter, but his, never: he was the lucky one.

*Too comfortable.* He enjoyed comfort and beautiful things, didn't he? Well, she could certainly do something about that.

Another phrase echoed through her mind. That old cliché *Get a life*. She dismissed that. She had the life she wanted, what else was there to get?

Missing him was like having toothache.

Perhaps if she changed everything here, that would change the balance of things. She walked down the long corridor, circled the reception room, once, twice, three times. And finally, dizzy with her own circular thoughts, lay on her sumptuous bed, still wearing the now creased negligee. The designer had been right. Ostrich feathers felt soft against the face, and the sheer sensation of silk could lull a person to sleep.

\*　　　\*　　　\*

Two hours after midnight, in total silence, Steven began climbing. The well of the building had been beautifully designed for his purpose: the drainpipes were ancient and fat, with solid brackets anchoring them to the wall, the window

85

ledges thoughtfully placed, and there were even small balconies jutting out from the kitchens and the remnants of an old, disused pulley system which had once been used to remove rubbish. He supposed, as he climbed, slowly and silently, keeping control of his breath, that in the heyday of this building there might have been a restaurant below, delivering meals to the apartments by a similar system. Those were the days when people really did live in style in apartments created to provide every service, and he was grateful for that kind of history as he clung to the metal stanchion of the old lift and paused for strength. Grateful for the fact that no one had ever cared about the well of the building, so that when new drainpipes had been included down one wall or another, none of the old had been taken away. It was a mess of foot- and handholds, because no one cared what it looked like and all the money would, of course, go on the front.

He worked upwards, to that open window. There were other open windows, but that was the one he wanted. Past the floor where Sarah lived, with windows closed, and on to the next. Convenient windows, too, big and old, with efficient sash cords, so that he could slip one open easily and swing himself inside. No burglar alarms at the back. They felt so *safe* in here.

Nothing much in this room. The torch showed a cluttered studio, as he remembered. He moved to the door and set off down a long corridor. How kind they were to him: even the floorboards did not creak. He toured the big room at the end, picking out the details. The curtains hid him from the silent street; every light was on. Someone had gone negligently to bed. He knew someone was there, he could smell it, but he did so prefer burglary with the occupants in residence. It seemed fairer somehow, and was more of a challenge. He liked to think how long it would take them to notice that something might have gone while they were asleep.

He went back down the corridor and tried three closed doors in turn. Boring bathrooms, etc. The last door, next to the studio door, was half open, a dim light beyond it. He pushed it open further.

Oh my God. *Zing*.

## CHAPTER FIVE

Steven stepped back out of the room, holding on to the door handle without relinquishing or closing it. There was a small vestibule which led to the three doors at the turn of the long corridor and with his back to the bedroom door he was facing a mirror, cunningly placed to maximise minimal light. He had retreated out of the room in order to go back in, but the sight in the mirror prevented him. He saw a smallish, skinny-hipped man with prominent thigh muscles, clad in black from neck to toe, with pale, chalk-stained hands, broad torso, and the heavy belt at his waist. He noticed the contours of too much muscle, normally invisible inside his usual loose clothes, and the ridiculous additional feature of a black rubber skullcap over his sandy hair. Left alone, that lighter hair would grow with the same unruly thickness as his sister's, but it was cropped, and his skull beneath appeared as a series of bumps and lumps belonging to some mutant beast. An erection strained the Lycra. There was no noise from the sleeping beauty in the room. He counted to fifteen, a random number slowly intoned under his breath, breathed deeply and quietly. Then went back inside.

*Zing.* He took another breath and tried a familiar trick. Compared the composition of her to *The Nude Maja* in the National Gallery, a painting he particularly remembered because it had been vandalised and repaired, and he had studied it closely. Here goes: a perfect composition, with her lying on one side, nicely centralised in the bed, with her visible eye central to the portrait. He took a deep breath and intoned to himself. *The eye of the onlooker is led first to the breast, half covered by the arm, and then to the profile, and then to the brilliant, dizzy curls of the hair, and then travels back, via the shoulder . . .* and then took another, similar excursion, this time noticing the peripheral details. A few, floating feathers on the pillow, the hand supporting the head, and then back down to the feet, via the knees, demurely together under the gown so tightly secured round the waist. Oyster white against purple, he noticed. A fantastic harmony of brilliant colours, deliberately enhancing the pale skin tones. He approached and touched the nightgown. Always did love fabrics. He wondered what the title would be, nothing pretentious or allegorical he hoped. Something simple, like *Woman Sleeping.*

She stirred and moved, while he did not. Turned a full half circle to lie on the other side, revealing more of her face. Now it was the right eye that was central, and more of the calf revealed, and the slipper shoe stayed on the same foot, but as for composition, still excellent. Beautiful light in here, softening already soft contours, accentuating shape. The only thing bothering him were the feathers on the pillow. That was slightly contrived, giving an unnecessary hint of conflict and decay, although otherwise the tableau was fucking stunning. He was disturbed by those feathers, hated it when the artist overdid it, but he was moved by the visible trace of a tear on her cheek.

One more time, then, just to get it again. Out of the room; breathe, count, and then back in, the way he did it with paintings. They had an aura, and if that did not work more than once, the critical faculty went into overdrive and the *zing* died. You did not want to look at them again. Somewhere in this apartment there was something to steal and rescue, but it was only this scene he wanted: shamed himself for wanting to rape and punish her for having this violent effect on him, wanting to possess and admire and then kill her, so that she would never move. It was his own reflection in the mirror that made him pause, but it did not stop that terrible beating of the heart, which pounded in his head, louder than a deafening electric drill. He wanted her to remain perfect. After a longer pause, he pushed open the door, waiting and aching for *zing*.

The room was empty. There was the stirring of a diaphanous curtain at an open window, a single slipper on the floor, but she was not there—she simply wasn't there. He was exposed in a room, facing rumpled bed covers, with feathers on the pillow, and she was not there. *Shit.* He was losing it,

89

losing everything to an illusion. He stumbled towards the window.

'*You cunt.*'

The voice hissed from behind his back. He felt the cold shock of a sharp blade digging into his buttock. 'You *bastard.*'

Steven stood very very still. He was so inclined; it came naturally. Everything about him shrivelled.

'Oh Christ,' she said. 'Wrong bastard.'

The way she removed the knife hurt. Not that it had penetrated far, but it still hurt. It would bleed inside the Lycra and stick it to his leg. He regarded the tableau of the empty bed and continued to stay very very still, and slowly raised his arms above his head, pausing to pull the skullcap further over his forehead. It made a slight, snapping sound. She heard it and he felt the point of a blade in the small of his back. The erection died completely. This time the blade felt dangerously close to the base of his spine; he tried not to squirm.

'Don't move. Put your hands on your head. It's a very sharp knife.'

The voice was harsh and calm, increasing his fear.

'Sit on the bed. No, don't, you might bleed. Sit on the window ledge. Slowly. *Go on.*'

He felt as if he was in a film; it was not a role he relished, and for all his fear there was a bewildering disappointment that he could not see her and the feeling of *zing*, dependent on seeing her, had temporarily gone. He turned and sat on the window ledge. The large sash window behind him was wide open and the material of the curtain tickled his hands. Sitting there with his hands above his head, unable to support himself, felt precarious.

He tried to visualise the street below and knew it was a long way down. He was balanced on his small, muscular buttocks, one of them bleeding.

'Keep your back straight. Don't move your hands. Just *don't*.'

He kept his eyes shut to assist his balance, holding his spine stiff, and then opened his eyes.

The sash of the gown was still knotted tight, but the gown itself was skewed sideways. The hair was a glorious mess. She held the knife in one hand, extended outwards, with her other hand gripping the elbow to keep her wrist steady. The knife was only a do-it-yourself Stanley knife with a tiny, triangular blade. They were indeed sharp but she couldn't do much harm with that, although she could certainly hurt and scar. He felt marginally better, until he remembered how easy it would be to fall out of the window if she stuck it in him. She moved closer to him and he felt worse.

'What do you want?'

*You. I want you . . . ZING.*

He could not speak.

'What do you want before, before I cut your nose off?'

His voice emerged as a strangled whisper.

'I'm only a burglar.'

'How did you get in?'

'Climbed through the window at the back.'

The high falsetto was part nerves, part disguise. He hoped it made him seem harmless.

'Through the studio?'

'If that's what it is, yes.'

She started to laugh. It was a rich chuckle and did not go on long enough before it stopped and she adjusted her hold on the knife.

'A *burglar*? Just what I need.'

She moved dangerously close, waving the knife with a steady hand.

'A bloody burglar, hmm. How timely. Perhaps you were sent from heaven. Look, why don't you just take it all and save me the trouble? Richard needs shaking up. I just don't want the bastard being so comfy, OK? And I thought you were him, sneaking back for a quick poke to make everything all right. Take it all, and maybe we can start all over again. How soon can you move it?'

He was still trying to expel his own breath, and it felt like *umphh*, and he let it out, slower than slow.

'Take *everything*? Oh, whenever.'

She adjusted the robe, tightened the sash, and was all business. With an hysterical gleam in the eye which showed she wasn't. She was suddenly very pale with sculptured white cheekbones, vulnerable and lovely, even with the knife.

'Oh Christ,' she said.

'What's the matter?'

'Never could take drink. Lousy with it. Feel sick. Look, just take that sodding picture, for now, come back another time with a van, and we'll forget the whole business. Just take the picture and get out.'

'Which picture?'

'The one on the easel, of course.'

She was a bit mad, and looking ill, and admitting weakness: now was the time. Steven braced himself, ready to spring, already planning the route out, thinking, I know what's happened, she's fallen asleep drunk, might not have set an alarm, might not have locked up, don't want to hit her. She moved faster, dropping the knife and punching him hard in the stomach. His back sagged back through the window and he screamed, arms flailing and grabbing for the side of the window, feeling himself move out into space, carrying the scream with him. Then he felt his right arm grabbed. His head banged hard against the frame and he was hauled back just as he thought he was gone, was pushing himself forward until he was a crumpled heap on the floor. He did not know how he had got there. The sound of frightened, stertorous breathing filled the room. Steven no longer cared about the knife. He sat up, shakily, flexing the damaged hand. She was sitting back on the bed, panting, gazing at the hand.

'Oh my God, I didn't do that, did I?'

'What, kill me?'

'It wasn't me took off your finger with this knife. was it? Did I do that?'

'No, of course not. It's been . . . like . . . that . . . since I was four.'

Perhaps it was relief made him smile. Or just the sight of her, which made it all come back with alarming force. Another perfect composition, the same colours, the same force field. *Woman Sitting . . . Zing*. He had been going to plead with her, threaten her, and what he said in his usual, pleasantly deep voice was: 'You are absolutely one hundred per cent, drop-dead gorgeous.'

A profound silence fell. He could hear the ticking of the alarm clock by the bed. She looked at him, quite the most fearless woman he had ever encountered, increasingly lovely and inviolate. He would have gone to prison for life rather than strike her. She sniffed, then eyed him up and down, the grin spreading over her face, and that chuckle beginning in her throat. The roving eye took in the

93

shape of him and ended with the skullcap, which covered his head and furrowed his forehead, pushed his eyebrows together, making him squint.

'And you look completely silly. Oh, bugger, wait a minute.'

She raced from the bed with her hand over her mouth into the en-suite bathroom. There was the sound of retching, of taps running, and groaning. Steven walked over to the window and shut it halfway down. She would need air, but not that much. By the time she came back into the room she was less pale, with pink patches appearing on her cheeks. She did a double-take when she saw him sitting on the window ledge, and her eyes went straight to the floor, where he had left the Stanley knife untouched, exactly where it had fallen. She sat back on the bed.

'Sorry,' she said.

The word startled him. It was, in the circumstances, so entirely inappropriate it almost overbalanced him. What was she, this divine creature, who apologised to someone who must have given her the fright of her life? Was she so schooled to please she said sorry for being sick to a thief? He felt desperately foolish and ashamed, and, perversely, still smarting from being told he looked silly. She still looked magnificent.

'Don't say that,' he mumbled. 'It's me who should say that. Shouldn't have done this. Sorry. I thought you'd have some big, hairy-chested man in here with you.'

She giggled.

'If only. Now what was it you wanted?'

He cleared his throat.

'I really only came to explore. There's something

I'm looking for, you see, and I thought you might have it . . .'

'You *climbed* in?' she asked.

'I said so.'

'Can you climb out?'

'I suppose so, but I was rather relying on immobilising the alarm which doesn't cover this bit, picking a lock if need be, I'm good at that, and going out the door. If that's all right with you.'

'Fine,' she said. 'But you've got to take that bloody awful picture. Is there anything else you'd like?'

He thought, sitting on the window ledge, one leg crossed over the other, with one foot wagging.

'I hadn't actually had a chance to look. I was rather distracted by you.'

He could no longer disguise his voice. The neutral accent would never give him away. The richness of her voice surprised him and added to her charm.

'Another time, then,' she said, getting to her feet, tapping his shoulder and leading the way out of the room. Her touch was electric through Lycra. His bum was stiff; the cap was still over his eyes. She would never know him again. He followed her into the vestibule bit where he had waited for *zing*, and watched as she went into the room through which he had entered and came back smartly with a small painting wrapped in a towel. She deposited it in his arms, and he stood awkwardly with his arms wrapped round the thing. She led him down the long corridor to the door, opened it and stood back from it.

'There's one of those buzzer release thingies for the front door, so I'll give you two minutes to get

95

out, buzz it and then it closes all by itself. So you'd better be quick, Mr Burglar. Just get rid of it. Goodnight.'

He went. There was no choice but to go, fumbling down endless stairs where he would otherwise have run, clutching the *thing* to his chest. And he did not want to climb. He was shaking like a leaf in rain and his muscles seemed an impediment, so he had to get out and breathe air and ... On the bend of the wide stairs, level with Sarah's door, at which he looked longingly and said no, he heard voices. Oh Jesus, that gorgeous bitch had called for the cavalry, buzzed them in instead, and here they were, coming to collect him. A posse of boys in blue, quicker to respond to the calls of the rich than the poor, thundering upstairs to find a damsel in distress and a man in a silly cap halfway down with a stolen *thing* in his arms and no nerves in his whole body. Oh, shit.

Only it did not sound like the cavalry. It sounded furtive, a posse of people coming upstairs without putting on the lights. Sarah's door to her smaller, almost forgotten flat was recessed, with a small security light next to the bell. He flattened himself against it, obscuring it, looking towards the dim light from the window which, at this point, also led into the well of the building and gave blurred, indistinct light. He imagined himself as a doorstop and crouched alongside Sarah's door like a dead dog. She had a huge letterbox low in her door which he could feel through his shoulder blades. The movement towards him seemed to have paused on the stairs. Steven uncrouched, shoved the painting through the slit, pushed the surrounding towel after it, put the black gloves back on his hands and crouched again, with his gloved hands over his face, first and second finger V-signed, showing only his eyes.

Like the eyes of a cat on a country road, ready to reflect, if only there was light to reflect. The shuffling continued towards him and he had an inexplicable conviction, based on nothing at all, that it had nothing to do with him. The shaking stopped; he simply shrank. Inside the cap, his head was damp with sweat. Steven only ever sweated from his head. A posse rose up the stairwell into sight. The posse consisted of a couple, dragging the reluctant form of a girl by the armpits, while she grunted without making any more protest than non-cooperation, so that her feet dragged on the ground and the stairs barked her shins but she still stepped, one in three. Steven had done that stuff at school when he had been bullied, pretending to be hurt when he wasn't, but he knew he could not judge if this was voluntary. There was a slight *clink* from a bright chain round her neck. He wondered if she was thumped or drugged, opened the slit of his fingers. Level with his own, he caught the other set of eyes of the woman, dragging, pretending to be dragged or being dragged upstairs. Minty. The eyes met: hers blinked and closed; his remained open, so fixed he imagined them as spotlights. The posse of the couple, and the man in the rear with nothing to do but pick up Minty's feet, wearily continued their dreary process out of sight.

It was Minty, even though he had not immediately remembered the name. The only thing he remembered about Minty was that she had a paintable face and a story and she was the same girl he had seen once, sitting forlornly with Fritz

97

downstairs, and he had been briefly bored by Sarah talking about her. He had not shared her concern, could not see why the girl couldn't just *go*. But the sight of a woman being dragged was shocking, sinister with overtones of rape and savagery, except for the fact they all looked so tired, more like a sullen family bringing home an errant daughter. They did not act as if they were embarking on any kind of party. It was more the fatigued footsteps of work being done en route to a funeral. Still, he stood and waited, outraged enough to race after them yelling *Oi, what do you think you're doing?* until he realised what he was. The burglar in the building, looking one, dressed like one, with a skullcap on his head and a burglar's implements strapped to his waist and stolen property shoved through a letterbox.

Steven raced downstairs to the empty foyer. The front door was unbudgeable smeared glass: he had missed the time slot the Vision had given him. She would not be standing by her own front door waiting to let him out, she would presume him long gone with relief . . . she would be putting that knife back under her feather-strewn pillow. His alternative clothes were round the back by the dustbins. There was a way from here to there, but he could not think of it.

The shaking started again. Post-climb nausea. He was hideously visible in front of the glass door, as exposed as if he was naked. The traffic outside passed slower than by day, but it still passed, the noise of it insulated. It would be easy to bypass the lock, if only he were not so ridiculously visible through the glass door, and if only he could concentrate. Instead he slunk back upstairs again.

Shivering and shaking, he leant against Sarah's bell. He had lost track of time.

He was leaning against the door and the bell, normally used only by Fritz since all other callers announced themselves at the front door. Hurt stung his eyes when Sarah did not reply. Surely she knew that the times he stayed with her he also desired to protect her? She *should* be there when he needed her. The refrain, what about me, what about me, was beginning to echo as he slumped against the door, until it opened so suddenly he fell across the threshold on to the painting he had posted through, landing against it so that the sharp edge of the rudimentary frame of the canvas dug into his ribs. He groaned and rolled over, exposing belly and groin, legs outside the door, torso inside, and looked up to see his sister looking like an avenging angel in that dressing gown, with a knife in her hand. Not a discreet knife, either: a big, fuckoff kitchen knife, suitable for sawing raw meat, and all he could think of to say was, Oh God, sis, not another one. I'm in love. Forget everything else, I've just had *zing*.

*     *     *

Love. A subject men rarely discussed, John thought long after the tail end of a meal best consigned to memory for its culinary insignificance, late service, poor quality and startling price, which his companion Richard Beaumont did not question, just waved away in the manner of a Londoner. They had begun late, in this wretched hotel where 'late' meant resentment, because John had been called out, did not get there until ten, an unheard-

99

of hour to eat in these parts, where the curtains came down and the closed sign was up long before that. True, they were a little slurred, the pair of them, at whatever the hell hour it was in the morning, alone in a restaurant with a view of the sea and bright moon, magnificent through clouds which disfigured the power of the thing and made it all wonky. The staff had long since given up on them and gone home. It was that nice degree of inebriation, all loose tongues and freedom of speech, and nothing to care about except the comfort of communicating with someone of the same sex and like mind. John told himself it was brilliant, and then amended his own description to stimulating. Brilliant conversations were those one had with women. It was the utter and complete frankness of the man that was so appealing, and the raving honesty it inspired in himself.

They had begun to order and eat when the others were ending. The hotel aspired to the old-fashioned, not to say outdated, standards of service which insisted that the waitresses wore black dresses and white pinafores while not insisting they knew anything about food or how to put it on the table. There was one smart French lad who knew better and was clearly loathed and feared by the rest. Their own table attendant, when finally allocated, redeemed her clumsiness by a pretty smile and plenty of leg. John had noticed how Richard looked at her and the other two girls, who were quite different in shape and size. He watched their movements as they advanced and retreated with unabashed curiosity and attention. It took a long time to get their attention, so there was plenty of opportunity. John watched Richard watching

100

and was amused by it, wondering if any of them would notice or complain, or offer to slap the customer's face. But then, they were in a bit of a cleft stick, he supposed. You could not say you had noticed a customer looking at your legs when you were also pretending not to have seen him yet. Richard Beaumont also watched a group containing two women as they left the restaurant, intently enough to be making an inventory of what they wore, leaning over to watch them until they had gone. His attention to them was curiously impersonal. Then he looked at the waitress's feet as she went away with their orders.

'I do wish they still wore high heels,' he said wistfully. 'But I suppose it's bad for their feet.'

'Would you like stockings and suspenders, too?'

'Of course. Wouldn't you?'

'I have to confess, I would like to imagine it. But what I would do if actually presented with the sight, I really don't know. Do you always look at women so closely?'

Richard sighed, and bit into a bread roll with good strong teeth.

'Yes. They fascinate me. The form in all its varieties fascinates me. I'm afraid it embarrasses my wife. Not my previous wife, who understood it for what it was, but my present wife who is ridiculously young and finds it insulting. Which is terribly odd, don't you think, for someone who is always the most beautiful creature in the room or the street. I forced myself to stop doing it for the first year or so of being married to her, but the habit's ingrained. Live models are hard to find, you see. You have to watch all the time and imprint them in memory.'

101

'You could be had up for being a dirty old man.'

'I suppose I could, but most mature women know the difference between looking and leching, and I find it extraordinary that anyone, male or female, should think themselves defiled by the simple fact of being looked at, especially when, in my case, it's invariably with admiration. Whatever age or shape, I love looking at them.'

John nibbled, and smiled.

'Being stared at could be threatening. I don't dare do it. But that might be because I don't want to be reminded of how frustrated I am. How much I'd like to bed one of them, and be good at it.'

'It could be construed as threatening, I suppose. But it is the nature of the male beast to observe the other, and the nature of an artist, even a not very good male artist, to look wherever he's allowed. I mean, just look at the shape of that leg.'

A plump leg skirted by their table en route to the kitchen. A slab of leg, John found himself thinking, leading beneath the black skirt to a wobbly bottom, not something he found appealing.

'It's the variety that is so extraordinary,' Richard went on. 'And you simply can't afford to miss another variation. You need it for the memory bank. And you should do something about this frustration. Lack of sex addles a man's mind, just as much as too much of it.'

He leaned forward to take another bread roll from the basket, his third. John doubted if it would affect his appetite. He felt he was issuing questions like a parrot, but he supposed that was habit, and he was invigorated by the responses.

'I thought you painted landscapes.'

'I do, but I'm enamoured by the idea of a female

form in a landscape. Have you ever noticed how a landscape curves? Dips into hollows, seems to move? Often seems to mirror the form of a body. I see women rising out of landscapes. That's why that body on the cliff seemed entirely natural. It was as if she had grown there. I felt I was seeing what I'd seen before. Maybe it's a boy's dream, coming across a pliant body in long grass. This must sound perfectly weird.'

He laughed, a loud but musical sound, refreshingly unselfconscious. The same waitress arrived with the fish, smoked trout in his case, salmon for his host. Neither looked particularly appealing, but Richard ate with the enthusiasm of someone who did not care what he ate as long as it was food, pausing only to look at her as she retreated.

'Are you married?' Richard asked. John nodded with his mouth full. The food was better than it looked.

'Was. She died.'

'Tell me about it.'

Oh no, men did not talk about their marriages. They did not, in John's experience, talk about the intimate side of their lives. In all the years of talking to Edwin, did he know if the man lived alone, or with another man or a woman? They would talk about their children, rarely their spouses. He chewed thoughtfully, then answered. The wine Richard had ordered was far better than the fish. Let me do it, he'd said; we'll just have the best.

'I'm married to a ghost. She died of cervical cancer, three years ago, never bothered me with it until it was too late. My daughter blames me. Says I

103

should have cured her. And I should have been able to. Very stoic and efficient, my wife. The guilt comes from the fact that we'd scarcely communicated for years. I bored her, and kept her. I shouldn't have taken so much of her life without honestly loving her. Or thinking ahead, instead of just wallowing in work and a comfortable enough status quo. And despising her for not being able to leave and try it on her own, just like I couldn't. So she lives with me still, in my guilty conscience. And from beyond the grave she encourages other women to torment me. About which I do nothing, and can hardly blame her.'

'Oh, what rubbish. Guilt's useless. Say sorry and get on with it. But see here, loneliness gets to be a habit. And it's no basis for making a choice, although that's the way we normally do it.' He paused, with a sudden gleam in his eye. 'You need a transitional woman. I should introduce you to this friend of mine. You need a kind, sexy lady to clear your mind. Worked for me.'

'At my age? Chance would be a fine thing,' John laughed. 'She'd have to be a listener and bloody patient. She'd have to be ... never mind. She doesn't exist, not here. They think I'm a depressive misanthrope in this town, and they're halfway right. I feel as if I live on the other side of the glass. Not like you. You seem to be sorted.'

'Different for me. I'm the marrying kind. I loved being married, didn't want anything else. If I'm brutally honest, I *need* to be married, need a woman in my life, just the one, perfectly bloody incomplete without, blundering around like a drunken bull after my wife died. Hopeless without sex and a female ear. Then Sarah, she's the friend I mentioned, looked after that side of things and knocked some sense into me, so that I was freed up to make a proper choice. I'm going to introduce you to Sarah.'

He grinned and waved his fork. He was a man who could eat and speak at the same time without one interfering with the other. He spoke like a person short of time, but not impatient.

'She's the sort of tart who sorts out your body and your mind, and puts things into perspective. Not wife material, thank God. Anyway, I fell in love with beauty and had to marry it. And no, I may not have been fair to her, and she'll probably leave me, but she will at least be well off. Do you think women can be bought?'

John chewed carefully, feeling slightly giddy.

'None I've ever been able to afford. No, I don't think they can be bought. And I think they need us less than we need them, if only they realised. They have the power, if only they knew.'

Richard nodded, and sighed.

'That's what I'm hoping mine will realise. That I don't own her, or she me. And yet she wants to be owned. I've only got a lease on her. That's all you ever have.'

Beef arrived, slightly cold and past its best. John wondered what his wife would have thought of Richard, could see her disapproval, and almost smiled at the thought. His mind was floating free. How strange to be talking about these passionate, mysterious creatures so dispassionately, and how cold-bloodedly accurate to equate depression and a sterile existence with a simple lack of sex.

'I began by wanting to paint birds,' Richard said. 'Of the feathered variety. But then I looked up and saw women floating among the clouds. And now it's shapes I want to paint. I think. I might go back to birds. I have, in a manner of speaking. Only I know so little about them. What do you know about ravens?'

John was becoming accustomed by now to the sudden changes of subject, even enjoying it and imagining that by the time they reached brandy and dessert they should be well into the realms of astrology or physics, and felt he was in the presence of a man who had smatterings of knowledge along a dozen lines and had waited until the brink of old age to find himself the victim of insatiable intellectual curiosity about life, the universe and everything. The artist, and that was how John described him to himself, was wisdom and naivety, impertinence and courtesy, all in one: a man who had confessed already that the greatest regret in his life had been the gaps in his education. He had read all his life, he said, not always wisely or well, and he had drawn, but never seemed to find an answer to any question without asking someone else. John found his own enjoyment invigorating and outrageous. Any subject would do.

The beef was tough and slower to be eaten. Richard's three bread rolls in advance of anything else were slowing him down.

'Ravens? Why ravens? Afraid I'm the softer type whose interest is flora, though birds have to come into that at some level, simply because their habitat and their habits might lead me to something I might see. You need Edwin on the subject of ravens, if he ever consents to talk to you, which he might, once the person who killed that girl is found. Or she's identified. Not yet, though. Why do you

106

want to know?'

'It still might have been *me* who killed her,' Richard said softly.

John ignored him. He liked to answer questions and he had been asked about ravens, and he was, as he rarely did, enjoying the sound of his own voice. He was floating on all this free-moving speech, the eclectic range of subject matter, the effortless chat. He was high on being heard.

'. . . Ravens are the subject of myth and legend, liking and loathing. They are the hardest birds to know because of their cleverness. They were celebrated by Edgar Allan Poe. remember. Quoth the raven *nevermore*, although it probably said *quork*. Noah sent a raven out from the ark to discover land, in advance of sending the dove. The raven did not come back, possibly distracted by carrion. It will eat any dead animal. Preferring not to kill the animal itself, it can pinch the kill of others, already dead. It will master its own environment and exist on fruit and grain, I understand. It will also kill other birds, or their young, if hungry. Its tribal allegiances are difficult to detect, Edwin says, except among cousins of the same genetic inheritance. I wonder if the only real loyalty is blood and genes? I doubt it. I like you tremendously, by the way. Ravens can certainly kill rabbits, but they prefer to find carrion rather than kill it. They'll approach the carrion with suspicion. How long were you up on the cliff before the rescue team came?'

'I don't know. It might have been hours. It was light and then it grew dark. Tell me more about ravens.'

'Oh stop, I'm almost at the end of my slender

knowledge. When there were sheep kept on the clifftop fields, a hundred years ago, they'd be guarded at lambing time because the ravens were famous for swooping down and taking out the eyes of a sleeping lamb. All I can really say is they would like what's on our plates, but they might not eat it all. They are hungry and cautious and curious, they like bright things.'

'Brutal.'

'Oh yes, what isn't?'

The doctor and the artist were objective enough to discuss the scavenger while eating what the scavenger would eat in a raw, disintegrating state. It did not affect Richard, who chewed agreeably, but John noticed he was concentrating more on the potato and the damp green cabbage that surrounded it.

'They're so beautiful, though,' Richard said. 'That sheen they have, like black ice.'

'The beautiful and the wicked tend only to go together because of their genetic inheritance of power,' John said, sententiously, putting his knife and fork together over his plate. It had tasted a great deal better than it looked and he realised he was pleasantly, controllably mellow, as well as being, for the first time in a long time, content to remain ever so slightly out of control. 'And it is always a mistake to make comparisons between the kingdoms and habits of birds and those of ourselves. We behave like ravens, rather than the other way round. No need to be shocked. We take our habits from the animal and bird, not the other way round. We're on the same spectrum and they were there first. They must laugh at us.'

'Thank you for that.'

Richard's uproarious laugh filled the now empty room.

Two hours later, they were still there. All the waitresses and their legs had gone home. They had touched upon another tangent, and then another, not yet including the tide and the stars they could see from the window. There was the view of the port, the sea and the sky. The food was long since forgiven. The artist could eat; got second wind on the choice of a stiff pudding and went at it with a will, while John stopped at that and toyed with coffee. Please, just bring us the port and the brandy, will you, John had said amiably to Miss Smiley face with the legs. Put it on the bill, it'll be all right, go home, why don't you? And watched her as she walked away. They were back, or was it forward, on another topic.

'Something you said earlier,' Richard was saying, slowly but unhesitatingly, 'about the beautiful and the wicked going together. On account of a genetic quantity which has always given them power. And I suppose you meant beauty equals power, and power corrupts. I don't buy that, but then I've never been beautiful, only powerful. My wife is beautiful, though. Will it make her wicked, do you think?'

'No, of course not. Although beauty creates temptation.'

Richard had his head resting on his hand, staring out at the sea.

'Oh good. It would be nice if she had that propensity, though. She's so keen on respectability, disgraceful in one so young. And she thinks someone like me embodies it. It must have been part of my appeal. I've grown into it, I suppose. With a suit on, I look like what I am. Financier, founder of insurance company, person who serves on committees, consultant to charities. But they don't know how I started. How I got the seed corn to start a business.'

'We were all boys once, and shall be again, won't we?'

'It was easy in the seventies. I got a balaclava and robbed a bank. Best moment of my life. Better than sex.'

John had the strange feeling of having died and gone to heaven.

'You never did.'

'I did so.'

Then they were giggling until it hurt. Snorting and spluttering with it, shushing each other on the way out through the silent foyer, perfectly delighted with one another. Phone numbers already exchanged, and changes of subject almost de rigueur. And so they parted, slapping each other on the back, lightly. A gesture of friendship which was never going to include platitudes.

Hitting the night air as they waited for John's taxi, suddenly more serious, they hugged one another fiercely.

'Don't leave me, John, not now I've found you. I've needed this.'

'You don't get rid of me so easy. And I've to come and see this friend of yours, and that painting of yours. Soon. I'll miss you.'

The taxi hove into sight.

'Bloody soon, John, you daft sod. Make it soon.'

John smiled as he tripped over his own doorstep. Soon sounded good. A good word, *soon*. Washing his face, it occurred to him that all the sudden changes of subject could be the result of defective memory, and thought, that didn't matter at all. The man was a life force.

Tomorrow was soon enough for duty.

And then the image of the girl came back.

Ah, yes, another woman would be nice, to displace her.

## CHAPTER SIX

### *Respect all wildlife*

Sarah Fortune, for all her habits, knew the difference between night and day, and left almost all conversation with her brother until breakfast. An early breakfast, by which time she had retrieved the clothes from beyond the dustbins, dusted him down. She was a night owl, but not that much. Nor did she share his capacity for instant sleep. Her own in the intervening three hours had not been refreshed by indigestible, now calmer rage, slightly mollified by the fact that Steven was also a little pale and wan and exhausted by his rushed explanation of events. She let me out, I couldn't get out, so I came back, was how he had ended it. Sorry.

The picture with the rough frame sat propped up against the back of a chair, next to the boiler, while both sat facing it in the kitchen, eating fresh bread and butter, like they had as children at tea. In a minute the phone would ring. Sarah knew it was going to be that kind of day. She was unspeakably angry with him, but for the time being it best remained unspoken. The knife was back in the drawer.

They looked at the painting.

It was highly coloured in the centre, brilliant reds and flesh tints. Beyond the centre, nothing to do with anything, there were vaguer blues, the suggestion of water, and a small clutch of pink, all of it littered with dark splodges.

'I wish he didn't use so much paint,' Sarah said. 'It's distracting. Like he was carving with it and hadn't finished yet. It needs a strong light and a different angle. Shoving it through a letterbox and covering it with a towel hasn't helped either. The paint's so thick, it's scarcely dry.' She picked off a thread of dark-blue towelling from the corrugated surface.

Steven nodded speechlessly.

'Haven't you got to go to work today?'

He nodded again. She rose and poured another cup of coffee. He was dressed in his loose-fitting suit, with a plaster over a small, sore puncture wound in his buttock; she was wearing her dressing gown, the colouring of which suited them both. They both turned back to the painting.

'It's not finished,' Steven murmured, mournfully. 'I sort of like it, but it scares me. A figure surrounded by vultures. I hope she wasn't sunbathing. And I'm very sorry about damaging it.'

'There's not much damage, and never mind that,' Sarah said, drily. 'You broke into the flat of the wife of an almost millionaire and stole it. It should frighten you to death.'

112

'I didn't steal it. She gave it to me. I told you. And oh, Sarah—'

'I know, I know, you talk in your sleep, and you're in love. With someone who could put you in prison and is probably thinking of it as we speak. Now, look at this thing . . .'

'It isn't a *thing*, it's a painting. Don't you dare call it a thing.'

'Listen, Steven, you're a hopeless aesthete, and so blind with the looking you can't see anything. Does it move you at all?'

It moved her, although Sarah reserved her most intense responses for real faces, and only occasionally for paintings. Such as the cow in the field in the next-door room, too big for its place, too intrusive, which was there because it inspired an absurd amount of daily happiness. There must be a word for a response like that.

'No. It doesn't *zing* to me because it's interesting but foul.'

'Doesn't *zing*. Therefore it's a thing without meaning for you. And for the first time in your pathetic life you've got a real buzz from a real woman, probably because she looked like a poster of those old film stars you loved. I am sincerely pleased for you. A little lust never comes amiss. Well, maybe you were hyped up at the time, but you have to accept it warped your judgement. Why on earth did you take this away? There's a fine collection of glass, some highly saleable paintings, plenty for a common little thief—'

'She asked me to take it. And come back for the rest. Sarah, she was lovely, I can't tell you.'

'Yeah, she stabbed you.'

He ignored this as well as the rising tide of anger

113

which made her want to get the knife back out of the drawer and stab him again wherever it would hurt most. Instead, she pointed at the painting.

'What do you see?'

He considered it.

'A naive palette. He's not good at mixing colours. Relies on primary, and building them up, like walls against what he sees. Too much physical matter. He's making defences, and he's trying out stuff as he goes. I don't like it, much. Amateur. Good, though.'

'Yes, but what do you *see*?'

He considered, with maddening swiftness.

'I see a mess. Done by a painter on a learning curve, long before peak. And I can see why she wanted it out of the house. It's only small, but it's powerful and unpleasant.'

He was on his feet, straightening his tie, preparing to leave, turning away from the thing as if it had nothing to do with him. She hated all men at that moment.

'Sit down.'

He sat. The phone rang.

'Stay there while I answer it.'

Steven sat gazing into space, gazing anywhere where he did not have to look at the thing, conjuring other images into his mind. *Oyster white and purple, red lips.* A tear rolled down one cheek and he brushed it away, half hearing Sarah's voice murmuring in the other room. She came back and leant in the doorway, blocking his way out.

'Right, dear, now here's a conundrum. Richard Beaumont, painter of this *thing*, husband of the lovely Lilian, that's her name, by the way . . .'

'Lilian,' he murmured. 'Lilian.'

114

'Is on his way home and wishes to call here for a chat this afternoon, possibly with a friend. Steven, you shit, why did you have to choose *here*? I suppose you were thinking of just buggering off and leaving me with this? What if you run into the lovely Lilian on the way out? She'll recognise you for sure. Fritz knows you. How am I going to get this painting back?'

'Lilian doesn't want it back,' he said indignantly. 'She wanted it taken away. And she won't recognise me. Not without a skullcap furrowing my face and making me look like a monkey, no hair and, oh God, what did I look like?'

'But what about Richard? *He'll* want it. *He* painted it, and he probably hasn't finished it. Am I to sit and talk to my old friend with his latest work of art on the premises? Or talk to Lilian, for that matter, without mentioning her burglar? Oh Christ, what a mess you've made.'

'I was looking for something special, and I found something special. She won't recognise me,' Steven was repeating sadly. 'She'll never know me again.'

The thought was so terrible it made him choke on the words.

'Never,' he repeated.

'Oh, shut up. No, she probably wouldn't; observation's not her strong point anyway, but what about me? What am I supposed to do?'

He took her by the shoulders and moved her to one side.

'You'll manage, sis, you usually do. And you won't give me away, will you? You'd never do that.'

'And the advantage to me is that you can never come here again.'

He pecked her cheek. 'I love you, too, sis,' he

115

intoned bitterly, which left her fuming with the usual feeling it was all her fault. As the front door closed behind him she ran to it, opened it again and listened intently until his footsteps had faded away, then stood there listening to silence. There were a couple of feathers on the hall carpet, disturbed by the draught. Fussily, she picked them up, hearing more footsteps coming towards her. They were the weary, wheezy footsteps of Fritz, with the post. She went back inside, counting on her fingers.

Supposing he had lied ... Supposing he had attacked Lilian, he was capable; supposing ... No, he had not lied, no one, not even he, could invent what he had described; he had been too tired to lie. Lilian would still be asleep. Lilian never talked to Fritz. Fritz already knew Steven as an innocent, irregular visitor. Richard Beaumont had never met Steven. Lilian was playing some game with Richard, the hell with them all. Back in the kitchen she picked up the painting, carried it through to the living room and propped it on the floor. Leaving the curtains closed, she focused one of the spotlights on to the surface and stood back.

Seen from this angle, with the light raking and raising the contours of the paint, she could see what he was about, and the central image of the painting assumed sudden and startling shape.

It was a corpse; that's what it was, unmistakably a corpse. Hideous in its dead certainty. And nice, worldly-wise Richard Beaumont was coming to see her later, announced by the phone call, bringing a friend he wanted her to meet. Richard, who seemed to have crouched over this corpse, pimping for a friend. He's very nice, Richard said. He needs someone like you. Life was rich.

*     *     *

The problem with having a good time and drinking too much was the morning after, when John struggled to describe to himself how he felt. 'Corpselike' seemed appropriate for the colour of his skin, until he remembered that corpses were devoid of feeling and retained only the capacity to inspire it in others. And he was not without feeling, this morning, far from it. He was stuffed to the gills with feeling, and it was mainly loneliness. Not an unhappy loneliness, but a symptom of what companionship did: made you lonelier later. Until, with the remembrance of pleasure and laughter, the guilt came in on the wake and you remembered duty, towards the living and the dead.

In the absence of any other, more original escape mechanism to clear his head, he got in his car and aimed for the cliffs, avoiding the car park and the normal route, finding one of the other, less known accesses to the cliff path, a mile further on, where his was the only car parked on the edge of a field. He was deliberately choosing a treacherous part of the cliff route, Cable Bay, where the cliff had partially crumbled two years before. The walkers' path was re-routed inland to avoid the massive fissure. There were danger signs, warnings of further erosion which he deliberately ignored. It was time to get off the path. And yet he felt light-hearted and happy, talked out, renewed, all inhibitions gone. Wanting life as well as mistrusting it, wanting *more*.

And yet there was a path of sorts, looking like the

117

work of a single man or animal, slithering into a new valley. What was it Richard Beaumont had said before they parted? Something along the lines of: 'Don't leave me, John. I don't make many friends, not in my world.' And one of them saying, 'You don't get rid of me that easy. You call me whenever you want, whatever you need.' John was resisting the urge to call him right now, just to say hello, are you as bad as I am? Come on a walk with me, please. Falling into liking was a bit like falling in love. He missed the bugger and worried for him.

Wrong fucking word, but it was the friendship, the artless intimacy, the free-ranging sometimes daft conversation he had missed for so long, the bloody honesty which had been such a joy and which made him so lonely now he simply wanted to continue where they had left off. Why can't *men* phone one another like girls do? He was angry with the women in his life who had persuaded him at various times that they were all he ever needed, when perhaps all he had needed was a man friend who talked with all the shamelessness he had always associated with women, but remained a man, without guile, for all that.

Shamelessness: a fine, gothic word that echoed in his mind as he walked down a steep hill, faster than usual for all the frailty created by his headache, but energising with the dull thump of it, so that he had already walked further than usual in an unfamiliar piece of landscape before he let himself pause. The sun shone. He associated sunshine with headaches and welcomed the fact that the light hit so hard it went straight through his eyes, like a laser, towards the source of the pain. Loneliness was biodegradable into physical energy, he decided; it had a purpose in life. It brought him here to a different and deserted part of the cliff route where he rarely came, half looking for something that might be an answer, and lo and behold, to his left, he saw the common spotted orchid, beginning to mean business with its glossy, purple-spotted leaves, and then further on *Brassica oleatracia*, contrastingly tall and straggly, with grey-green leaves, the unconvincing ancestor of the cultured cabbage he never liked to eat. There were the tight-fisted buds of yellow flowers. The knapweed with its spiky red head, ready to flower later in the year, something to look forward to, and further along this route he remembered that the path dipped into another valley. Where the flowers that had once flourished on overgrazed land now gave way to small trees and shrubs. While he mourned the displaced flowers, the tree he loved best was the holm, a rare, evergreen oak which never grew tall, simply wide, and then hawthorn and blackberry, and the ones he called the friendly aliens, growing bravely from seeds and berries transported from distant, cultivated gardens, into which they might have arrived from the other side of the world. There were pathways and airways for every living thing.

He was feeling physically better now, although not wholly so, and was planning to walk one more quarter mile and make himself go down to the water so that he could walk back *up* the broken chalk and then scramble upwards from the shallow slope he remembered from last year, and that would finally restore sanity through sheer physical effort. And besides, he had a sudden desire to be right by the sea and drowned by the sound of it, looking back at the cliff rather than always looking down. He found this a sympathetic place, where the cliff had obligingly shown itself to be vulnerable, crumbling clumsily and spreading outwards into a shallower outline. New life grew here: fresh creatures would find residence. He was scolding himself as he moved: why did he not come to this spot more often? Poor Edwin warned him off, but that did not explain why he always walked the same part of the route. Because that was where there were people. He hated himself for having to admit that he usually came to the cliffs not to be alone but for company, and it was probably he who had sought out Edwin, rather than the other way round. For company. Now that was a thought, such as who needed who in this world? He must make more effort with Edwin. No one else ever did, but then no one ever knew him. A shadow crossed his path, almost blinding him. Edwin, stepping out from behind a shrub where he must have sat to be so invisible, looming so close that in miles of open land they almost collided. His fists were clenched.

'Are you following me?' he asked, belligerently.

For a small moment, John was frightened. His welcoming smile faded.

'I've just seen *Brassica oleatracia*,' he said. 'It's cabbage, you know. It's really rather pointless.'

Edwin unclenched his fists. He fingered the scarf round his neck, loosening it as if he was hot. There was the rare sight of perspiration on his brow. Edwin never broke sweat, even after the usual fourteen miles. Perhaps it was a disappearing hangover, like his own. He was thinking, briefly, of how little he had tried to know Edwin. Edwin didn't drink, smoke; this Edwin was a stranger, in

120

retrospect, another person he had failed. Perhaps the only people he did not fail were those who were bullies, demanding his attention.

'And why should I be following you, Edwin? You know I'd never keep up.'

Edwin relaxed further, unknotted the twisted scarf and used it, still twisted, to mop his brow. John gazed at him, fascinated by the tremor of his hand and the intimidating harshness of his voice.

'I told you not to come here, and I don't want you going any further. Where's that friend of yours? That fucking artist? Only it looks as if he might have been at it again, the bastard. *Don't* go any further down this path.'

The path was fitter for a dog or goat than a man. Some of it was covered with bramble.

'All right, I won't. But why not? You don't own the pathways, Edwin, and you shouldn't spit at people, like you did yesterday.'

'Why? You want to know why you shouldn't go down? Well I don't want to shock you, Doc, but there just might be another body down on those rocks, and it just might be something to do with your friend. He's a fucking jinx on this place. Anyway, there's something wedged in the rocks, came in with the tide. Something nasty.'

He looked at John's white face, appeared to relent, stopped fiddling with the scarf. 'Only kidding, Doc. But I tell you what there is. There's a raven's nest under the cliff, over there.' He flung out his arm. 'Ravens with babies. It's the first I've ever seen here, first ever, the darlings. Took 'em weeks to build. They nest early. Fucking wonderful. I can't have them scared, and I can't have anyone knowing, see? Not yet, not till the little ones can

121

manage on their own. Soon. Anyone sees, anyone disturbs, they'll never come back. I'll kill anyone who scares them. Come on, Doc, come away, and don't come back.'

He paused for breath and began to reknot the scarf.

The intensity of his voice was as sinister as the movements of his fingers. John kept quiet for the beat of a whole half minute, while Edwin finished with his malodorous piece of cloth. He fancied he could smell the perspiration of months of wear on Edwin's scarf. There was no one else in sight. Why had he never noticed this aspect of neglect in him? Or was it new? Edwin had his good clothes. Or had he never cared enough to notice? Edwin put his hands on his hips.

'All right. That fucking artist never came this far. Wouldn't know the fucking way, I suppose, little short legs on him, anyway. And if it is a body down there, I reckon it came in with the tide, from somewhere else. Likely it's a sheep, I don't give a fuck about it.' He hesitated, and John got the impression he wished he had never spoken.

'But the ravens, that's another matter. They're a fucking miracle. Get out of here, Doc, before I throw you out.'

Edwin did not care for human beings; he only cared about birds. John knew this already, but it was uncomfortable to have it confirmed, as well as his wilful ignorance of the man, and he had the fleeting thought that if he himself had not appeared, with the look of a person aiming for the rocks on this calm day, Edwin would never have mentioned the existence of a body. If there was a corpse, Edwin would have preferred it to remain as

122

it was, out of common sight, a possible feast for a family of ravens. Ravens would be rarer than hen's teeth on this part of the coast. They would draw crowds and destruction; Edwin was keeping them secret. Maybe even keeping them fed. Ravens ate rodents, birds, fish, carrion. John was dredging back remnants of knowledge about *Corvus corax*, forgotten knowledge surprising him as it had last night. There was a slight memory of a newspaper article about dozens of ravens, roosting in the next county and flying away. About how they were cautious and shy but incessantly curious, took away meat and hid it, were drawn, like magpies, to bright things. Another, appalling image came to mind.

'So what do we do, Edwin? You'll have to call the police and etcetera, even for a sheep. It'll have an owner and its own infections. We can do it now. I've got a phone.'

'You would, wouldn't you?' Edwin said bitterly. 'I've got one, too, only I don't know how they work.' He tapped at a phone in his breast pocket. John was surprised. Edwin and a mobile phone simply did not go together.

'Why did you have to come this way today? All right, I was kidding about the body.'

'Does anyone else know about the ravens, Edwin?'

'No. The botanists maybe, but they know fuck all and I saw them off before they went. Told them the cliff here's still likely to crumble. Told them it was dangerous, and it is.'

John took his phone out of his own pocket, levelling Edwin's stare.

'Well, why do the ravens have to be mentioned if I call the police?'

'Oh God, you're a fool, you really are. As soon as *anyone* comes the news would spread like wildfire. They'd fly and maybe die. What would it cost you to say nothing at all?'

He made to grab the phone but John, for once, was quicker, putting it behind his back and behaving as if Edwin had never lunged for it. This close, it was not only Edwin's scarf that smelled: he reeked. The lined face was runnelled with sweat. For a split second John thought Edwin would hit him. He spoke quickly.

'No rush, then, is there? I'll just go, shall I, Ed? Would that be better? I haven't seen you, haven't seen ravens, haven't seen a body, OK? And when you get to the other end of the line, *you* report whatever it was you've seen. In your own time. But you must report it, OK?'

Edwin nodded.

John looked once at the sea, and retraced his steps. The path was slippery, as if it too sweated anxiety, and suddenly he hated it all. The sun, the sea, the sky, prissy plants and flowers, everything. Loathed it. He tramped back up the headland without looking back, and once on the path broke into a shambling, energy-wasting run that was short-lived and left him breathless. *Ravens, bright things, carrion, shameless.* The cliffs were no longer a solace. Edwin was not a friend, nor he a friend to Edwin: he was just another failure of the dry years, and he longed for the presence of giggling crowds. He wanted faces and voices and he was glad he had brought the phone.

\*     \*     \*

Two hours later he was sitting in a train opposite Richard Beaumont, both on their way to London, watching Richard bite into a sandwich. The man was uncanny.

'I don't know why,' Richard was saying, 'but I knew you'd phone. Perhaps I was just missing you. I'd already made arrangements. Easily cancellable arrangements, but arrangements. Presumptuous of me, I daresay, but that's what I'd done.'

'Why?'

'Why' seemed be John's favourite word. The story of his life. Always 'why', never 'how'.

'I'd been thinking of you and your wife problems. Believe I know all about those. And I thought, what John needs is a break away from everything and a day or two with crowds. And I told you, I wanted you to meet this friend of mine. She's very good at straightening out men's heads. And we did say soon.'

'I don't want my head straightening out. It sounds painful.'

'You want different scenery.'

'Yes, I do.'

He was calmly forceful and John could see how the man could have manipulated both people and money.

'And you knew that if there was a second body that might have meant the police coming round to see me? Not that there's any connection, but they might make one. Was I up there, sketching when this one came ashore? Is it me brings them in? Something like that. So it's best we're both out of the way.'

John nodded, took the other half of the proffered sandwich and put it down. The colour of the tomato was horribly vivid against the dead white of the bread.

'Yes, that did occur to me. It was an excuse to phone. And there was something else . . . I wanted to see that painting.'

'Don't make excuses, John. You're allowed to be spontaneous. Otherwise, I would have had to phone you. You were on the edge of a breakdown last week. Run away, why don't you? I know what you need. Female company and sex works a treat. Forget everything else.'

Such a cold, kind man. John Armstrong sat back and wondered if either of them was mad, or both. The body of the girl haunted him, Edwin haunted him, new life haunted him. He wanted to go with the flow.

*     *     *

Lilian rarely telephoned before deciding to visit Sarah. It was always a spur-of-the-moment thing, frequently because she was early for whatever she planned to do and killing twenty minutes with Sarah was as good a way as any. And besides, although Sarah was not always in residence, she was more often than not in the mornings, and it was mornings that Lilian was anxious to fill. Quite apart from that, this morning she was full of guilt of an unusual kind, and Sarah had a natural knack for assuaging pangs of conscience. Oh Lord, what had she done the night before? Was it a nightmare or a good dream? Anyway, Sarah had nothing better to do and always seemed pleased to see her, although, oddly enough, this morning there seemed to be a deal of hesitation. Maybe Sarah felt as weird, and wired as she did, although Lilian could not imagine why. She had nothing to do, poor old thing, but she looked as if she had not had enough sleep, and Lilian could empathise with that. Along with the guilt, she was suffering from a strange excitement. The place smelled pleasantly of coffee. Tidier than usual, Lilian noticed. A pity Sarah could not afford more nice things. Told to wait in the living room and not follow her into the kitchen since that was too messy for words, Lilian waited, tapping her foot, and avoided looking at the cow on the wall. Then she remembered her other resolution to try and appreciate painting, and looked at it more closely. Nothing flickered. It seemed to be inviting her to leave. She really did not like it.

'Nice to see you,' Sarah said. 'You're looking, how can I put it? slightly academic this morning. Are you meeting a professor for lunch? Or is it the new look?'

'This? Oh no, but since Richard won't deign to be back until much later I may as well be casual today.'

'Casual' to Sarah meant old clothes for the housework that had subsumed her energies and driven her mad with dislike of it for the last two hours. It was a reaction to events. Domestic chores should be done by men to quell their aggression. It was difficult to feel anything much after polishing wooden floors and scrubbing the floor in the kitchen, but it had improved her mood, ultimately, which was all it was for, and why men should try it. You could take the girl out of the small-town terraced house, but you could not take the clean-

127

doorstep mentality out of the girl, even if she was more naturally a bit of a slut. This was Lilian's thought about Sarah this morning. Otherwise, she was rehearsing a story, and she needed to tell it out loud.

The casual look, in her case, was an immaculate trouser suit with slender-heeled boots, a blouse buttoned almost to the chin, and somewhat severe, half-moon spectacles perched on her nose. As far as Sarah knew, Lilian had no problems with eyesight. How mean of her to hope that she did: would be useful, especially now, if it made it difficult for her recognise people. The painting, hidden in a kitchen cupboard, felt like a hot coin burning a hole in her pocket. It was only the spectacles that made Lilian's appearance relatively severe, and the trousers, since she usually wore short skirts, and with legs like that who wouldr't.

'I didn't mean academic, now I look at you,' Sarah said. 'I think *businesslike* would be more appropriate.' It was obvious that Lilian had not arrived in a hysterical state about being burgled in the night, so Sarah was beginning to relax. She had feared otherwise.

'Look, darling, I took your advice. Something had to be done.'

'What advice was that?'

'The other day, darling. You said I made Richard too comfortable. Something like that. Anyway, I took your advice about it. And now I feel bad. Tell me I was right, will you? Pretty please?'

She was sounding very little girlish, which Sarah had come to interpret as a bad sign, at least as far as Richard was concerned. It meant she was denying responsibility, looking for something to

128

blame, mimicking childhood behaviour. Not a luxury she had ever had, although there were men who loved this stuff. Never mind.

'My advice, was it? Making him uncomfortable. You'll have to tell me what you did to reduce the comfort level. I wouldn't approve of ripping up his clothes, for instance.'

'Oh, I'd never do that and he doesn't care about clothes anyway, but I'm afraid I got one of his paintings, messed it up and stuck it out with the rubbish. The rubbish has gone, hasn't it?'

'Yes, early this morning.' She had met them, down at the bins. 'Was it a recent painting?'

'Yes. I hated it. So I didn't do *much*, did I? Just enough to make him see it isn't always safe to leave his rubbish lying all over the flat.'

'Yes,' Sarah said faintly. 'I suppose that might do the trick. Only it might be wise to see what the reaction is before you do anything else.'

'And then he rang,' Lilian went on, 'from where he is, this morning. Told me he'd been out for dinner with a *man* he'd met in the hotel where he stays on the coast. Lovely man, he said. I can't tell you how relieved I am, Sarah.'

'Because it's a man? Well, you knew there was no question he was having a relationship with a woman, didn't you? Not his style.'

'Yes, of course I knew *that*, but it's always nice to know that if he's away and lonely ... well, you know. Anyway, then I started to feel guilty. And I thought of the other part of your advice.'

Sarah felt faint with relief, ready to hug this silly bitch. So that was the story, then. No man, particularly no brother of hers, had climbed up a series of drainpipes and burgled the rich wife upstairs. Lilian had not thrust a picture of a corpse at a Lycra-clad burglar, and even if she had, was never going to admit it. Steven was safe. The rich wife was telling a story which completely excluded him. Sarah felt vaguely hysterical.

'*You* said that I should try and understand Richard's passions. I mean, his painting passions. So I thought I'd go and look. At paintings and stuff. Today, tomorrow, all week. Do a few galleries. Get the gist. Then I can talk to him about it. Stop him feeling cross with me. But how do I say I got rid of the painting by mistake?'

'You went into the room and it fell on you,' Sarah suggested, not having the faintest idea which room she was talking about. 'I suppose it's large?'

'Oh no, not at all, it's very small. I could blame the cleaning lady, though she isn't supposed to go in there. Say she knocked it over by mistake.'

'Good idea, provided she doesn't get the sack.'

Lilian shivered at the very idea. 'Never, over my dead body. I can say *I* knocked it over and it broke, and was ruined, so she threw it away. That way it would be both our faults. Richard's too nice to sack anyone.'

'Paintings on canvas don't break, Lilian. Say it got smeared or something.'

*Shut up.*

Lilian hauled a live and vibrant body out of the armchair, drained her coffee and shook her legs to readjust the trousers until they fell just over the little tippy toes of her boots. Stop this, Sarah told herself. Shut up; be grateful that this is the version of what happened to a painting. What a lovely woman. And then, just as Lilian reached for her cerise, lightweight pashima and wrapped it round her elegant shoulders, she dropped another bombshell.

'Sarah? He did say, Richard I mean, that he was bringing back this nice, old doctor he had dinner with, to stay the night. I gather this doctor's single at the moment. And part of the reason for bringing him was that Richard thought you might like him. Isn't that nice of him? I'm sure he's not too old for you. But then I thought, Rich and I could probably do with a bit of time alone. I mean, there could be a bit of an argument and a bit of making up. Any chance he could stay with you?'

Oh God. The most unlikely people collaborated, without even knowing. Sarah was now furious with Richard. And because of Steven, she had to keep everybody sweet.

'I expect so. Tell you what, if he's a nerd, deaf dumb and blind, you have him, you've got more space. If he's OK, he can put up here. Only I charge sixty pounds per hour, plus VAT.'

Lilian trilled with laughter. It was an irritating version of the usual seductive chuckle. She picked up a duster she had found on the floor and placed it neatly on the table, still laughing.

'You're so funny, Sarah, really you are. You're a scream. Must go and look at art. Oh, I tell you what, why don't we go together, sometime? You wouldn't blind me with science, would you? And you should get out more. You always seem to be here in the morning.'

Lilian's mornings began no sooner than 10 a.m, at a time when Sarah might only just have got home. Well, they both lacked a work ethic, and the less Lilian knew of her neighbour's lifestyle, the better.

131

'Yes, I'll come and look at art with you. Next time Richard's away. I do it anyway. Hang on, I'll come down with you. Need to buy food.'

Need to check on Fritz, too, and what *he* might have seen and heard. He was there, polishing the mirror, smiling at first, and then nodding a formal 'good morning' to Lilian.

'Really,' Lilian said in a stage whisper as soon as they were outside, 'he might do the stairs as well.'

When Sarah came back with tea and whisky, cheese and wine, Fritz had gone. Good: there had been enough conversation for one morning. She was feeling totally outmanoeuvred, blackmailed by everyone into being *nice* to everyone so that Steven would be safe, and she was even going to have to be nice to Richard Beaumont's bloody friend. It was going to be a long day. She was very, very cross.

They sidled in in the late afternoon, Richard and his friend John. Richard was mellow and John was shy. Sarah made them tea. There was an exchange of pleasantries, where Sarah asked John if big cities were a shock after small towns. He said they were, this one most of all. He was tongue-tied. Sarah checked a sigh of impatience. Richard winked at her; it didn't suit him. She smiled and went out for more tea. Stood in her kitchen, furious.

Sarah Fortune knew very well how she augmented her income, by being a tart with a heart, as naturally promiscuous with her affections as anyone on the planet. It just came naturally, was all. Never a question of why?, but why not? At the moment, she resented it. Richard Beaumont might be a friend and a kind man, but he would always see her as a tart, and he was pimping for his friend, there was no doubt about that. Probably wanted to help him, somehow, and didn't know a better way. *Got a friend, Sarah, needs looking after, know what I mean?* Loaded words, and not the first time she had heard them, and she could always refuse, but what with Steven, and Lilian, and that blasted painting, it might be difficult. And she wasn't going to be doing anything with Mr Tongue-tied out there unless she found something to like. That was the rule: they had to be worth the effort.

John, the doctor, was gazing at the painting of the cow with the reverence of an acolyte, his face slowly and unconsciously changing expression, raising an eyebrow, wrinkling his nose, frowning then smiling, as if he was having a conversation with it. She watched him out of the corner of her eye as she spoke to Richard, as if it was a vicarage tea party and John was the mad one in the corner. Instead of a man experiencing *zing*. Then John knocked over the milk jug and did not seem to notice as he rose to look closer, and Sarah relaxed. This was familiar territory. He was another William, another Henry, another nice, awkward man. Richard gave her another wink, an imploring glance. 'Goodness,' he said. 'Must go.' It was hardly subtle.

'Well, that was hardly subtle, was it?' Sarah said as the door closed noisily behind him.

'No,' John said, faintly.

'Do you really like the cow?'

'Yes, I really do.'

There was no point in pussyfooting around, it never worked. It was usually better to trust people and take the consequences. He was a likeable man, reminding her of a bemused bird. There were enough good vibes with this fellow to allow instinct

133

to take over.

'What did Richard tell you about me?'

'Well, he gave me the impression you were a friend, and a sort of . . . counsellor.'

'For which, read amateur tart. Does that bother you?'

His face went white, then pink, and then he laughed, loudly and honestly.

'No, it doesn't. They were always my favourite patients. Only I can't afford you. Nor can I perform, I seem to have lost the knack. That Richard, he's a cunning bastard, isn't he?'

'Yes, he is. Don't worry about the tart angle. Richard told me you needed to talk. And I'm the kind of person who needs to listen. I've got a terrible addiction to talking, too. Shall we have a drink? I'm sick of tea and coffee, been drinking it all day.'

He shook his head, back to tongue-tied. There were purple hollows beneath his eyes, etched lines of weariness. She liked him, waited for him.

'Speaking for myself,' he said, 'I'd like to talk about Richard. He's been a marvellous shot in the arm for me, but I don't know him. And there is something the matter with him, you know. He worries me.'

'The memory, you mean? Yes, I've noticed. Do you always worry about people?'

'Oh yes. It's a habit. Thought I'd shaken it off, but I haven't. Wanted a quiet, pain-free life, and now I don't.'

They liked one another.

'Fine,' she said. 'We talk about Richard first. And what a cunning bugger he is. Call it tit for tat because, you see, I desperately need to know about *him*, and what he's been up to.'

'That's fine by me,' John said. 'I'd really like that.'

'Good, because I doubt if he'll be back. I'm afraid they might be having an almighty row upstairs because, as far as I can gather, they might love one another but they never talk about anything at all. Mind you, it's the hardest thing to do when you live together. Much easier with strangers.'

He could see a path between him and her. He had nothing to lose. Richard was right: he had been losing his mind.

'Keep my seat warm while I get some wine. Or would you prefer whisky?'

'Please.'

'I have it.'

He gazed at the somnolent, lumbering, grazing cow in the oversized painting, thought the scale was quite right and felt unaccountably content.

He felt safe. He forgot the cliffs, the bodies, everything. He was adrift, not at all in control, and safe.

Tomorrow was soon enough for everything else.

*       *       *

Edwin stank. He had waited for the low tide. Then he had gone out over the rocks, slashed at the corpse with an axe. It took a long time to dismember it. The business disgusted him, but it was bloodless. Food for *them*.

He pulled parts of it ashore and let the tide take the rest. There was no light except the reflection of the moon, and the torch. On the horizon there were still the boats coming into port, and halfway

135

between, the signal.

Don't you dare, he told them. Keep away. All of you keep away.

## CHAPTER SEVEN

### *Fasten all gates behind you*

There was not enough light.

Fritz paused outside the door of the penthouse flat and watched the city dawn through the window of the landing, with a duster in his hand as an alibi. Go check up there, his wife said: too much coming and going for anybody's good, all those parcels, people coming and going at night, but it was futile to check like this. No sound penetrated into the corridors from behind these doors and he should know, he listened all the time. Then, as he watched, the door shook, as if someone was pushing it from inside. The brass handle on his side of the door turned vainly back and forth. The door gave slightly but held. The rattling went on for a minute. He felt he could hear sobbing. Fritz fled.

\*       \*       \*

Lilian could not sleep. She had been so pleased to see him and Richard told her she was always a joy to behold. He dropped his bags where he stood, looked round, breathed a sigh of relief to be home and hugged her. Told her he thought his doctor friend was better off with Sarah, and what they should do, just the two of them, was go out

136

to dinner. He could eat a horse, he said. Richard could always eat. Puzzled but relieved by his casual abandonment of his friend, Lilian let herself be led, her own worries giving way to a mild anxiety about him at dinner. There were the occasional lapses of memory she had noticed before, such as when he could not remember what he had ordered and was surprised when it arrived. And when they emerged from the place, and he did not seem to know how they had come to be there at all. It was if he was still elsewhere, but it passed and it did not matter; he was jovial and affectionate, talked about the children and where they should go in the summer. Italy? Turkey? Should they include her family, too? No, she said, firmly. She was desperate to tell about the burglary, but she could not. If she told him the truth about what had happened, she would have to explain why she had let that muscular burglar out of the door with the only thing in the flat which had no value. She would have to explain that she had been drunk and not frightened, and she had an inexplicable but determined instinct not to mention the ridiculous garb of a man who had let her overpower him and then admired her. And Richard forgot to go into his daylight room. Maybe he would forget the painting, too, in the pleasure of shared sleep.

Then he woke her, early in the morning. Not forcefully, but by sitting on the big bed beside her, shaking her shoulder gently until it was obvious he was not going to stop. One look at his face told her he had not forgotten anything.

'Lilian, what happened to the painting?'

'What painting?'

'The one on the easel.'

She was wide awake now, about to bluster and pretend she did not know what he was talking about. All the variations she had rehearsed scrambled in her mind, coinciding with the realisation that she was afraid of him at the moment, and had been denying to herself the fact that she had been worried to death about exactly this.

'I took it to a dealer, it fell on me, it broke,' she said.

'Paintings don't break.'

She wondered about bursting into tears. Too late for that, and it would not work.

'I'm sorry. I was cleaning up in there. I knocked it over by mistake. It stuck to the floor. It was ruined. I threw it out, so as not to upset you.'

'So as not to upset me,' he repeated, slowly. 'Was it smeared? I thought it was dry.'

'Sarah said . . .'

'Sarah said what?'

'She said paintings don't break. Nothing. I told her about it. I was worried. Oh, Richard, I'm sorry.'

He was silent. She could not bear it when he was silent. Rowing, shouting, reacting any old way was better than silence. Quietness made her lose control.

'It was an accident,' she screamed. 'And I hated it. It's horrible. Why did you paint it? Why?'

He would not look her in the eye. Disconcertingly, he patted the shoulder he had shaken. She would almost rather he had struck her, then she could have retaliated. Instead there was a long pause before he replied, and his words were like sighs.

'I drew her, sweetheart, because she was there, and I painted her to fill in the gaps of what I saw. Do you hate all my paintings, or just that one?'

It was so mildly spoken it surprised her into truthfulness. Not a time to admit how much they hid from one another.

'I hate them all,' she muttered, 'but that one in particular. It was obscene. Yes, I hate them all, hate the bright colours, hate the fact you do it at all, hate the smell. I don't understand. You're no good at it.'

'Ah, I wondered if you'd noticed. About that.'

He walked out of the room and left her. She followed him to the door of the daylight room. A second realisation, worse than the knowledge of wounding him so profoundly, struck her as she looked over his shoulder into the room itself. The room was as messy as ever, showing no sign of anyone attempting to clean it, and there were no marks on the floor by the easel. It was all bathed in that awful daylight from the blue bulbs he used to illuminate the darkest room, an unflattering light to everything. He looked an old, defeated man in this light.

'Can you at least understand why I want to try?'

'No, I don't. You can buy a painting. You don't have to make it yourself.'

'I suppose you're terrified I might want to hang them up on the walls.'

'I'd hate that, too. They don't go with anything.'

'I need to get the anger, or something, out of my soul, Lilian. I need to try to paint the images in my mind, because I know I see things other people don't see. I'm transfixed by certain things, can't rest until I've explained them, by this.' He gestured at the empty easel. 'I'm no longer sure of what I see until I try to paint it. Being good or bad isn't the point. I have to do it.' She was quiet, shivering in her nightdress. Not the oyster white.

'And it's difficult, Lilian. It's hard and frustrating and maddening . . .'

'It doesn't look hard.'

He shrugged, aiming for nonchalance, trying to control himself.

'I don't need you to appreciate what I try to do, darling, but it would be nice if you tried to understand why. Perhaps if you ever tried to understand what goes into a painting . . .'

'But I do understand,' she protested. 'I love pictures. I love beautiful things, you know I do.'

'You like *pretty* things, Lilian. They have to be wrapped for you. You only see beauty where you expect to see it. You have so much of it yourself it no longer disturbs you. I wish you knew what it was like to see it everywhere, not pretty beauty either. It's like being on one long visual assault course. Always confused and amazed and feeling punched in the eyes. And wanting to remember it, and not being able to.'

The sadness in his voice made her want to cry. She felt deficient, and then confused and defensive. He never talked like this: it frightened her, she wished he had not started.

'And the paint itself,' he murmured. 'Oil paint. Such gorgeous, tactile, lovely stuff, unbearably beautiful all by itself. The agony of mixing it, going too far, watching it turn into sludge. And then, that fatal little stroke that ruins the whole thing.'

He kicked at the pile of canvases to his left. They remained immovable.

140

'Don't do that,' she said sharply. The violent movement frightened her. He turned and smiled at her, shrugged his shoulders and put his hands in his pockets, the way he did when he wished to end a conversation.

'Don't worry, Lil. You're probably right. It doesn't matter. It might be just as well, but I wish I'd finished it. There was something else to go in there. Something I saw out of the corner of my eye. And it might be the last memento of someone dead. Like a gravestone. Never mind. We'll just have breakfast, shall we?'

He moved to put his arms round her, held her briefly. It was a distant embrace, but it was still forgiveness, and more humiliating than anything else. She knew he knew she had lied, but he did not know how much. She would not cry; she would *not* cry.

'I'm sorry, Rich, I'm *sorry*. I'll try and understand. I'll go and look at paintings until I understand. I've already started. I shall, I promise.'

'No, don't force yourself. Doesn't work.'

'. . . And I'll try to get it back, that thing.'

'I thought you threw it out.'

'I did, but I can try and get it back.' He was patting her gently as if she was a child with hiccoughs.

'That would be nice, but don't worry. What's gone is gone.'

Lilian knew he was referring to something other than a painting. Something vital in their relationship. It would be so much easier if she did not love him. She padded down the long corridor towards the kitchen, angry again, wishing for once he would lock himself in the daylight room and

141

leave her to her own thoughts, but now he followed her, sat and watched her, irritatingly, as she fetched crockery. She was used to him watching her and usually enjoyed it, but now it unnerved her.

'I tell you something, Lilian. You aren't so bad at art appreciation, at that.'

'Why?' she asked, bending into the freezer, letting him see the fluid lines of her behind beneath the black satin slip of nightdress.

'Because at least you could see the vital thing about that painting of mine. You may not have much brain, but you do have eyes. It *was* obscene.'

\*     \*     \*

'That wasn't so difficult, was it?'

'No. You made it easy.'

'I have a theory,' Sarah said to John, 'that if men knew more about women, it would be a very bad idea.'

'It's the basic conflict,' John said. 'The basic dilemma of human relations. One sex cannot possibly know what it is like to *be* the opposite sex. To *think* like the opposite sex. Therefore, complete understanding is always impossible. I could deliver a dozen babies, and still not know what it's *like* to have one. I don't know what your orgasm is *like*. I never knew what my wife was *like*. It's like living parallel lines you can never cross.'

'Does that matter? Why do men always concentrate on the differences, instead of what's the same? Same pain, same lust, same needs, same old bruises.'

'Only different.'

'No. Just different levels of intensity at different

142

times. What you bloody men tend to suffer from is this dreadful need to know. I think it might have something to do with power. Needing to know what the hell is going on at any given time. And you can't.'

'You seem to.'

'No, I don't. I just respond.'

'I noticed.' He felt incredibly, ludicrously comfortable, lying on Sarah Fortune's bed with Sarah, so comfortable he wanted to pinch himself. This was not him, it was someone else, aeons younger, cheerfully irresponsible, lying on a bed with a woman fifteen years his junior and twice as wise, talking his head off and not giving a shit. This was not Dr Armstrong. It was a man talking to a woman about everything and feeling entirely natural. It could not last, but then it was not supposed to do so. That gave it the freedom. He felt very grateful to Richard Beaumont, and that reminded him.

'We never did get around to Richard Beaumont last night, did we?'

'We touched upon the subject, among other things. You said you were worried about him. So am I. I stopped when I realised you scarcely knew him. I was wrong, I think. You do know him. We talked about other things.'

'And drank too much.'

'Not too much. Just enough.'

John felt a faint stab of envy that Richard knew Sarah better. That Richard might have *used* Sarah, just as he was doing, but no, that was all wrong. Sarah was not used by anyone. She gave; she was not taken from. The envy was also about Sarah knowing Richard better than he did. It came and went like a frivolous storm cloud, and he knew she could feel it.

'Am I taking up too much of your day?' he asked.

'The day's young yet, and it's yours as far as you want it. But I expect Richard will come along at some point and scoop you up.'

'What am I going to do about my life?'

'You'll know what to do about your life when the time comes. I expect you already know. But for what it's worth, I think you're too young to compromise and hide away, the way you are. Now, about Richard, your friend.'

'My new friend. Your old friend.'

Envy again.

'Old friend, old lover, same thing in my book, whatever. He's a husband now. I think he needs help, but I don't know what kind. You never even told me how you met him.'

John's sense of responsibility came back. Responsibility to that other world, to other people; the innate sense of responsibility for that girl at the foot of the cliff, the odd responsibility he felt for Richard ever since he had met him. He closed his eyes, but no, it was all right. He could share this one, too.

'I met our mutual friend because I was called to see him. He was sketching on the cliff near me, you must see it some time. A girl either fell or was pushed from above him, literally fell past him, or so he recalls, although he cannot remember how he got where he was. She was killed, of course, although perhaps not quite as instantly as one could wish. Instead of raising the alarm, he sat where he was and sketched her. Probably for hours. He was, understandably, suspect. I was

144

called to assess him.'

'And what did you assess?'

'A humble, likeable, honest man. With that ice chip in the heart that doctors and artists might share, perhaps. The ability to be objective, opportunistic, even, in the face of death. My professional kind carve up the cadaver after death and sometimes find it beautiful. We know when there is nothing else we can do, and so did he. He sat and sketched it. We understood one another, I imagined, at a rather profound level. And he was sure he had seen a chough. It's a rare bird, black with a red beak, by the way, and he couldn't possibly have seen it. And he suffers from vertigo. I can't imagine how he ever made himself go down that path to where he sat, unless he was desperate to hide. Avoiding someone? And he isn't as well as he looks, or what he seems.'

He was going on too long. She was not prompting him, which was reassuring, so he resumed.

'As I grow even older, I find I trust my own instincts more. Am able to fall prey to sudden likings and believe what I find. Perhaps it's a feature of being alone. It's liberating, or this has been. Richard could have pushed that lass, and then gone down to his overhang to examine the result. Deliberately stayed hidden. In my dreams, I thought she might have been some awkward mistress who'd followed him up there, and he simply dispensed with her and forgot. His memory lapses are worrying. But that's wild conjecture and I don't believe it. I believe he could be violent, but not that way.'

He loved the way nothing surprised her. It was infectious.

145

'Hmm. Pretty wild. I don't see the mistress angle. He's monogamous by nature, a one-woman man with newish, gorgeous wife. And Lilian might not know much, but she'd know about that, I bet. And if Richard had a mistress, he'd acknowledge it, I think. That's the type.'

'On less intimate knowledge of them, I agree. But there's an absence of any other theories. And this peculiar lack of identification—no shoes, no bag, as if everything had been removed from her. Maybe a fight before she went over; maybe a deliberate depersonalising, as if it was important that no one should ever know who she was.'

He paused again, feeling her rapt attention spurring him on.

'It's that which haunts me, you see. Everyone has something that says who they are. I can't bear her to be buried without a name. She sort of brought *me* to life, poor girl. And I *know* there must have been something. And I have this feeling that Richard knows, or he saw something he may have forgotten.'

She was silent, horribly moved, against her will. So much for the peaceful life.

'Was she injured before she fell?'

'Difficult to say. She was, how shall I put it?, rather broken up, but there might have been a pre-mortem wound to the abdomen. Not enough to kill her. I've seen mortuary photos. They couldn't do them at the scene.'

He rubbed his hands over his eyes.

'That's the puzzle and pity of it; nothing to identify her. Thus no one to avenge her, no one to mourn her or tell her father. I found myself carrying a copy of Richard's sketch of the body, and I found him again, haunting the same spot, because I wanted to ask him what more he had seen. And, of course, I wondered why he came back. And I wanted to protect him, because the ice chip melts, you know, and he was shocked and someone had hit him. He had told me he was going to make a painting of the sketch, that's the way he works. He was the one who studied her. Maybe there was a necklace, maybe there was something. Something he saw. She moved me because she was like my daughter with her bleach-blonde hair.'

Their arms were touching. Sarah had become very still.

'Stay where you are. I want to show you something. No, come with me. We need the right kind of light.'

*     *     *

She lit the painting as she had before, in the east-facing, always shaded living room of her flat. There was a shortage of natural light in all the apartments except for the one at the top. She had noticed how the painting faded into garish insignificance in such ordinary light, and then transformed itself into something entirely different and horribly decipherable when strong light was played upon it from above.

'Is this familiar?' Sarah asked. 'Is he looking *down* at her?'

'Yes, obviously. I wish he didn't use so much paint,' John said.

'Do you? I like all that paint, I've decided. Although I want to pick it off, and see what's

147

underneath. See what he intended, supposing he knew.'

John walked backwards away from the thing, then towards it, suddenly excited.

'That's her, all right. I can see the sketch, but it's not like the sketch. Look, he's looking down, but out of it. And the body's not in proportion, like he's magnifying what mesmerises. The head's too big; she has no eyes. Tiny feet and huge, ripped-up torso. And there's something round her neck . . . yes!'

'So there is. Yellow, or is it white? And did he imagine the black bra and knickers? A slight, pornographic touch?'

'Oh no, they were there, and why is there always something suggestive about black underwear? Because men like it best?'

'What's this?'

She was pointing to the right of the bloody corpse, to where almost backing out of the painting bottom right there was a large, roughly elongated, circular blob of sheer black with a spume of red emerging from it.

'That's his chough,' John said. 'He swore blind he'd seen a chough.'

'The black bird with the red beak?'

'Yes. Spelt C.H.O.U.G.H.'

'Could he have seen such a thing?'

'No, but he was sure he did.'

'And the other black bits?'

There was so much black and red, the more she looked the more they were submerged. Into a ghastly, eyeless turmoil. She leant forward, still holding the light. In what she took to be sky above the corpse there were black, winged creatures,

148

obscured by the bits of lint from the towel that stuck to the raised surface. The paint was pointed here, even thicker than elsewhere, blunted by mistreatment.

'The texture's like cake icing,' she said.

'I wouldn't know about that. I'm surprised you do.'

They were making light of it.

'I don't, but my mother did. What are the black things?'

He did his backward, forward routine, almost dancing. Nimble on his feet, she noticed. A fine man, hardly in touch with his own intelligence. Discovering spontaneity. The phone rang. She left him holding the spotlight to go out into the hallway to answer it.

'We can ask Richard,' John was saying. 'All we have to do is ask Richard. Where did that thing round her neck *go*?'

Then he stopped, hand on mouth, moving closer, looking again.

Distorted abdomen, slashed. Black blobs of paint, oh no.

'We must ask Richard,' he repeated as she came back.

'He wants to speak to you. I said you'd phone back, in a minute.'

She sat, very firmly, on her sofa, looking small in it, and lost. His eyes were dizzied with the savage colours of the painting. She was another mix of colours altogether, passionately calm.

'You cannot ask Richard. You absolutely must not ask Richard. And I'll tell you why.'

'Don't be silly, Sarah. I must.'

'Yes, you must, but not yet. You cannot ask

Richard, because my brother stole this painting from him the night before last, with the connivance of Richard's wife. And he can't be told that, can he?'

She told him not why, but how, and odd though it sounded, he believed every word of it. After all, there was no other logical explanation for this painting to be in this flat. It all made sense, once he got to grips with the fact that everything in this alternative world was screwed. Nothing was going to shock him ever again. It made sense to him, because nothing made sense; it made sense because loyalty to a brother was second nature, and it made most sense of all because he could entirely see why a wife would do anything at all to get this painting out of her house. The story ended.

'That's it, as far as I know,' Sarah finished.

'Hmmm. See what you mean. Better put it away then. Until we find some way of getting it back. Put it out of sight. What does Richard want, anyway?'

'He wants to know if his cunning plan to get us together and sort your head out worked. Which I think it did, if you don't mind my saying so, do you agree?'

He nodded. She grinned. He grinned back. 'It's been great,' he said. 'It's great to be trusted, you know.'

'Don't worry, it's free. And a pleasure. You could call it an unrest cure. You've entered the world of amoral eccentrics. Oh, and by the way, Richard says he's sick of female company already and wants the male kind. He's anxious to spirit you off somewhere. I think you'd better go.'

'Can I come back?'

'Oh yes. We've unfinished business. As long as

150

you don't tell Richard you know where his painting is.'

'Yes, I can see why I can't do that. But I think I need it, this painting.'

'Take it, then. Not now, later. I'll wrap it and leave it behind the porter's desk. You can collect it. Better with you than with me. I've got your number and you've got mine, so come back soon, friend, I like you. Richard's flat is one flight up, number fourteen. Keep your face straight when you see the wife.'

\* \* \*

The flat was empty and still clean. Sarah showered and went back to look at the painting. She chose her clothes carefully, and went back to look at the painting. Retreated, brushed her teeth again, and went back to look at the painting, falling prey to an old habit of counting on her fingers. Then she made the third cup of coffee and sat with it in front of the painting. Finally, she found it moved her to tears, so she got up, fetched a handkerchief, told herself to be sensible and then sat, staring at it again. Then picked it up and carefully removed the traces of lint that still adhered to the surface. It was not *zing*; it was pity. Admiration for the sheer effort of it, which moved her. The hours it had taken, the use of all that paint. The uncertainty of it: the artist not sure what to include or omit, altering and maybe ruining it as he went along, risking the advantages and disadvantages of rich oil paint. The things he had included out of his imagination, because they could not possibly have been there. The red beak of the bird in the corner, as if it had risen beyond what else he could see, level with his eye. The disproportion of the body, as if he had tried to bring parts of that dreadful anatomy closer. Did he remember details he could only have seen through binoculars? Details he could never have seen from this distance? The necklace, a line of yellowish white . . . could that hold the clue to identity? And finally, the corpse itself and the overwhelming pity of its isolation. The reminder of dying in terror and misery, never to be acknowledged or mourned, no time to think of someone, somewhere, waiting for this child to come home.

Who would look for me? Sarah asked herself. All the lovers? I don't think so. I sidle in and out of other lives. I don't belong. Nor did she. I owe her something. I have a trivial, lucky, feckless life. John cannot be the only one who owes her something.

She looked one more time at the blacks and reds and wondered who the girl was. A younger alter ego, dying in terror. An awful memory of the twice in her own life when she had known that terror, and lived. Then she wrapped the painting in brown paper, attached a label with the doctor's name.

*Don't want to get involved. Don't want anyone else's pain. Want a quiet life.*

It was too late. She had seen what she had seen, heard what she had heard, and it was too late to back away, although she tried. Brush hair. Go out. Find noise, find people, get these images into proportion. Down in the foyer, Fritz sat at his desk. She had the impression he was waiting for something and she hoped it was not her, since she was not in the mood for mournful Fritz, who looked as if he, too, might have been crying. But he waved, and once she was reluctantly within earshot of his whisper, she could see that the guess was right.

'Hi, Fritz, how are you?'

'Oh, Sarah, what are we to do? What are we to do?'

She immediately thought he was going to say he knew all about Steven, braced herself.

'What are we to do, Sarah? Minty's back.'

'Minty?'

'Either Minty's back, Sarah, or they've got another one locked in there.' Shit, shit, *shit*. She handed to Fritz the picture of a dead girl, which could have been her, could have been Minty. And knew that a long and happy spell of not *quite* getting involved in other people's lives had finally gone down the pan.

'So tell me about it,' she said, 'before I remember I don't want to know.'

She felt profound relief. If Minty was back, then Minty could not be the girl in the painting, led to her death by a lecherous artist.

# CHAPTER EIGHT

## *Do not uproot any wild plants*

When Dr John Armstrong got back to his house late in the evening, he was tired in the pleasant way of being tired, which meant pleased to feel that way. Still buzzing with images, novel interiors and beautiful women, and still full of food from the afternoon meal with Richard. John had eaten ravenously, perhaps, he thought wryly, because the evening before with Sarah had not featured much by way of food. The late luncheon had been fish and chips and John took it as a return to the health of optimism that he should suddenly think about food at all; he had got out of the way of that. Depression suppressed appetite; uncertainty suppressed everything else. For God's sake, eat, man, and all else follows was a mantra he often repeated to patients. He was humming to himself a ditty he had repeated to Richard who, ready to laugh, had done so.

*Always eat when you are hungry/Always drink when you are dry/Always scratch when you are itchy/Don't stop breathing or you'll die.*

An adequate philosophy. What a day, what a two-day wonder. Alive, all over again. He had made friends and made love.

John even quite liked the sight of his own house, a nice contrast to the grandeur of the Beaumont abode. He could not live in that size flat, with that great, long corridor, even with the Beaumont wife he had met so briefly and found sulky. In fact, it

154

would not do to live in any flat, or even a city, or at least not all the time. And Sarah, oh Sarah: he was tingling.

The thirty hours away added perspective to the view of his small and over-cosy dwelling, with neutral walls and excessive tidiness. Plain colours, hardly a pattern in sight, as neutral as a surgery. Now whose idea had that been? He had never really thought about his own house before. The decisions had always been someone else's, wherever and however he had lived since memory began. There were no paintings on the walls. The place was only distinguished by its garden. A bland house, the symptom of the marriage he had mourned because he could not make her happy. He felt as if he had entered a decompression chamber in the last few days and now he was free. He had even learned deceit.

The only tricky bit of the day had been not mentioning *painting* to Richard, either as subject or object, but that, in retrospect, had been avoided because Richard had avoided it, too. He had been anxious to shuffle him out of the place where his pictures were. Then, in a way that reminded John of two boys let out of school, they had gone down to the river as sightseers, hopped on the London Eye, with Richard pointing out the sights, yelling *Isn't it bloody marvellous?* and John agreeing. Yes, he tingled, but he was glad to be home. The second tricky bit was saying goodbye to Richard, who was going on somewhere else, and then, guiltily, going back himself to the block where Richard and Sarah lived in their disparate styles, picking up the brown-paper parcel which contained the painting from the gloomy man at the desk, who handed it to him as if

155

it was contagion. Which it was, in its way. John postponed thinking about it, having carried it back as precious cargo. Then he thought of Sarah Fortune with downright affection and looked forward to seeing her again. For the moment he strolled around his own house as if he had been away for weeks, noticing how blasted ordinary it was, preserved as his wife had made it. Whisky in hand (this was getting to be an excellent habit), he looked at beige walls and imagined them in reds and blues with hot paintings, emerald-green blinds and useless ornaments. A dour but faultless leather three-piece suite glared at him sullenly. He wanted clutter and colour. He was already starting to imagine it that way. He would make it something uncompromising, vivid, make a virtue of living alone and throw open the doors.

There were a few telephone messages. He was on call to the police station tomorrow, might learn something. Reality was seeping back. Devotion to his own life did not mean he could abnegate all other duties. He still had an obligation to the dead.

Drawn to it like a magnet, John looked at the painting again. He was right. There was something round the neck, and birds pecking at the body. He remembered Edwin's ravens, and the whole of the other, city world slipped away.

He counted the black splodges. Six. Four young, two adults, perhaps. About right. Ravens had between one and seven chicks. They would nest once, early in the year, sooner than the other birds. *Put it away.*

He looked at the local newspaper, which had hung, crookedly, through his letterbox. No report of another body; no further reports on the first. The absence of that, the way other news had overtaken the murder of a stranger, brought back the old, guilty fury.

Tomorrow, he would go back to the cliffs, only slowly, carefully, calmly. It was too late today.

*       *       *

Steven Fortune considered his name to be a distinct disadvantage and had often thought of changing it. Fortune meant fortune cookies, good fortune, a knack for making a fortune; it meant jokes in school. It had not meant good fortune for his deserting father, whose name it was, or his mother, whose name it became, or his other sister, who had died in a crash. Normal family life. No wonder there had been no time for him. Girls, in the Fortune family, always took precedence over boys. Their lives were far more dramatic. A boy had to introduce drama into his own.

'Fortune' also suggested a sunny, sweet-natured, easy-to-get-along-with *fortunate* disposition, a boyish charm, which he could summon with ease, thus belying his more customary self-effacement, or scowl and a reputation for cleverness. Those with whom he worked assumed the swings of mood between cynicism, laughter, silence and occasional sheer unpleasantness coincided with either his apparent need for exercise, since climbing was his avowed passion, or an ache in his missing finger, which everyone noticed without comment or question, until they forgot. A driven man was a man admired and the ability to make people laugh, at least once in a while, was an effective disguise. He was one of those who went

157

round with a chip on his shoulder bigger than a parrot carried by a pirate, and since the parrot rarely spoke, he was most of the time an easily forgotten individual, who might well have been gay, since he was also crazy about art and timid with women. He engendered no more than a faint uneasiness, paid his way at the bank, he was brilliant—there was nothing else anyone needed to know, including his erratic hours. He also dressed well in those over-loose suits, bless him. And a passion for art, even more than one for climbing, was a tame distraction. He could have been looking at potential investments by looking at paintings and sculpture, whatever he did, and he could always be got on his mobile, although one reply to a query about where he was one morning had brought a sharp, obscenely phrased response. No matter: he would work until midnight, if required.

They simply did not get it, and he was long past supposing they would, or caring if anyone did. He knew he lived for *zing*. The gorgeous feeling of not wanting to be anywhere else other than where he was, the end of all restlessness as he stood and gazed at a painting he might have seen a dozen times before, the sense of being lost in the force field created by it. When he tried to define *zing*, all that came to mind was the electric charge that shot out at him, then flowed back, just as quick and vibrant. A current exchanged, flowing back and forth like a supercharged dialogue, escalating until either his hair stood on end or, as in front of the Tiepolo, his jaw dropped in astonishment. *Zing* was when eye contact was fired, and a vision imprinted itself on his retina and wormed its way

158

into his brain. *Zing* gave a greater degree of delight than he ever felt in the so-called real universe he occupied. Odd, then, that the paintings that soothed him most were the genre depictions of everyday life, executed to a level of perfection, an interior by Vermeer, for instance. That Tiepolo drawing was different, oh that drawing, all form, all purity, but with the same effect. He would always remember that Tiepolo: it was gone and he would never, ever forget it.

Here and now, he wanted to step inside the canvas, or melt himself into the paper, and he wanted to bow before them. It was, he told himself, his own way of seeing the world, through the prism of far superior eyes. Paintings and drawings never grew old or changed; they were timeless and generous and never let him down, they simply went on revealing more. But today, as he stood in the Cou tauld Gallery, it was different. You're a bloody great failure, mate, he told himself. And you are in deep dark shit. Because the *zing* factor simply did not work today: it was agonising in its absence. Other images got in the way. He simply could not *feel*. He was lost.

There was a picture on the top floor, by Manet, entitled *A Bar at the Folies-Bergère*. It was of a girl standing behind a bar, with the mirrored glass behind her showing what she was seeing herself as she stared out over a crowd. She was idle for a moment, indifferent to the spectacle and to the wonderful lace and velvet fabric of her own tight bodice. With her corsage, and her sad and beautiful face, looking at the lives immediately in front of her, and the life ahead, either completely distracted or realising just how bad it was going to

159

be. Reflected in the saloon mirror behind was an excited audience of spectators, men and women, drunk on entertainment, the globe lights on the pillars of the vast room glowing softly, and in the far left corner of the painting the tiny, dangling feet of a trapeze artist. The girl was watching a circus, indifferently, mirrored from all sides and defenceless, vulnerable, lovely, hopeless, her corset probably uncomfortable, realising in that moment that the world was not kind. She would lose her job for not smiling: existence would go on, close around her, until she was extinguished and too tired to fight. On other days, Steven could imagine her life unfolding otherwise—she was caught in a moment, that was all—but more often her ennui moved him to tears. Today nothing moved him at all. She created no flicker of response and he felt he betrayed her. Her face became another face, her clothes became other clothes, and all he could see was oyster-white and purple and feathers and a creamier complexion. Another, far less vulnerable-looking beauty, but all beauty was vulnerable.

He sat on the thoughtfully provided bench, and began to panic. He had revisited the smaller Rubens, strolled past his favourite Modigliani nude, and this was the third time it had happened. No *zing* on seeing, as if there had been something else superimposed on the canvas, or as if it was lit by a series of wrongly angled lights, which stopped him seeing it at all. Yes, that was it, as if someone had turned out all the lights, or turned them all on, creating a harsh reflection on the surface of the image which stopped him seeing anything at all. All the faces turned out to be Lilian's.

The bench he occupied was hard on the bum. He was in the long, tall gallery, sitting in lonely splendour, with his head in his hands, unable to see. Anything. Wondering what the hell had happened, and where he could go next. It felt as if life had ended. There was nothing to love, nothing to do, nothing. He was utterly lost and dazed in the memory of Lilian Beaumont. He had even forgotten the Tiepolo. Lilian had taken everything, she had taken his eyes. It was love at first sight, continued for all the hours in between when it had grown like a tumour. Dear God, if this was love, no wonder men went mad and blind.

Then, from the bench further down the deserted gallery, he sensed, rather than heard, the quiet sound of sobbing.

It was a dream, surely a dream. Twenty yards away sat a woman in a severe trouser suit with silly high heels, tapping against the wood. What kind of wood made these benches, he wondered, beech, mahogany? They always looked as if they had been there as long as the floors, a long time. The woman raised her face, not to look at the painting in front of her but for the single purpose of blowing her nose. It was Lilian, clothed. The confusing vision of Lilian. He put his head back in his hands, quickly. His heart began to thump. There was an overpowering desire to go and sit next to her and somehow end those gulping tears, tell her that whatever was wrong would be right, do anything that would make it right. And then reality struck. His head remained in his hands while he thought about it. He struggled not to go on looking and tried to stop his heart making all that noise.

This was a woman he had burgled, who had taken

161

a knife to him and tried to push him out of a window. She would not recognise him, but he could not approach her, even as a stranger. The second thought was Christ, get outta here. And then the third thought was, go across to where she sits, a soul in misery, and put your arm round her. *She is absolutely gorgeous.* She Zings.

Steven chose to leave, although not immediately. The racket of his heart forbade it. Sneaked a glance at her, watched her retrieve another handkerchief from her small handbag and blow her nose, again, with an ungainly sound. There was a terrible privacy in public galleries. The viewers of paintings invariably treated one another with great politeness, murmuring *sorry, sorry, sorry* if they got in each other's way or trod on each other's toes, and in the same way signs of emotion were treated with distant respect and ignored, unless the sufferer actually foamed at the mouth. These were places for understated feelings and personal revelations best left unexposed, perhaps like cathedrals. While moved by Lilian in distress, Steven found he was far more moved by her inelegant blowing of her nose. Each of them had made infinitesimal movements, glanced at each other, which was all viewers ever did. A posse of Japanese with a tour guide came in from the entrance nearest to where she sat. They cackled like a subdued crowd of hens with the sound turned down. Steven got up and left by the far door, making himself not hurry.

This fantastic gallery led from one room to another, with the same wooden floors. They creaked, comfortably. He moved to the next room, stood in contemplation of something else

162

he did not see, then moved on, going faster. Fear of discovery itched uncomfortably; he wanted out. She would never recognise him, never, better to be sure. He stuck his hands in his pockets and comforted himself with the thought of his soundless shoes. He moved to the next room and the steep set of stairs that led out to the ground floor and the street, faster still, and then realised that behind him there were the staccato footsteps of a woman in heels, first walking after him, then as he went faster she did too, until she was running noisily, the sound of her like the arrival of the fire brigade, the noise of her steps like a series of orders, tap, tap tap, close behind him, though she was confused about the way out and where to go and he could hear when she faltered at the top of the stairs and looked down the spiral, lost.

He was running now, touching the banister for balance as his feet moved faster, keeping his head down until he made the mistake of looking back and seeing her, framed up there, the golden hair catching the light from the chandelier, her hands gripping the banister rail, leaning over it dangerously but elegantly. There was a brief and glorious moment of sheer *zing*, followed by more reality. What on earth did he think he was doing, running away from the creature who had haunted his every waking and sleeping thought for more than forty-eight endless hours, dreaming of seeing her again? He was running *away*, running from everything that mattered.

So he stopped and went back two steps at a time, as fast as he had descended, in case she should disappear, slowing down only as he approached, to a stroll, remembering he was a stranger she would

163

not recognise. She remained standing where she was, looking down the spiral, without losing hold of the rail, seeing nothing and only turning when he was close.

'Are you all right?' he asked, softly. 'Can I help?'

She squinted at him, smudged mascara giving her eyes a panda-like effect that was enormously appealing. Quite unexpectedly, she smiled and let out a deep, juddering sigh.

'Oh, thank heavens it's you. I thought I'd lost you.'

'Do I know you? Do you know me? I was simply asking . . .'

She was looking at him impatiently, her voice high with relief.

'Of *course* you know me. Anyway, I know you. I'd know you anywhere.'

He felt a momentary, irrational sort of pride in hearing her say that, as well as a desire to tell her to lower her voice. These were not gallery tones. The feeling of pride in being so memorable was shattered when she pointed to his damaged hand, which gripped the railing alongside hers.

'Your hand,' she said. 'I couldn't forget that, could I? Especially when I thought I'd done it.'

And then she smiled again. There was no calculation or falsity in the smile: it simply went on being a smile, as if she was delighted to see him and it acted like a blessing. His heart lurched: fear and zing; he could smell her perfume. The buttons on her severe jacket were done up wrong, she had probably fastened it as she ran. He was lost for words. Lilian was not.

'This is really sort of lucky,' she said. 'I couldn't ever have imagined I'd see you here. Are you casing the joint? Only I've been thinking about you for the last two days—is it that long? Yes, it is. The thing is, you've got to help me.'

'Anything,' he said, faint and fervent.

'And it wasn't just the hand I recognised,' she went on. 'It was definitely the body. There wasn't much to remember about your face, but you've got a great body.'

'Thanks,' he said, even more faintly. He was horrified to feel the beginnings of a blush.

'Do you think we could go for a cup of coffee?'

Strong drink would have suited him better. His mobile phone went as they descended the stairs and she waited while he answered. 'Not now,' he said, 'I'm with a client.' They went towards the exit without another word and out into the street. Perhaps she would disappoint him when he saw her in daylight, but she didn't: sunlight and traffic noise improved her. Inside Caffé Nero she told him to get a seat and asked what he wanted to drink. He wanted to get it, he was like a puppet; she insisted, a tussle easily lost, so he chose a seat by the window where he could see her better and watch her move back from the counter, carrying clumsy mugs on saucers with ease. She had nearly as much aplomb as his sister Sarah, and Steven wondered, irrelevantly, how often he made comparisons between other women and his sister, decided it was often. The heart rattle was down to a steadier beat.

'Well,' Lilian said. 'Here we are. Like I said, you've got to help me. I've got to get it back. That painting I gave you to take away, I've just got to get it back.'

'Ah. That might be a bit tricky.'

'You haven't sold it, have you? Who on earth

165

would want to buy it?'

He was calmer now. May as well behave as she did, but his hands shook.

'Why do you want it back? I thought you wanted it stolen, as well as everything else.'

'I want it back, because it wasn't mine to give away.'

She paused, stroking the side of the mug with a long finger, struck by another thought. 'Mind you, if I'm honest, nothing is mine to give away, not really. Or to keep. And I'm going to lose everything at this rate.'

'Such as?' he murmured, taken aback by the rush of words and the complete confidence she seemed to be reposing in him. It made the blush rush to his head, but that could have been the mere sound of her voice. He ached to hear her laugh.

'Oh, just my life, my husband, just everything I've got. Well, borrowed, really. I've had to do a lot of thinking in the last day or so, especially since he's gone off again. He doesn't like me much at the moment. And he won't, until I get that painting back. He painted it, you see. Or if I can't get it back, I've got to learn to understand stuff, so I can talk to him on the level he functions at, if you see what I mean. Only I can't. I just don't get all this art stuff. That's why I was crying.'

'You're gorgeous,' he said. He felt as if he had scarcely listened, but remembered every word.

She threw back her head and laughed. It was utterly infectious; he thought his head would burst.

'Am I? I don't feel it, I just feel stupid.'

'What is it you don't understand?'

'Why anyone would want to paint pictures when they can't make anything pretty, and keep on doing

166

it. Or spend hours looking at them, like he does.'
The husband went up in Steven's estimation.

'Oh, I see. So you came here today to learn. Is that it?'

She nodded, vigorously. The golden hair danced, the eyes were brilliant green, he decided. She sipped the coffee gracefully, a blob of foam attaching itself to her lip, as if this was a conversation she could have every day. Sweet. It was never utter perfection one wanted in a painted face, it was perfection with a flaw. The *zing* factor kept on returning, making him stare. She turned her attention on him.

'What about you? What were you doing, sitting in front of a picture with your head in your hands? I was sorry for you. Made me sorrier for myself.'

He was shy, but encouraged by example, cleared his throat and gave up any attempt to make sense.

'I go there often. It's one of the few places where I feel completely happy, although any of the large collections would do. My spiritual homes. Like other people might go to churches or temples. I love looking.'

She shrugged. 'I thought you were a thief.'

'I am, but I don't steal, I liberate. I get hidden stuff to people who will love it. I probably only steal because I hate things to be hidden and I love looking.'

'Teach me,' she said. 'Teach me how to look and love looking.'

There was a pregnant pause until his mobile rang again. He ignored it, but knew he could not ignore it for ever. Her hand covered his. Warm, dry skin, like an electric shock.

'You could teach me,' she said, forlornly. 'You

167

know what I'm like. Will you? And will you get that painting back?'

'Which comes first?' he said. 'They'll both take a bit of time.'

'I've plenty of time,' she said, 'but not much brain.'

'You don't need brain. You need courage and feeling. I reckon you've plenty of those. I think we should start by looking at bodies.'

They were gazing into one another's eyes, his brown, hers green, locked in a challenge. *Zing* was never quite like this.

*          *          *

He needed courage. John was not thinking about bodies per se, but a single body. The possible second body no one cared about. Easier to care about a young girl. John parked the car where he had before, ignored the wind, and wondered why a day which had begun so refreshed by sleep could alter so fast in a matter of hours. A patient had told him once: *I feel so down, Doctor, that the only decision I have to make when I get up in the morning is whether I do the suicide before my dinner, or after.* He had told the man to eat and think about it. Grim as he felt as he strode towards the crevasse of the cliffs, John smiled at the memory, because although he was angry at Edwin, and all the old guilt was back, it was controllable and, in its own way, stimulating. It was not a day he did not wish to live through. There was none of that dullness, only excitement, energised by such sound sleep and the existence in his mind of a number of jigsaw-puzzle pieces inviting interconnection.

It had begun when he had gone to the police station in response to a call. A sad youth in a cell, sat with a blanket round him, speaking in broken something or other through an interpreter. Afghan, thin as a rake, bruised, hypothermic, traumatised, immediately consigned to hospital, he would have been enough to depress the best of days, although he was not entirely unusual. It was what he had said, when he could speak at all, before John ended any attempt to question him, which lit a fuse. He said, as much by gesture as by words, that he had come in over the cliffs, out of a boat, and been left behind, weeks ago. That was all he could say.

Hanging around the police station, a yellowed institution of many locks, barred doors and paper-thin walls, John waited and listened. He never left until the ambulances he requested had actually arrived, and in the waiting time, if he was not with the patient, he was either being consulted by the police about minor ailments or was universally tolerated, included in conversation sometimes, more often than not. In the listening interval today, conveniently coinciding with lunchbreak in the canteen, he had paused with his bad coffee and listened to gossip. Someone said the girl body was now officially classified as suicide, but that was only because there was too much else to do to call it murder. Someone else said the pathologist could not make head nor tail of her, an unintended pun which caused rueful laughter. They were tough, but not tasteless; they knew when they were beat. There was no mention of a second body, although someone had talked to Edwin the day before. That was when John's hackles had begun to rise.

Then the regular sergeant who had mentioned Edwin eyed John and told the others to shush. Gradually conversation died and they froze him out.

The story of the illegal asylum-seeking youth was not taken seriously. Why land on that lethal bit of coast and scramble up over cliffs when you could cross in a choice of transport whoever you were? And, if the choice of lorry or train were denied you, wouldn't you take the risk of a boat which could land far more easily a few miles further away, on flat coast, with no cliffs to climb?

He had listened to their incredulity, but did not share it. The problem with all of *them* was they were, like himself, half afraid of the cliffs and would do anything to avoid going there. But the cliffs were just another pathway. If you were desperate for freedom, or a chance, or a dream, or for profit, any pathway would do. Theories formed and reformed in his mind. No one would want to know them.

What made him mad was Edwin saying nothing, because of the ravens.

The second body might exist. It might have been Edwin's tease. So John drove himself to Cable Bay.

It had rained in the night, and now the wind blew hard. Again, his was the only car parked in the field, but he noticed when he got out that the grass verge at the side of the road was churned with tyre marks. He tried to remember if they had been there the last time and could not. A signpost, warning of danger and pointing out the deviation of the coastal path inland, had been tilted sideways by the wind. Nettles grew round the base of the sign. Absentmindedly he pushed the sign upright, pulled at it with his full weight to make it stand straight. Then he embarked downhill, ignoring the flora, concentrating on his feet. He wore his stoutest boots, taken from the boot of the car. They were soon caked and heavy with mud.

He slipped and slithered, despite the tread of his boots; the fresh mud made a sucking sound.

He was remembering what Edwin had said about pathways creating a new wilderness. They closed down and protected what lay on either side, rendering it impenetrable. Until accidents created new pathways, new vistas, like the fall of the cliff in this particular place, revealing a fresh view of the sea, and a different accessibility to it. Also, a new point of access to the land, as soon as anyone saw the possibility of a path. He went on into the valley which led down to the sea. It was late afternoon now, the sun fitful and spring-like, more rain threatening at the same time. White horses danced on the water. There was no hovercraft sound today. Perhaps those sensitive machines could not function in rough seas. A ferry ploughed across the horizon. John concentrated on his feet.

The same, scarcely created path, for the sheep and goats that had once grazed the headland and thus created a habitat for birds like the chough. The chough had thrived on overgrazed land with bare patches for scratching. It lived sparingly on fly larvae, beetles, earthworms, cereal grains, and the barer the land, the greater the access. The chough required a combination of agricultural land and wilderness. John knew that: he had looked it up. Richard could never have seen it round here. Remembering the joyful conversation of yesterday and the day before, the

171

product of Richard's grasshopping mind, John wondered as he walked if this random selection of topics reflected not only true freedom of speech, but the inability to remember what he had said last. Certainly the rapid succession of ideas and observations and preoccupations was infectious, and presently confusing, adding itself to a cocktail of ideas. John made himself concentrate, first on his own physical progress down towards the sea, and then on his purpose, which was in itself an amalgamation of several superimposing images, leading to uncertain conclusions rather than ideas. He was beginning to see images were as important as ideas.

He hoped he would not see Edwin. Edwin had become frightening because he was unknown and ignored, but John was not going to think about that. Edwin could not be everywhere. John paused to massage his temples and count the priorities of what he wanted to achieve. C'mon, man, what was the purpose? To find the body Edwin said he had found, and failed to report, get it dignity, whatever it was, while avoiding the terrible thought that it might be a human body. Then maybe to see these mythical ravens, which were unlikely inhabitants of this part of the coast, although more likely to occur than Richard's lonely, freakish chough. He counted backwards. He had to see if Edwin had lied either about the body, or the existence of a raven nest, or both. His suspicion was that Edwin had not lied about the body, but had lied about the ravens, and his overriding thought was that Edwin would lie about anything to keep everyone away from this part of the cliff. Which certainly begged that repetitive question, why?

Squinting down he could see that it would be possible to bring a boat in here, although dangerous, even for the most experienced navigator. There could be high seas, there were certainly strong currents, and there were rocks. Again he had the overpowering desire to be down by the water, looking up, instead of the other way round. He was beyond the point in the path where Edwin had materialised last time and began to feel safer, spurred onwards by raw curiosity, scolding himself for ever feeling unsafe. The greatest danger here was falling rock. Fresh boulders and fragments looked incongruous among new green. He could imagine the sound of a new fissure forming, like a giant groan, the earth grumbling and coughing, like massive indigestion.

This time, just as he began to feel almost carefree, with the pure attitude of an explorer, he almost stumbled across Edwin, sitting in that uncannily still pose that only Edwin could hold, looking as if he merged with the ground. The shock rooted John to the spot, although, for God's sake, there was no reason to be shocked. Edwin could always have appeared from almost anywhere, that was his habit—but John had not wanted to see him today, not until he had seen something else for himself, and he had persuaded himself that Edwin would be miles away. Edwin was looking out to sea but the notion that he had not heard John's approach was fanciful. He must have sounded like a herd of elephants in his clumsy progress. Edwin would have felt him coming, let alone seen. Play it by ear. John stood still. Edwin got up and dusted his trousers.

'Why didn't you report the corpse, Edwin?' John

173

asked, raising his voice over the noise of the sea. 'That was the deal. I said nothing on the basis that you reported. And you didn't.'

He tried to keep a note of recrimination out of his voice, to speak more in sorrow than in anger, although anger was beginning to percolate, replacing the fear. Edwin spoke over his shoulder, as if throwing away the words.

'Body? What body?'

'The body you said you didn't want me to see. Remember?'

His voice had risen to a shout. Edwin shrugged. He turned to face John and his fingers went to his own neck, fiddling with the scarf. There was some of the perspiring anger of the other day, mixed with weariness and cunning. John felt as if Edwin's responses were somehow rehearsed.

'You're losing your mind, old man. Getting on in years, happens to us all. What body? I never said anything about a body.'

He continued to finger the scarf.

'You got bodies on the mind, ever since that girl. This one's nothing but a dog. You imagine things. That's what I'll say. I've already had a word with the police. Told them I was worried about you. Being friends with that artist and all. Dining with him, too. It's a small town, you know. You're imagining bodies everywhere, you.'

'You told me there was a body,' John insisted.

'Me? I said no such thing. It isn't there now. Never was. You've been imagining things.'

Anger blocked John's throat. He watched, speechless, while Edwin unknotted the scarf, as if irritated by it and needing to retie it, instead pulling it taut and yanking it straight between his

174

hands. The material looked cleaner than he recalled, freshly washed and strong enough to use as a ligature. Edwin seemed to have renewed all of his clothes but he still smelled as he stretched the scarf as if testing it for use.

'Forgive me, I must have been mistaken,' John said, as the scarf, having illustrated its own strength, was twisted and wrapped tightly round Edwin's sinewy neck. 'But did I also hear a myth about the existence of ravens?'

Edwin turned his face east, shaded his eyes, watching the broken end of the cliff, then turned back. There was something like adoration in his eyes. He began to shake his head, then stopped. *He cannot lie about birds*, John thought. Nor can he not boast.

'Yes, there are ravens. Four young. They'll be ready to go soon. Look, I only told you about a *body* to put you off. I can't have anyone going near the nest.'

John did not believe him, which did not stop him being mortally afraid.

'Where's the nest?'

'Over there. They've built so big, under the overhang, I'm scared they'll pull it down. Not long now, though, before they can all fly far away.'

John followed the direction of Edwin's outflung arm.

'I want to see it.'

'You couldn't. You have to climb from the other side and get above. Wouldn't see nothing of them just now anyhow, they go a long way to forage. Listen, Doc, do you want to be fished out of the sea ten miles up the coast? You say a word, it'll happen.'

175

John stood his ground, but he knew his fear was as clear to Edwin as the colour of his coat. And he wanted to live. Yes, Edwin would kill him without a second thought.

'The young need a few more days, and food, and then they'll be OK,' Edwin was murmuring. 'And now, since I don't have a car, perhaps you could give me a lift home.'

*He would kill me now if he hadn't remembered the car. Someone would find the car. Edwin cannot drive. Cars are harder to hide than bodies.*

John nodded and let Edwin lead the way back up the narrow, muddy path. There were so many variations of insanity. He recognised Edwin's to be of the kind that switched on and off, like a light, with no known limitations.

They drove back, wordlessly, Edwin sniggering and triumphant, alpha male. The car was rank with his smell and his triumph.

'Here will do,' Edwin said. They were at the car park where the path began. An inaccessible mile or three from the ravens. Edwin's mood seemed to change. A return to the old camaraderie; now that he had got his way, remembering an old respect. It was as if he did not like to see an old friend so beaten and cowed.

'Look,' he said. 'I don't like threatening you, you know. We're mates.'

John remained silent, bracing his hands on the steering wheel to keep himself steady. *Oh no, we were never that. You wanted to be friends. It was I pushed you away, as well as everyone else. Just get out, for fuck's sake.*

'But I can't have anything disturbed up there. Not until the chicks can survive. Any time now. I don't

176

like doing threats, Doc. I'd rather trade. Tell you what, you keep quiet, I've got something to give you.'

'There's nothing I want from you, Edwin.'

Edwin shuffled. He smelled of blood, sweat and madness.

'Oh yes there is. Something I found. *Maybe* from that girl. Something from that girl. *They* found it. My beauties. *They* found it and gave it me.'

He was gone.

When John finally stopped shaking, he helped himself to whisky from his cocktail cabinet, thought of his options and knew he had none. He turned the car round and went back, beyond the field where he had parked before, until he found a space. This time he went north of the broken headland, where there was no path, forcing his way between bramble and hawthorn, trudging through wilderness, until he was at the edge where nothing grew. He was good at measuring distances, translating the map into metres and landmarks. Ignoring vertigo he walked almost to the edge, and when within feet, with the wind, thankfully, blowing hard off the sea, shoving him back rather than forwards, he crawled the rest of the distance on his hands and knees until he gripped the very last bit of damp springy turf and looked over. He estimated that the nest, if it existed, was immediately beneath. Down below, there was a plateau of rocks, just above high tide, invisible from any path, perhaps accessible on steady feet when the tide was low. He pressed binoculars to his eyes and watched. *If* the nest was below, it would be invisible from this angle, and the scramble to reach this terrifying point was futile. Then he saw them.

177

The birds were sleek and black, and feeding. The juveniles were uncertain and much smaller, screaming and yelling, hopping with outstretched wings on the rocks, but the parents were entirely focused. With concentrated industry, they pecked at the ribcage of a narrow torso, flesh bleached faintly pink. He guessed it was the remains of a large dog. The tip of the cliff seemed to shake as the sea ate away at the base with a steady breathe-in breathe-out impact. John could feel the tremor of the onslaught of water, could not take his eyes from the ravens. He crawled backwards and was sick in the grass.

There had been a second body. Part of it formed the ravens' meal.

They had practised on the first.

He needed to go back to the painting.

*       *       *

An hour to midnight and lonely, Steven wanted to speak to his sister, but whatever else he felt, he could not initiate it. He could not do a single bloody thing, except dream of tomorrow, in between occasional bouts of sheer anxiety about what kind of fool he must be to give Lilian his mobile phone number, like making himself a hostage to fortune, the final insanity, apart from arranging to meet. When his mobile went, his feet left the ground. It was a disappointing relief to hear the voice of his sister, issuing a single, surprising command. Get here.

He was only a street away, unable to do anything but haunt the vicinity where Lilian lived. Lilian, whom he would see again tomorrow. Sitting in a

178

pub, nursing a single malt, and dreaming, when he was not also thinking of his sister and how to prise that painting back without facing her anger, and there she was, obliging him. God was kind and the world was marvellous and everything would work out.

He went to Sarah's, and was inside in ten minutes, horribly, deliciously conscious that Lilian was upstairs, and he felt a fool for blowing a kiss down the hallway in that direction.

Sarah ushered him into her tiny kitchen.

'Listen,' he gabbled, 'I'm *sorry*, I'm really sorry. But I've got to have that painting back. I've met Lilian, and she wants it, I've got to have it.'

So much for diplomacy.

She seemed to understand the whole situation without further explanation and she smiled. She could terrify him when she smiled, and her face, in the harsh light of the kitchen, was hard.

'Ah, I did rather hope you might say that.'

'Pardon?'

'That you *really*, *really* wanted it back.'

She pushed him ahead of her into the living room, where Steven found himself opposite a tableau of people sitting on her old sofa, facing the cow. It was a real work of art, he always thought, definitely gave zing, but not now.

'You want that painting back, darling,' Sarah said, 'you have to climb.'

179

# CHAPTER NINE

## *Do not leave children unattended*

Not quite a tableau, but the two of them had spread themselves on the sofa. Steven recognised Fritz, from a nodding acquaintance, and waited for an introduction to the woman who sat next to him. Sarah provided it, doing the rounds like a hostess.

'Fritz? You've met my brother, haven't you? Steven, this is Fritz. Not his real name, I think, but that doesn't matter. What's in a name? Often wonder what fool dreamt up Fortune. And this is Mrs Fritz: Mrs Fritz, my brother, Steven. He's a thief in his spare time, but not too bad otherwise. Would you all like more coffee?'

There were two sets of nods. Steven sank into the armchair, gazing at Mrs Fritz. She looked like a gypsy, and he was distracted by her face, wondering why he made that assumption, trying to recall the memory of a painting somewhere featuring gypsies. A slightly insulting generic term, he thought, and then he was remembering a Modigliani painting, *Gypsy Woman with Child*, yes, she was a little like that. Modigliani's gypsy had bright red cheeks and that was where the resemblance lay, although in Mrs Fritz's case, there was nothing gypsy-like about her drab clothing, and she would have suited a scarf round her neck to go with the flushed planes of her face. In face, at least, Mr and Mrs were an unlikely couple, he rounded and pale beneath a coffee skin, she squared and rosy. They looked embarrassed as well as determined.

'Steven, dear, don't get too comfortable, and drink your coffee soonest. Do you need anything to eat? I do hope not. I know you prefer to climb on an empty stomach, and we do need you to climb.'

Sarah filled the china cup he was nursing in his hands. He could feel the heat of the liquid through his fingers, sipped it. There had been far too much coffee today. He put the cup down on the floor and waited for whatever might happen next, fingering the fabric of the chair in which he sat, disapprovingly. It was something to do with his nerveless hands. He looked at his sister. Her face turned into Lilian's face.

'Climb?'

'Burgle, climb, however you put it. Come on, Fritz, explain.'

Mrs Fritz stirred, restlessly, clasped her fingers and leaned forwards, earnestly.

'Is Minty,' she said. 'Upstairs.' Then nodded, as if that said it all, and sank back on the sofa. Steven thought he had seen worse, far more obscure films than this. Her accent was indecipherable and he looked at her with greater interest. These days it was impossible to define people by nationality. Modigliani had already proved that.

'Over to you, Fritz,' Sarah ordered.

What a silly name. He looked like . . . he looked like . . . They all looked like Lilian, since that was the face imprinted on the inside of his eyes. He had to get that painting back, then he would hear her laugh. Fritz cleared his throat as if for a speech. He spoke peculiarly imperfect English.

'I know you, Mr Steven, 'cos you come here. And I know you are doing this climbing, maybe burgling business up the back when you lose your keys. I tell

181

her,' he nudged his wife, who nodded vigorously, 'and she is saying, OK, what harm, he is being Sarah's sister. Having jokes. No complaints so what the hell, hey?'

He tried to laugh, but he was far too miserable.

'I deny it,' Steven said. Fritz spread his hands.

'OK, OK, is someone looks like you. Only a coupla times, OK? No worries. You climb, he climbs, who cares? No security at back. Even on top floor. So, you go or that other bloke who looks like you, he goes.'

'Why and where do you want me to climb?' Steven asked, mildly.

Sarah took over.

'Steven, dear, in the top-floor flat, a sort of penthouse, lives a strange Chinese couple, running what is loosely described as an import–export business. For several months they had a servant called Minty. They locked her up most of the time, until they seemed to trust her not to escape, but even so she was more of a slave. They are alternately sloppy about security or paranoid. Haven't yet established who she is, except she's probably a Romany from the same part of Kosovo as Mrs Fritz, here. The most stateless persons in the world. I told you about Minty, to your great disinterest, and I must confess I did little enough to assist, figuring people usually find their own way out. Anyway she escaped, with a lot of help from these good people, who put us to shame. Only, it seems, she's been got back. And now she's really locked up.'

Steven remembered the girl stumbling upstairs with her captors while he crouched in Sarah's doorway two nights before, felt guilty, remembered

182

in time to keep quiet, because there was another face he remembered better. Revealing such a sighting and his own failure to do anything about it would put him at a further moral disadvantage and he was feeling thoroughly outclassed as it was. He was struggling to remember the geography of the block, a jumbled map in his mind, jarring alongside the deep feeling of shame for the fact that he had forgotten the girl on the stairs, and the fact that his climbing up and down the well of the building had never been secret. Who thought he was so clever then? Wouldn't want Lilian knowing that. Shame made him blush. On top of all that, there hovered the sweet sensation of her, one floor away, and how much he needed to retrieve that sodding painting of her husband's she valued so much, to prove himself. This was bargaining time, and with the scent of her so near he did not give a shit if he was being asked to ascend into heaven without a rope, or descend into an icy hell with crampons. His mind worked overtime. He brushed his hand through his hair. It stood up in short spikes.

The phone rang. Sarah ignored it. Mr and Mrs Fritz sat to attention.

'Mr and Mrs Fritz believe Minty was brought back the other night,' Sarah went on, reverting to the voice of the lawyer sent upon earth to clarify things to befuddled fools. 'Certainly there's someone up there wanting to get out. And a lot of coming and going in between. But without proof of nefarious activity, slavery or whatever, it all gets a bit difficult. Could be a crying child—'

'Who turns the door handle,' Fritz interrupted.

'Or Minty, or someone else,' Sarah continued. 'But we can't call the so-called authorities, for

183

obvious reasons. So be a dear, Steven. Just go up there and find out. You don't even have to start from the bottom. You can start from here.'

'Doesn't Fritz have keys? He's the caretaker.'

The phone rang again. Fritz was shaking his head.

'No, I don't have no keys to flats unless people give 'em me when they go away. But if you got a burglar alarm, like the Beaumonts do, and the Chinese do, you gotta post a code with me, so I can turn it off from downstairs if it goes on and on. Security firm comes automatic, but I can make it quiet. Chinese don't know that. I fix with security firm 'cos it kept going off. And there's no alarms at back. Too pricey, looks safe at back, not worth it. You know that,' he added, nodding at Steven. 'Sorry, man who climbs up and down there, *he* knows that. *He* gets in back, comes out front, OK?'

'I don't quite understand,' Steven said. 'Why not call the police?'

Mrs Fritz exploded into a stream of expletives and gestures. They all listened attentively.

'Mrs F was saying earlier,' Sarah translated, 'that the Chinese would get them the sack if they did that, and the police would take Minty away. And they might mention someone climbing up the walls.'

Steven ignored the latter part.

'Sounds as if she'd be safer if she was taken away. They wouldn't get sacked if *you* called the police,' Steven said.

'And if I tell the police, where would I have got my information from? Where else but the caretaker? Oh for Christ's sake, just get in there, you're good at it,' Sarah said impatiently. 'And if

184

she's in there, bring her down without disturbing anything.'

'They'll know if Fritz overrides the alarm.'

Fritz shook his head, confident about that.

'I don't steal people,' Steven said, helplessly, but still feeling a surge of excitement. 'What language does she speak, this girl?'

'Romany,' said Mrs Fritz. 'Gypsy to you, bit of English.'

'Jesus, that's all I need. Who the hell else speaks Romany?'

'I do.'

'Nobody's asking you to *steal* her,' Sarah interrupted. 'If she doesn't want to go, leave her. Get on with it, there may not be much time.'

'Oh for God's sake, don't be ridiculous. I can climb up there, probably, but bring her down? I'm not a sodding rescue service. I'd need harnesses, three men and—'

Steven, nobody's asking you to bring her down the drainpipe.'

'What are you asking then?'

Sarah sighed in exasperation. He was supposed to be able to read her mind.

'We're asking you to get in secretly, see if Minty's there and what state she's in. If she'll go out of the place with you, then you pick the lock on their door from the inside where it won't show, and bring her down here. In the meantime, you smash a back window or something, make a mess, or whatever, and make it look as if *she* went out by climbing out and down. See? There's even ropes up there, over the balcony. A broken washing line, even. Make it look as if she shinned down. Then no one else is implicated.'

185

'Why can't I just pick the lock from the outside with you standing guard? And what makes you think I can pick the lock?'

'You grew up around me, Steven. You can pick any lock, you did it at school. And if you pick it from the outside, it might show. And if they come back, you'd be stuck on that landing with nowhere to go. Anyway, Fritz says it isn't a special lock. Like he said, they're paranoid, antisocial, but cocky. That's what they are. They've got used to no one interfering. Or noticing.'

Steven sat back, arms crossed across chest, hands hidden beneath his armpits, feeling the sweat. Mr and Mrs Fritz leaned forward, simultaneously.

'These fucking Chinese by way of being out, just now, Mr Steven. Whole bloody lot. Place empty, but for crying Minty. I bin up there. I got no key, no going-in rights, gotta job. But they in't there this minute. Mrs and Mr Beaumont, they out, too. Son's birthday. You go and look, please? They got line hanging over back balcony, Sarah's right. Messy people. They don't care.'

Despite himself, Steven could feel a terrible tendency to rise to the challenge. He had surplus energy and surplus guilt and other motives he was not willing to discuss. *Yes.*

'You can see the way from my back window,' Sarah said.

He wondered for a minute if she was trying to kill him, or had greater faith in his climbing prowess than he did himself. Still, he had climbed with great ease to the Beaumont floor, so what was another floor?

'I can do it, but I don't know how to get in. It usually needs some kind person with a preference for fresh air and open windows.'

Fritz had the answers, as if rehearsed.

'Window at back broken,' he chanted. 'Always was, before they lived there. They don't fix. They never fix. They don't let anyone in to fix nothing. They don't move ropes, neither. Lazy bastards.'

'Your gear and your climbing suit is in my bedroom,' Sarah said. The way she said it made it sound like a set of pyjamas.

'And if I do it, then will you give me the painting?'

She did not answer, but he trusted his sister to keep a bargain. She always did, in her way.

There were terrible flaws in this stupid plan, but he knew he would do it anyway. Those soulful eyes of Fritz, that sensation of being seen as powerful, Sarah needing him, all worked like an aphrodisiac. And Lilian's face: there was always Lilian's face. The glamour of a rescue mission. Steven surveyed the terrain as best he could. Then, dressed in his black Lycra with the gear neatly stashed at his waist, he climbed out of the window into the well, feeling this was insane, and also gallant. Someone might praise him for it. He ducked his head back to speak to Sarah.

'Wouldn't it be easier if I just gave her a box of chocolates?'

She shook her head and backed away. She could not watch.

Fritz went downstairs to turn off the burglar alarm. Then they sat and waited. The phone rang again. A small carriage clock in Sarah's living room struck midnight. Fritz leant forward and patted Sarah's knee.

'He's a good boy, he. Very good climber.'

'Have you watched him, then?'

'Oh yeah. Very good.'

'Didn't you mind that he was getting inside the flats?'

Fritz shrugged. 'Better the devil you are knowing. I think he is only playing. I am only the porter, why should I care?'

'What's your real name, Fritz?'

'None of your business, Fortune.'

They waited.

*     *     *

Steven chose the drainpipe route up to the next level, glad of its iron solidity, until he reached the balcony and hauled himself on to it. So far so easy. This was the window into the Beaumonts' flat, his previous point of entry, and his heart, already pounding, pounded harder. The window was firmly shut, with an opaque blind drawn across it, through which an eerie light seeped. It looked as if it was daylight inside, an almost blue light which somehow gave him the feeling that Lilian had left it to guide him. Would Lilian approve of what he did now? Surely. It was crazy, but in his way, he was doing it for her. So that he would survive until tomorrow, when they were going to meet and study *zing*. So that he could get back that painting, which would make her happy. He stood on the balcony rail, placed his right foot into a space between the girder of the old lift arrangement and the wall, and his left against the drainpipe. There were old brackets in the wall. Rust crunched between his toes. His taped fingers, dusted with chalk, were glad of the friction created by rust. He jammed his

188

fist into a crevice created by broken brick. He never looked down, kept his face level with the brickwork of the wall until he was spreadeagled safely. He tested his toes in his rubber-soled slippers. A heel hook to the ironwork on the side, then he eased his whole body to follow. Then the drainpipe, which held. Another fist jam. He moved to the second pipe and the metalwork left from the old lift. Then he looked up. The rope hanging over the balcony was almost within reach. Now he had to commit, leap for that thing just out of reach. It was dark up there. His hand clutched at the rope, a slippy, plastic-coated line, as strong as wire, which bore his weight as he wrapped it round his knuckles and pulled. He climbed, hand over hand, then pushed himself away from the wall so he swung into space, and as he swung back, caught the balcony with his hands and hung there. Slowly contorted his body until his heel was above his head, holding on.

My next trick is impossible, he told himself. I wish someone was watching.

Someone was.

He saw the face behind the cracked window as he hauled his way on to the balcony. Small and pale with a mouth shaped into an O! before she moved out of sight. There was a pile of old clothes in a basket. He threw them out of the way, down into the well. The window was dirty and cracked. Fritz was right: they were messy. They made it easy. He was beginning to feel contempt for the owners, recognised that as dangerous. Get in, open window, rearrange rope first. Smash glass from *inside*. Get on with it, you great, soft bastard. It's the best job you ever did.

Downstairs, they waited. Sarah had begun to pace between the front and the back, and from the back, heard the glass and began a slow gnawing of her fingernails. Then she went and stood by the front door. Then came back. It was better not to know what he was doing. They were both a little mad.

\*       \*       \*

John paced up and down, waiting for daylight. It felt as if it was the darkest hour before the dawn, but midnight was still close behind so there was time to go. He had got it: he had finally cracked the code. Sleep was out of the question, despite the exhaustion. He had slept too much for too long.

There would be regret, too, for the whisky consumed as he paced, but that was not important. Overindulgence was better than going out of doors and hitting people, which he might otherwise have done.

John had consulted his library, that much-loved, often ignored collection of books on plants, gardening, birds, explorers and medicine, excluding a single unreal story or anything frivolous. He had always assumed that most of his knowledge came from the dry pages of books, and that knowledge thus acquired was the most important kind. He had never rated the more instinctive knowledge he had acquired through prolonged contact with sick human animals as anything like as important, and at the moment he wanted to shoot himself in the head for the realisation that the opposite was true. If only he had trusted himself: he was a walking encyclopedia on human behaviour. He had eyes, for God's sake. It was his eyes and his ears and his daily experience that truly informed him. Another slug of whisky. He was full of useless energy and sleepy at the same time. If he slept, there would be nightmares, and it was disappointing that Sarah did not answer her phone, but what did he expect? Just because he wanted to talk and refine his thoughts, and she was suddenly the only person he could think of. He wanted to say out loud that it was unpleasant to conclude that Edwin was homicidal, that Edwin was a friend he had come to loathe, and then he was angry with himself for being so vulnerable to his new friendships that the isolation he had once enjoyed seemed to have turned against him.

Sleep beckoned. He resisted it with the irrational crossness of a two-year-old, beating at it with fists and cries for fear of being left behind and missing something. Squinting at that damn painting, with the light at another angle, vowing that this dram would be the last, he repeated his own conclusions, dredged from the paint, and the books, and everything he thought he never knew. He thought of his own daughter and how much they had wounded one another; thought of Richard Beaumont, and then thought back to his daughter, and how much he preferred the status quo to the bottomless pit of horror that would exist if he did not know if she were alive or dead. *I can't make it up to you. I can to her.* The love of a child put all other loves into perspective.

He looked at the oil painting through a haze of smoke. The cigarette made him dizzy. He was still imagining this room with bright colours, gracefully faded by nicotine, bad habits and good company.

He would do it, when this was over. Never again would he live in his former sterility, or neglect a duty dictated by passion. He would reach out, he would interfere, he would instigate, instead of waiting. When this was over. As he grew calmer, he realised again that he owed a terrible duty to that pathetic body at the bottom of the cliff because it was what had awakened him into a new lease of life, opened his eyes to the pity he had lost, made him want to be in some small way useful, and unique, because others would forget. And he owed it in particular because he now knew what no one else did, and knowledge always imposed a duty. Knowledge imposed dangerous, inevitable obligations. He was not sure he was up to it. That was why he phoned Sarah, ashamed to admit he needed a woman and there was no one else. For the last three years he had shunned his friends.

'You were a sweet lad, once,' he told himself. A bookish lad with a great knowledge of birds. A boyhood passion, until he became bored with it, like he had with the stamps and the music. He had come to be wary of them. So, back to the volume containing *Corvus corax*.

There were the ravens in the painting, surrounding the dead body of the girl, the smaller ravens hopping and dancing as they had today, the larger adults slashing and pecking and carrying away. He was confused about what he thought he could see and what he had read. Adult ravens carried away flesh, hid it for future consumption. Babies were nervous, followed examples. Ravens were discriminating, charming, yet the omens of doom. *And the raven, never flitting, still is sitting, still is sitting . . . And his eyes have all the seeming of a*

192

*demon's that is dreaming, And the lamplight o'er him streaming throws his shadow on the floor.* They were all crows. Carrion was carrion: flesh was food, and the more scarce the food, the more they pecked. They did not kill: they found what was already dead.

And they liked bright things. They went for wide open eyes, anything that shone, the tawdry and the precious, as long as it glittered. Thieves. Something about the punctuated thread of gold around the neck of that painted body failed to convince. John remembered the dog he had once walked on the cliffs. It had careered after a rabbit, caught it and then, unable to arrest its own headlong pursuit, went straight over the edge, to be found later, dead, broken backed and bloodless on the rocks below, with the rabbit still gripped in its spaniel jaws. Perhaps the body at the bottom of the cliff also held something in her mouth, or in her clenched fist.

He had a brief moment of pity for what Richard Beaumont had seen, and then it was temporarily displaced by an acute dislike for anyone who could have sat, sketched and dispassionately absorbed the terrible sight of Edwin's ravens pecking at a young body. It was the work of a ghastly voyeur, with blood the temperature of ice or an enjoyment of revenge. Not only had he watched and sketched, but he had, painstakingly and with loving clumsiness, transferred it into paint. The bastard. But oh, the painful shock for a man with such a soft and sentimental reverence for innocent birds, to see what they could do. Take out the eyes, widen the wounds, tear at the flesh and remove what glittered. John struggled to remember his huge

193

liking for Richard Beaumont, contemplated the perils of any friendship. Friendship was love of a kind and involved accepting what you could not understand and forgiving it. Artists were different anyway. They viewed selectively; they were mesmerised and blinkered by turns; they were intoxicated by the visual, like boys on drugs. Maybe Richard was not aware of what he had seen. Oh yes he was. Perhaps simply paralysed. And he thought he had seen the chough, because he had dreamed of seeing it, and because it was infinitely better than what he had actually seen: the carnivorous brutal raven, raping flesh. Far better to have seen the gentler chough, with all its optimistic associations. When he had had the clarity of just enough alcohol, John was sure he had also discovered the mystery of this red-beaked thing, which crowded into the right-hand corner of this small oil painting. He squinted at it again, thick paint, rough shape. The black bird with the red beak and red feet. The thing that Richard included because he thought it might have been there, or wished it was there, or wanted it to be what it was not. And it was not the ancient chough of his fond imagining, but a baby raven, with feet and feathers still bright red with blood. A bloodied raven, rising to a height, yelling at the parents to go, go, *go*. Enough to fool a man who was denying what he had seen, and preferred it to be the gentler chough, which fed on invertebrates, insects, crustacea, molluscs, spiders and worms, but never carrion.

John found he could not stop crying.

Brushing away tears, he looked again. Oh Lord, he had not cried in such a long time. The thing round the neck was simply white, a gap in the deep paint, where the canvas was visible. He thought of a ligature, and of the dirty pale colours of Edwin's scarf. Shuddered. The bright yellow speck by the hand was more significant. Something she clutched that might show who she was, or where she had come from. It was all there, in the painting. Edwin had something to give him. Something the ravens had taken from her hand. Or her neck.

Sarah would understand. He knew she would. Somebody must. She *had* understood. She said it was the mourners who lit a soul's pathway to heaven. Not greedy ravens. If that lonely girl had a father or mother, or sister, they must *know*. But not everything, no, not everything.

And yes, he could still like Richard Beaumont, and want to know him for ever.

\*          \*          \*

Sarah did not understand.

The bedraggled girl who sat on the sofa was not Minty, although there was a resemblance. Possibly the same tribe. She was a more beautiful, harder version of Minty. The tableau had re-formed. The girl sat between Mr and Mrs Fritz; Mrs Fritz held her hand. Steven sat on the floor, patently exhausted, resting his back against Sarah's knees. She kept one hand on his shoulder, not wanting to lose contact. There was a scratch on his face. They were two entirely separate groupings, the sofa and the floor. Steven seemed to have removed himself in spirit from all of them. He had pushed the girl through the door and run back upstairs, muttering about fixing the lock, then back down again, while Sarah ministered coffee, then into the bathroom, where she heard him, noisily sick. Mrs Fritz had taken charge of the girl. A babble of low-voiced conversation still ensued. Steven had returned in Sarah's dressing gown and sat where he sat now, utterly silent. The low-voiced conversation on the sofa went on. Sarah roused herself. At the moment, she cared for no one but him. And felt heavy with foreboding. 'Think you ought to go and get some sleep. You've done your bit.'

'I should go home.'

'No, sleep here.'

He turned his sweet smile on her. The smile which transformed his face from the nondescript to curiously attractive. It was when he smiled they most resembled one another.

'Come on, then. You can have my bed.'

They left the room; the babble went on behind them. Steven got into her bed; Sarah sat on the edge. His day clothes were strewn around the room and she remembered, inconsequentially, that he would need a clean shirt for the morning. Plenty of those: she kept them in reserve.

'Are you always sick, afterwards?'

He nodded.

'I shouldn't have asked you to do it.'

'Oh, I don't know. It was different. I had to hit her and she scratched, but it wasn't bad. What's the story? Who is she?'

'I'll have to find out. May take the rest of the night. You sleep.'

He was fading. 'We always reverse it, don't we, sis, you and I? Day is night and night is day. Perhaps we'll be reincarnated as nocturnal animals. There's a bird called the fire raven. Saw a picture of it once. You look like it. Red beak and claws.'

196

'I wouldn't mind being reincarnated as perfectly normal.'

'Too late, sis, too late. What time is it?'

'Early for us. Only one a.m.'

'Night's young,' he said drowsily. 'But I got things to do tomorrow. I'll take all my stuff away tomorrow. You know the difference between us two? You care about people. I don't. But I don't want Lilian to see me before tomorrow.'

'Lilian never surfaces before ten. Steven, are you all right?'

'Never better. Knackered. I was good, wasn't I? They'll never know about the lock, promise. Stupid, stupid idea, though. And Sarah, love, I tell you something, they're serious traders up there. Serious thieves. Serious good taste.'

His eyes were closing. She was worried about the flushed pallor of his skin, his hectic happiness.

'I think they trade in people.'

He was drifting into sleep. 'Paintings, drawings. Why are they always a she? Why ... are they always *shes*?'

She was quiet, holding the damaged hand he placed in hers. Hallucinating, surely he was. May have needed food; he neglected food. She pulled the covers up to his chin, as she had when he was a child, and put the hand beneath.

He withdrew the hand and patted her with it. All four fingers. Then woke up again briefly, suddenly urgent.

'Lovely day tomorrow, got to be well. Lovely Lilian. I'll take her back that painting and she'll love me for ever. Where is it? Only small.'

She hated to do this.

'I can't give it to you, Steven. Not yet. I gave it to

197

someone else for safekeeping. It was too important for me to keep. I'm sorry.'

His eyes closed again.

'Oh, sister Sarah, you bitch,' he said. And slept. And slept.

She checked on the balcony. Washing line, scarcely visible; the floor of the well littered. It would do.

She went back to the others. Night would be day and day would be night.


# CHAPTER TEN

## *No unauthorised access*

I want my sister. I want my sister. Angry weeping.

*I came here to this country the same way as she. In a boat, cold, cold, cold. We paid good money. Up a steep hill, out of the sea, cold. In the dark: man with a scarf and a torch. Remember he. Eight months ago. We got our phones, nothing else. We know the name of the first town, near the Cliffts. We all have these tags with number and address, like soldiers do, only in case we get lost. We want jobs, money to pay back. Go to one house, first, then London. To Chinese people in office, not here. They tell us what Jobs are. Like tarts. Minty don't want to be no tart: she won't do it. They take her somewhere else. Then no word. Nada. I work, I don't mind, but where is my sister? She lose her phone. Months, I worry, then angry.*

*Then Minty phones me. So pleased. Someone give her a new mobile phone. All she wants to do is go home. So homesick, has to go home. So she says she is going back to these Cliffts, the place where we came in. She's gonna wait for the boat bringing people in, ask them to bring her back. She has money: she wants only to go home. She want her grandmother, her father. I say, you stupid, where are you? She says she don't know how to get to Cliffts, but Mr Fritz tells her there is kind man who goes to Cliffts. Must be the same place. She is going to follow him, on train. Wait for me, I say. She won't: she is sick for home. No more words from her. So I come to find her.*

*Wait outside. Chinese people come. I shout and scream, where is my sister, where is my sister? They hit me and bring me upstairs. Say I must work instead of my sister. They lock me in. Take my phone. They say she will come soon.*

*Where is my sister?*

Sarah had written it down as it emerged, in broken phrases, over two hours. Throughout the girl fiddled with a gold-coloured chain round her neck, her only adornment, cheap and bright.

'May I see that?'

The girl took it off and passed it to Mrs Fritz, who passed it to Sarah. The girl's face was red and blotched; she swayed with tiredness. Sarah held the small yellow medallion in her palm, where it was warm to touch.

'Tell her,' Sarah said to Mrs Fritz, 'that her sister is probably—'

'No.' Mrs Fritz shook her head.

Sarah turned to Fritz.

'Did you tell Minty to follow Mr Beaumont?'

'Yes.'

'Did he know?'

'She like Mr Richard. He chat to her. Like her

199

father, she said. I think he look at her *not* like her father.'

'Her friend?'

'Yes, her friend. More than you.'

She remembered something Richard had said. *Live models are hard to find.* The bastard.

'Where can we hide her for now?'

'We do that. She ours,' Mrs Fritz said. 'Keep very quiet. And you—' she stabbed a finger in Sarah's direction. 'You lucky. You nice rich tart. You got flat. You got money. You got men friends. You lucky. Us, we look after this girl here. You find Minty.'

\*       \*       \*

Sarah went downstairs first, checking. Silent as a grave at dawn, traffic beginning outside. The girl and her new keepers disappeared into the basement. It seemed to her later, trying to snatch sleep on her sofa, that there was no one to tell, except perhaps the doctor. Her flat felt like a prison, suffocating in sadness. So much for non-involvement. She slept until eleven and woke up guilty. Steven was long gone; she wanted to crawl into the bed he had left and disappear. *Don't want anyone else's shit, anyone else's pain*, but there it was, like a big fat nail through the skull. Dangerous knowledge, about to grow into a tumour if left alone. Knowledge of girls bribed into slavery, into being servants or prostitutes. She got up, listened to the messages, cancelled her appointments, and enquired about the times of trains. Richard Beaumont's painting of the body haunted her as if it was still in the room.

200

There was no reply from Dr John Armstrong, only messages. Right. Go. The building remained silent from behind her closed door. No alarms, no sirens, no movement. She phoned the Beaumonts. No reply either. Just as well. Richard could not be trusted. What had he done? *How could you?*

So, go. Go and look at the sea. Something to do, perhaps, before telling a girl her sister was dead, but immortalised in a painting. Nevertheless, she did not move. Sat and tried to work it out, the whole of her slow with angry pity and lack of sleep. How little one knew about one's neighbours, after all. Who lived alongside her? The Smiths, who only took up residence at weekends; Hoffman, who was only there during the week. The Skoyles who came in late at night and left at dawn. People who respected the privacy of others, used their apartments as static vehicles for living, themselves always in transit, appreciative of the quiet and the empty flats which separated them from one another. An ideal place for hiding. Rich, mainly, and busy. A place half full of people who did not want to know one another, committed to peace and ignorance. The Beaumonts, living in safe splendour, he being the only other who talked to everyone, only to forget, while Lilian was contemptuous and disinterested in anything outside the door. Fritz, who either cared selectively or not at all, and would not care if they were robbed. They might as well all have been ghosts. They did not think about where they lived as Sarah did. This place was her refuge, her security, the heavyweight anchor of her life, the place to which she hurried to return, but at the moment it could have been anywhere.

She looked at the medallion in her hand. It was like a cheap identity disc, the texture of tin. What was it like to have no possessions, no identity, other than a piece of tin? And what was it like to want to go home, all the time, every waking hour of the day?

Sarah counted on her fingers, childishly, trying to concentrate her mind. The Chinese in the penthouse. Would they call the police and report another missing servant? No, not if they had imported her: too much to hide. They were the receivers of parcels and goods; they never came in or went out empty-handed. So, they were traders of a kind. Everyone knew that. Traders in things, possibly including people. Confident traders, not even trying to conceal. They were rude, dismissive, confident no one would notice or care. The building itself, with its indifferent occupants, shrouded them. Was it they who filled boatloads with displaced Romanies, lured into long-term payment by the promise of jobs and better lives? What was the difference in trading in chattels, or people? If that is what they did, they were arrogant enough to supply their immigrants with incriminating evidence. The medallion did not say who the wearer was. It simply told them where to go. A bright thing, like a thin polished coin. *15 Cram Mans W1 0207* ... the rest of the number blurred.

It was no good. The whole picture slid in and out of focus, although, with the help of her imagination, it was complete. She could not give that girl in the basement any clue as to her sister's whereabouts until she knew more. Could not say, I believe she is dead. If Minty had followed Richard to the cliffs where he painted, then she was the one who was dead. She was the broken, pecked-at body of Richard's painting.

Sarah had to see. Once she saw, she would know. The image that obscured all others was that of a girl so homesick that she would walk along alien clifftops, searching in vain for the boat which would take her home. Not wanting to get in, wanting to get *out*. Wanting to go home. Sick with it.

She roused herself from her doze. This was home, and it was time to leave it. Get out of the rut, feel as that girl felt: take another path. Remind herself of what she would feel if Steven disappeared for ever and no one ever told her. Incomplete, bereft, robbed. Better to know. Identifying and punishing. That was the small service she could offer the dead and the living.

Dr Armstrong, please answer your phone. I need to look at those cliffs. Need to see the pathways between here and there. Need air.

She would have to find trousers and boots and then find the doctor. Between them, they had the story. With the omission of whatever it was that could be supplied by Richard.

Who either led Minty away, or she merely followed. One version was wicked; the other merely cruel.

\*      \*      \*

The thing about *zing* was that it overcame everything else. Such as fatigue, rope burns on hands, muscle ache, hangovers and disappointments. It replaced all the energy that living took away. It made him happy. Standing beside Lilian, Steven *knew* he had never been

203

happier. True, there was a gnawing going on his gut, as if he had eaten a live rat, but anxiety about his own deficiencies, as teacher, lover, mixed-up human being with bad hair, were subsumed in a thrill of happiness. He had everything. Her profile was outstanding.

'It doesn't matter about you not being able to get back that painting yet,' Lilian was saying as they sat in the National Portrait Gallery. 'I don't think that's the problem. Not any more. The problem's him. Gone all quiet. Comes home, gives me a hard time about it. Goes out all day with his new friend. Comes back in time to be life and soul of the party, as long as his kids are there, like last night. Then he falls asleep, without taking his clothes off. Talks in his sleep. Minty, he says; Minty, go away. So much for not having another woman. Mind you, we were back late.'

'Oh dear,' Steven said, gazing at the curve of her nose. She wore her hair differently today. It looked as if all the mad, honey-blonde curls had thrown themselves upwards into a clasp, exposing the back of her neck, decorated with sweet tendrils. She frowned, deliciously, sighed in a way that made her chest heave. She crossed her legs and the short skirt rode halfway up her thigh. She generated, to his mind, exotic smells, but the favourite part of her was the exotic and vulnerable back of her neck.

'And today he says to me, sorry, Lilian. Can't talk. Got to get out. Never mind the painting. I'll do it again. Only he doesn't go out, he goes in his room and locks the door. In his studio, with nothing but a stuffed buzzard for company. Doesn't care what I do. So I thought, fuck you.'

Her eyes filled with tears and she blinked rapidly.

204

The tears made her eyes as bright as crystals.

'I think he can't stand the sight of me,' she was saying, with artificial brightness of voice. 'So there may not be much point in this. Anyway, shall we look at another one? I'm not wild about this woman. Is it someone famous?'

A painting to Lilian was always an *it*.

'It's Vanessa Bell, painted by Duncan Grant,' Steven said. 'She was famous, in 1918.'

'She's a bit of a slob, isn't she? Well, she could have done with going on a diet and getting herself a proper bra. Nice colours though.'

Sitting in the pub yesterday evening, all other thoughts suspended, Steven had planned this. The art tour for the uninitiated. He was perfectly capable of leaving in limbo everything which had happened between then and now, since that also made him happy. Better begin in here, he had thought yesterday, with all the portraits. Better to start with faces and costumes, lots and lots and lots of faces and fully clothed bodies. Begin the art course with historical figures, heroes and heroines revealed and illuminated by some of the most fantastic painters of the western world. And above all, fabric and faces. Pretty clothes and lipstick, truth and artifice, something, surely, to entice her with wonder.

'Who's she?'

'Virginia Woolf, painted by the same Vanessa Bell you saw just now. They were all artists, in their way.'

'I like that,' Lilian said. 'She looks like she's fallen asleep in her chair with her knitting. I like that orange chair.'

That was promising, but so far she was more

attracted by the inanimate objects which featured in the paintings than she was by the main subject. Inspired by a chair, or a colour—promising. They walked on. They had walked a long way. Steven was waiting for her, letting her set the pace, hoping she would stop only when she wanted to stop, when some distant cousin of zing got to her. So far, she had only experienced the palest of imitations of zing, but then, so had he, unless he was looking at the curve of her nose or the back of her neck, both of which gave him electric shocks. It occurred to him, treacherously, that he had never shared the painting *zing* with anyone else except his sister Sarah, and that Lilian might prefer abstracts.

They walked on.

'And who's this?'

'I don't know. It says Doris Clare Zinkeisen, painting herself in 1929. I love this, because of the shawl, but then I love fabrics.'

The portrait was of a pale woman, with ivory shoulders and half-exposed breast, holding against it the shawl which missed her shoulders and cascaded down her back. Half turned to the viewer, her hair was coiled, her eyes knowing, her cheeks powdered to pinkness and her mouth painted crimson to echo the vibrant red of the flowers woven into the dramatic black, red, blue and orange of the exotic oriental shawl which filled the rest of the canvas. Flowers bloomed on that silken cloth, leaves burgeoned; there were peacocks and humming birds crowding for space amongst the folds.

'Yes,' Lilian said. 'I like the shawl. I'd like to pinch it off her, as a matter of fact. But why did she bother with the rest? Why not just paint the shawl? Because

206

that's what it is, a painting of a shawl, and she's hiding behind it. Turning herself into a coat hanger, with a face made like a doll and a mouth to match the shawl.'

Steven wanted to cheer. She was right, she was bloody well right, she was clever. He patted her shoulder and grinned. She shrugged.

'Well, that's what we all do, isn't it? Hide inside our clothes, even when we aren't wearing very many. And no woman's going to paint a picture of herself to show anything nasty, is she? She wouldn't paint herself as she really was, would she?'

'She might have done.'

'I wouldn't. *She's* saying, look, I'm better off inside this shawl than I am naked. And she's painting herself as a bloke would like her to be, as well as herself. Slightly dressed in something a woman would envy and he could rip off. I tell you what, Steven, I'm sick of all these women. Let's go somewhere else. Where are the paintings of men with their clothes off?'

They were walking round the corner to the National Gallery, when she surprised him again.

'You know what I always associated with the kind of art galleries we got dragged to from school? Big and cold. And once you're in, you've first got big pictures of men, fighting, battles, ships, hunting and stuff. Then you've got men with dogs. Then you've got miles and miles of tits. Big women with bits of net over their pubes, and always these tits, standing up like pears, even while they're doing something like washing up or eating. It's all about men, art. Men painting what they want to see. Men painting what they've got. Nobody does it for women.'

'I think your art appreciation stopped long before the twentieth century and left out landscape entirely.'

'Probably did. Might explain why I prefer paintings of flowers.'

'There's a selection here you might like better.'

He led her to the series. It began with an almost life-sized painting, *Une Académie*, artist unknown. Followed by more, in a sequence of male bodies, students painted by a master perhaps. Four perfect young men, in less than innocently naked poses. One reclining on his side, back towards the room; one bent forward, as if to retrieve something from the floor. One with hands on hips, and one presenting a slender, muscled torso and glorious, tensed buttocks as he stretched upwards with one arm, accentuating the span of his shoulders. Naked men at work. No distracting genitalia, all viewed from behind. Touchable, vulnerable hair: men painted for men. The first one mesmerised her most. The spine flowed curved into the shoulders, curved down into the hollow of his back, oil paint turned into utterly tactile flesh.

'That's more like it,' Lilian whispered, clutching his arm. 'How did he do that? Oh yes. I love that bit where his back curves in. I could put my fist into that curve. God, he's beautiful. Look at that arse! How could anyone paint like that? Look, he *moves*.'

Steven smiled. He knew *zing* when he saw it, but then he found he did not quite like this response. It was making him faintly jealous. It was a very physical *zing*, not quite what he might have intended. It was not an intellectual experience for sure. She was almost swooning.

'He's got legs as good as yours,' she said. 'But you've got better shoulders. Get me out of here, will you?'

The day was bright and freakishly warm for April. Back in the open air, temporarily blinded by the light, Steven felt the return of happiness, mixed with anxiety. What was he to do with her, now he had found her? Run away from her might be best, but he could no more have prised himself from her side than he could have leapt over the moon. It was a perfect day, in which something had been achieved, i.e. an element of *zing*. It did not matter what she liked, as long as she was here, and liked him. He sat opposite her outside a café, both of them shaded by a canvas awning pulled down to shield them from the sun, bathing them in a blue light. *Zing*. Lilian was toying with a glass of wine. There was a slight sheen of sweat on her forehead.

'I think I get it now,' she said. 'It wouldn't help at all if I was crazy about art like Richard. He wouldn't like it if I knew too much. Then I might criticise. Then I might fill the house with stuff he hated. And if I had *real* paintings like those on the walls, I'd never get anything done.'

'What do you mean?'

'Oh, I'd just sit and fantasise.'

'What's wrong with that?'

'Because I'd rather be doing something. Looking at stuff would make me restless. Would stir up emotions I didn't know I'd got. I think I mean *horny*. Looking at those bottoms would make me horny as hell.'

She took a hefty swig of the wine, and pushed it to one side.

'No, I don't think it's painting does it for me. It's

209

real flesh does it for me. I don't like thinking. What am I good for? What am I good *at*? Looking nice and doing sex, that's what I'm good at. Not much cop for making a living if he leaves me, is it? Oh God, this heat makes me horny, too. Look what you've done. I can only think of bottoms. You shouldn't have showed me. Don't worry, I'll calm down in a minute.'

She sat back and looked at him shrewdly, and then gave that gorgeous, dirty chuckle of hers. There was either the chuckle or tears, he thought. She laughed so she would not cry.

'Sex and looking good is what I'm good at. Not like you. Am I right or am I right? You'd rather just look at stuff than touch it or do anything else. You'd like to go right inside a painting and never come out. You want to get lost in it. It's a sex substitute. Maybe a substitute for touching or being touched.'

He was silent, trying to work out an honest reply. There was no point being otherwise, and questions like this had vexed his mind ever since he had seen her and lost the ability for getting *zing* from a painting. As if he had changed his allegiance from canvas to flesh, but he could not remember a time before this when the canvas and the paint had not seemed more real.

'I suppose looking at thing ... looking at paintings is ... a substitute ... might be called a substitute. Not a substitute: an alternative love affair. I've never loved anyone, you see. Any woman, I mean, and it would have to be a woman. It might be different if I did. If I could. If I could love a *she* as much as an *it*.'

'You mean you'd rather moon over a painted face

210

than a real one? And what do you mean, never loved anyone?'

He felt himself go hot with shame.

'I mean I've never loved any woman, except my sister, and that doesn't count, does it? Perhaps painting's my substitute for lust, love, whatever you call it. It's a theory, anyway.'

He was still smiling at her, but his hand clenched the stem of his wineglass so hard he risked breaking it. She was looking at him, horrified.

'How old are you, Steven? Are you telling me you're a virgin?'

He blushed to the roots of his hair, stuttered.

'No, not quite. Made a fool of myself once or twice. Pretty humiliating. Not exactly *skilled*. Must have decided to devote myself otherwise. Climb, steal . . .'

The look of horror intensified into curiosity, then back to horror, then to determination. Her eyes seemed to be enlarged in the blue light. Green eyes, red mouth. She was breathing deeply.

'It's because of that silly hand, isn't it? You think it puts girls off, but it doesn't. That's absolutely terrible, Steven. With a body like yours. Such a waste. You're absolutely gorgeous.'

They were both breathing deeply. Then, that chuckle again. Her foot was stroking his ankle; their eyes were locked. *Oh zing, zing, zing*.

'There's a hotel round the corner,' she murmured. 'Tell you what. I teach you about love and you teach me how to be a thief. Much more useful than bloody art.'

\*     \*     \*

*She* had become *it*.

Richard Beaumont had forgotten the time. The morning had arrived after the restless night. He had spoken to his wife without remembering what he said. He had eaten something, hours since, and then he had painted. Time in the daylight room, like time within earshot of the sea, became immaterial and he only knew hours had passed when hunger reminded him. He could stand for hours doing what anyone else would call nothing, growing numb, brush in hand, knife poised over paint, postponing the moment when the brush would connect with the canvas, afraid to commit. It was not an activity he could describe to anyone else since he did not understand it himself and it therefore seemed pointless to try. Self-taught painter, attempting techniques described in books and ending, most of the time, in this stagnation, followed by frenetic application, random, hit and miss—hours doing *nothing*. Except when he painted *her*. She had arrived on the canvas complete, and then she had been lost and he wanted to create her again. *Woman at one with Nature*. The best, and only complete thing he had ever done.

The sketch was taped to the window, to the left of the easel. The canvas was best quality, but it did not help. There were the outlines of a figure on it, sketched in paint so diluted it scarcely made marks. He moved over to the sketch and tore it down. Memory, even the defective memory he struggled to control, would serve him better, but the canvas was the wrong size, he could not do it, the colours were too bright. The daylight bulbs in the room only mimicked daylight, it was still the darkest,

212

most enclosed room in the flat, even now in the middle of the day. Slowly, he painted the black bird with the red beak and claws at the bottom left of the canvas. In the last painting, it had been on the right. Perhaps if he reversed it, it would all come back, as if appearing in a mirror. The bird, the chough, came first, because it was an omen of hope, the rarest of crows, a noble creature, and although he doubted everything else, he was still absolutely sure he had seen it. Of all the other details, he was not so sure.

He wanted to paint the body again, because she had worked, the painting itself had worked. Painting it was the last time memory had worked. He wanted to create the black outlines of the underwear, or had that been a kind of prurient imagining, because he preferred the female body minimally clad, just like that? Always black. The body, with the bright thing at the neck, or the wrist, which reminded him of something else, a golden thread, a trick of the light. Instead, there was the thick black paint of the chough, and in the centre of the canvas he had sketched the upright outline of a tall man with a scarf round his neck. He could see it was a man; no one else would, and he was trying to remember where the man had come from. He put his hands over his eyes in despair; now he knew his mind was not his own.

It was impossible to paint the same thing twice. He could not imagine how anyone ever did so, even if a fortune and a reputation hung in the balance. No good: the best thing he had ever painted had faded and gone, and only the outline of the man and the red-beaked bird remained. He was losing his mind, and mourned it. He wanted his wife. He

213

wanted to apologise. He wanted people and yet he wanted silence.

There was that constant, wearing vacillation that went with painting and watching, that push and pull, between the craving for isolation, to be immersed in a scene, to be watching, to be doing nothing, so that he could *see*, then the entirely opposite desire. The awful contrast between the lovely, hopeful loneliness of waiting for an image to form, juxtaposed with the intense longing for the sound of a human voice to drag him away from the frustration of it all. The real tension of his life, that he was either running away, or running towards, a voice or a face. Friendly as a puppy, loving the company of others, preferably one at a time, but then behaving like a savage if they got in the way and did not leave him alone. Sometimes he thought he wanted to be alone so much he would have killed for it. Pushed someone out of the way, as if he had been afraid of them. When he wanted to be alone, seeking the image, people made him afraid.

There was a sudden clattering noise from the well of the building, audible through the open window of the daylight room. He put down the brush, flung the window wide and looked out, gripping the sill and pushing his head and shoulders through. It was always gloomy out here, even on a sunny afternoon. Turned his head upwards and felt rather than saw a washing line flick against his face. Craning further, he saw a face staring down from the balcony above. The face disappeared. Richard looked down. The floor of the well was littered with clothes.

It was the first time he had ever heard noise from here, and it made him angry. Wanting company did

214

not mean wanting noise.

He moved from the daylight room to the kitchen, looking for food to soothe the irritation. *Always eat when you are hungry* . . . You must always look out for the effects of low blood sugar, the doctor had told him, and it was a long time since breakfast. Lack of blood sugar will be death to creativity, and to memory. Standing there, chewing on a piece of bread, staring at the display of glass he had once created, lovingly, in the days when he cared about *things* and which now inspired nothing but indifference, wondering why it looked lopsided, he had the sudden sensation of something else being wrong. It was noise, a vague, intermittent thumping from upstairs, when there had only ever been silence: not loud noise, but the noise of objects being moved. Destructive noise, subtly disturbing, added to his anger, made him put down the bread, grab the keys and make for the front door.

In the hallway he paused. Here, silence resumed. The first instinct was to go upstairs, remonstrate and tell them to shut up, but he remembered what little he knew of them, namely horrible, unfriendly people, who all looked the same and kept Minty locked up. And all the other things Fritz had told him. Better tackle this in the more official manner: go downstairs and enlist either Sarah or Fritz. Richard padded down in his stockinged feet. He could never wear shoes when he was trying to paint in the daylight room.

The place was like a ghost town in the middle of the day, no reply from Sarah, and everyone out. You could do anything here, he reflected, as long as you chose the middle of the day or the middle of the night. Be a tart, or a trader, or a money

215

launderer, or an artist, anything without raising an eyebrow. Such was the character of a respectable block, full of strangers. He wanted to whistle to make a noise, so strong was the silence. As he approached the last flight of stairs down into the lobby, he felt it again, the sensation of something being wrong, and found himself going slower. Then he saw them in the mirror, at the same time as he heard Fritz sobbing. Richard stood by the bend of the stairs, one hand on the cold banister, watched.

In the mirror, he could see reflected the geometric pattern of the carpet and the backs of two men, who faced Fritz over his desk. Fritz was whimpering, without it being immediately apparent why. Richard saw through the mirror how one small man had hold of Fritz's tie, pulled his face over the desk and held a knife to his throat. The other stood by. There was a conversational hiss. They were all small men. All bad men, Fritz had said. *Never mind, as long as they leave us alone.* He retreated a few steps, and then came down the last stairs slowly, whistling very loudly.

The group had slightly re-formed as he came into sight of them all. Glancing at the mirror, he saw the one with the knife now held it behind his back.

'Afternoon,' Richard boomed. They all looked at him, blankly.

'What on earth's this?' he went on, in his best hectoring voice. 'Is this a hold-up, or what? Ha ha! Are we playing games here? What's going on? Fritz, old chap, have you seen my wife?'

Fritz shook his head. Out of the corner of his eye, as he gazed at Fritz, looking for a clue and seeing nothing but terror, Richard saw the man with the knife move round behind the desk and stand so

216

close to Fritz the cloth of their jackets brushed. Fritz flinched, gazed at him appealingly.

'Is there a problem?' Richard asked with loud geniality, turning to the man on his left. 'Can I help? Fritz here isn't always very helpful, are you, Fritz? Anything I can do?'

The man on the left shrugged and pointed at Fritz.

'You tell him.'

'Where's your wife, Fritz?' Richard said, gently.

'They . . . she's out.'

'That's all right then. What do they want?'

The man beside him nudged him.

'They say someone in here, someone in one of the flats, has stolen something from them. They want to find *it*.' He trembled with his own, nervous rage. 'They call it *it*. Bastards. They means *she*. I thinks they lost a *she*.' He faltered. 'They very angry.'

Richard turned to the man on his left with a wide, amazed smile.

'How absolutely ridiculous,' he said. 'Who on earth here would want to steal anything from anyone? Who do you think would do such a thing?'

The man said, 'Maybe you.'

Fritz spoke up.

'They think maybe thing stolen from their flat, this *it*, is in your flat, because of rope hanging down. Then maybe they think is in Miss Fortune's flat, because she has window open. They want keys to look.'

'Do you have Sarah's keys?'

'Yes. Gottem here. She always lose keys, she leave spare with me.'

Richard opened his arms in an expansive gesture,

217

embraced them all with another broad smile. He really did mean it: he really did not care.

'Well, what's the problem, then? We can't possibly have these gentlemen imagining that my flat or Miss Fortune's contains anything stolen, can we? I'm sure Sarah won't mind. I certainly don't.' He placed his own door keys on the desk noisily. 'I do believe I left it open, anyway. Give the gentleman Sarah's, Fritz, there's a good boy.'

Fritz reached into his pocket and produced a single key. Richard took it from him and handed it to the man on his left, winking, as if to say, Servants, dear boy, so slow on the uptake. He was the perfect personification of a stupid Englishman, ready to oblige. Age helped the impression: he was a genial buffoon, condescending to a foreigner he might otherwise have referred to as a wog.

'There you are, gentlemen, do go and look. Can't have you thinking the worst, can we?'

They were confused and undecided, overwhelmed, but cautious.

'Take him with you, I would,' Richard said. 'But bring him back safely. But I say, chaps, wouldn't it be easier to call the police?'

All three shook their heads emphatically, Fritz more than the other two.

'So what are you waiting for?' Richard demanded. 'Go and look, for Godsakes.'

It was their failure to speak more than a word at a time which made them sinister, as well as the little matter of the knife. They acted as if they had a single mind. The man with the knife behind his back came out from behind the desk, pushing Fritz ahead of him. The second man gestured to Richard to take Fritz's place behind the desk.

218

'Oh, I see, you want me to wait, do you? Jolly good. I'm retired, you know. Got plenty of time.'

He took the seat behind the desk as if he did the same thing every afternoon, hoping he was doing right. The second man leant against the wall next to him; Fritz and the man with the knife went upstairs. Silence fell again.

Richard flashed a grin at the man on his left, to no response, and pretended to read a magazine. He had no doubt of the presence of another knife.

Silence fell again. Then there was the whirr of the lift. The Chinese woman appeared, with an enormous suitcase, passed the desk with a venomous glance in his direction, exited the front door and hailed a taxi. As the door opened and closed behind her, there was a sudden burst of traffic noise. It was odd to be sitting still, whistling as if he had not a care in the world, all to aid an impression of innocent foolishness, looking out through the glass doors and knowing he could not move. Watching the traffic go past, seeing the nonchalant progress of people walking by, and knowing nothing could help. If he had been strong enough to deal with the small man standing next to him, adroit enough to evade a knife, nimble enough to run for the door, it would be different, but he knew he was none of those things. Once, but not now. He was an old man, who knew the determination of thieves with knives, knew an enemy when he saw one, as well as a friend, and knew his own limitations. Resourcefulness and patience were the best defences for age, he thought. You have to play games rather than rely on the brute strength which would never again work. Shame, he would have preferred to fight. He

219

did not feel afraid for himself, but oddly contemplative, which was, he supposed, another advantage of age. Or maybe the discipline of painting had made him so. You learned to hide the adrenaline, or convert it into something else, such as patience. His mind had not felt this clear in weeks. He was afraid he had a short-term lease on his mind.

There was the one recurrent anxiety that one of the women of whom he had always been protective, in his way, would come back: Lilian, Mrs Fritz, Sarah. That could be tricky. He willed them to stay away.

Fritz had told him about the Chinese. More than he had told anyone else. He knew to take them seriously. Bad people, Fritz had said, not wanting to say it to a woman. They trade. They launder money. Get money from bad trade, drugs, maybe. Turn it into other stuff. Loadsa money.

Speaking for myself, he had said to Fritz, I doubt if I ever turned an honest penny in finance: let them be. Don't tell. But keeping a slave was beyond the pale. Had to help Minty. Sweet girl, better for being not pretty.

He was not afraid. His mind was dying and there was nothing else to be afraid of. He mourned his lack of strength, briefly.

He had wanted company, although not of this kind. The sunlight struck through the glass door, revealing smears and creating a shaft of futile light on the geometric carpet, the way it did this time of the afternoon. Into the silence, as the man next to him shifted, ominously, there came the awful punch of memory, about a day when he had not wanted company because the light was so good.

220

Minty. The path beneath the overhang of the cliff, where he would never have gone, except to be alone. If he had wanted any company at all, that day, it would have been a man. Not some bloody woman. A man would say hello and go away.

Feeling unwell, the lost feeling, when he had difficulty in remembering the route, or why, but his fingers were tingling to sketch and he wanted to be nowhere else in the world than under that enormous sky. And like a fly buzzing round his head there had been someone dogging his footsteps, hiding and yet trying to get his attention. Someone he had spoken to; he spoke to everyone, but someone who was like girls are, thinking that if you do them a favour, they own you, or you own them, like his children thought. Minty. He had seen her on the train, or someone like her, not wanting to know. And then, there she was, or someone in a silly dress, running towards him on the cliff path. Not pursuing, but running as if she did not see him, running towards the man with the scarf who was coming in the other direction, the girl coming into sight as he began to get to his feet from his resting place behind the hawthorn. She was still some way off, coming from the car park and carrying a bag, and he was irritated with her for not wearing enough clothes for the weather, as if she had been his own daughter, and he did not want to see her and be bothered. He wanted *no one*, not when the light was good. He had helped her, surely that was enough. *Go away.*

So he shambled across the main path, seeing where the other path dipped out of sight near the cliff edge, forgetting vertigo, forgetting where he was in the desire to be alone, scrabbled down any old dry path, found that broad, dry, safe ledge, and sat again, feeling pleased with himself. Suddenly faced with the breathtaking view of the sea he had never seen before, forgetting everything else. Proud to have found this pinnacle, master of all he surveyed.

Oh poor bitch. As she sailed over his head, she became an *IT*.

*       *       *

There was the sound of footsteps coming down the last flight of stairs. Richard looked towards the mirror, which gave him the view of the stairs, the lift and the front door. They were heavy steps. Fritz came into sight, via the mirror, struggling along with a colossal suitcase. OK, Fritz, it's better to be a packhorse than dead. While he had waited, two other men had exited, swift and fully laden. He had never realised how quiet and deserted the place was in the afternoon.

His eyes went back to the door. Late afternoon sun. Lilian was on the other side of the heavy plate glass, inserting the key. He could see her, caught in the light, which blinded her from seeing him. He thought he had never seen her more dishevelled or lovely, tousled and gorgeous and uncertain, as imperfect as any painting, and wished he had ever been able to paint her. She looked vibrant, incredible, happy. He knew why. It was only a matter of time. He was on his feet, shouting, *No, no, nooo . . . go away.*

The man by his side hit him, once, a solid punch to the stomach.

Fritz handed the suitcase to the second man. A

third had joined them, equally burdened and inscrutable. Lilian opened the heavy plate-glass door with a sigh of relief. The posse pushed past her roughly to where the taxi stood outside, so that she was forced to stand, holding the door open for them. A young man stood hovering behind her, as if uncertain whether to go further.

'How bloody rude,' Lilian said as she wiped her feet on the carpet, checking the heels of her shoes. She looked up.

'What are you doing down here, Richard? Bored again, are you, darling? RICHARD, RICH, RICHARD.'

# CHAPTER ELEVEN

### *Do not attempt to capture wild animals*

John had needed company, but only of a particular kind. He had fretted away the morning, cleaning the bloody car, for God's sake, tidying the house and hanging out washing, like a good, fussy, widowed bourgeois, conscious of the neighbours. Re-exerting control over his environment, tending his garden, deploying all the displacement activities he knew were appropriate for an indecisive coward. But when Sarah finally phoned he was pleased he had done all that because he would have been ashamed of a dirty house.

She had phoned from the train, and although John loathed the tyranny of mobile phones, this afternoon he could have kissed it. For the next hour, he imagined her here, inside his plain living

223

room, and found it difficult. The room was so plain, he picked pansies from the garden and placed them in a vase. The overnight wind and rain had freshened everything, and he was wondering if it was that which had also cleansed his mind and made him realise that he was mortally afraid to go to the cliffs alone, and he was postponing, waiting for the strength that might occur when there was absolutely nothing else left to do. When her taxi arrived at his house (her choice: she refused to be met), he was mightily glad to see her, and shy. That had not lasted. They looked at the picture, best in the afternoon light, and he had told her what was inside it. And about Edwin.

Now they were on the cliff path, and she was entirely the right kind of company. She was allowing him to feel superior and in charge, which indeed, in this setting, he was. It was his territory and he was leader. She did not say much; even the purpose of the expedition was ill defined, but she walked smartly and let him talk. He felt he had known her for ever. The wind had died and the sea was gloriously calm, murmuring sweet nothings. It isn't usually like this, he told her. Her clothing amused him: the town person's version of country clothes, immaculate cord trousers, shiny boots more suitable for pavements than muddy paths, more like slippers with laces, and a broad belt around the waist. He found time to admire her waist; if she slipped and fell, he would hold her up by the belt. The black rainproof with the red lining she wore would be useless in a storm, but all the same, she walked like an athlete with a dancer's figure and step, and he had the uneasy feeling she could outpace him whenever she wanted. Yes, she was entirely the right kind of company. She encouraged him to explain what was on his mind by not prompting, and whatever was there tidied itself into lines.

The cliff paths seemed deserted most of the time, so that a single figure stood out, but John knew that was an illusion. There were multitudes of people, he told her, hidden in the folds of the land, lost in the size and scale of it. They hid off the path; they sat out of sight; they became sticklike insects in the distance, but they moved, they crawled, they explored, because it was there. The warmth of the last few days and the lessening of the wind brought them out. It was only the dream of the preoccupied, lone walker that no one else inhabited his domain. This was not unexplored territory, only felt as if it was because most people kept to the paths.

John had woken that morning with a fixed idea in his head, which had taken root before he went to sleep, when he heard the wind howl round his bare, snug, book-filled house.

'I don't think Edwin's ravens could remain a secret,' he told her. 'I don't see how they can. Not from predators.'

He had gone to bed clutching a book on the subject of *Corvus corax*.

'What, in particular, could harm them?'

Oh why did he love giving explanations? Should have been a teacher rather than a doctor.

'They only nest once, far earlier in the year than other birds, even other crows. Lay eggs in March, when the others are only thinking about it. They've a single chance of raising progeny in a

225

year, so they build an elaborate nest and take time over it. And because they build so early, they don't compete for territory, like other birds. They have a choice. Especially here. But when the chicks hatch and grow, they're far more liable to attack from a larger predator, like a falcon, perhaps, because he's in search of good protein to fuel *his* own mating and breeding.'

He paused for breath, thinking out loud.

'Then again, the dearth of birds on these cliffs means a dearth of that kind of predator. Maybe why the ravens chose their spot.'

'So they're fairly safe. What else could harm them?'

'Gapeworm, perhaps. A parasite, breeds in the throat. Asphyxiation from wire or something they've gathered to fortify the nest. Act of God, wind or storms, lightning strikes on the exposed edifice of a big, clumsy nest.'

The wind had yelled in the middle of the night, but he knew the degree of it. A noisy, fussy wind, which would churn the sea into protest, not gale-force and not really trying. An undestructive wind, in a mild spring. He went on, as much for his own benefit as hers.

'No. The danger to Edwin's ravens would be human. The man's a fool to himself and the birds if he believes that no one else has seen them. Edwin stays blind, most of the time, to other people on the cliffs, because he'd rather they weren't there. He shoves them aside and ignores them. He'd kid himself that no one else went off the path, except me. It's usually human danger. Anything rare is in danger. Rare birds in the wrong place attract collectors and murderers. There's a market for

226

ravens. And by now the young are ready to leave. They only need a few more days. He's done well.'

He looked at his feet rather than the sky. In his garden, the daffodils had turned rusty and brown at the edges. Their optimism was repeated up here where the celandines exhibited bright chrome-yellow petals that shone in among the still-low grass as if they were glazed with wax, looking like flashes of gold, glistening wetly in the sun. He kept to the path to avoid them, and had a brief moment of not wanting to be anywhere else. The premonition of what he might find, further down the path, made no difference. Sarah was tiny, but she made him feel safe.

'What about the chough? Could Richard really not have seen it?'

'No chance, I told you. Not this century. They thrived here once, and they've started grazing sheep again on the headland on the other side of the port, which might provide the right kind of habitat in time. There was talk of a scheme to lure them back, but . . . no,' he said, roughly. 'He saw a baby raven, covered in blood.'

'You sound as if you hate the poor ravens.'

'I do. I hate what they did.'

'They did what was natural to them.'

'They savaged her. They took away something that might identify her. Yes, I hate them.'

'And this man, Edwin, loves them.'

'Oh, you bet, better than life. He'd kill for them.'

'I think a passion as strong as that has to be admirable, doesn't it?'

'You can admire it, I don't. Not any more. '

She had the medallion in her pocket, safely concealed, and as yet unmentioned. Nor had she

227

told him anything at all about Minty. She had to *see* first. Had to know how it all fitted into the landscape and where all the connecting paths were.

'I never asked you, Sarah. Why exactly did you come here? Are you being kind to me?'

She was pretending to be out of breath and he knew she was pretending.

'I came because I lead a shallow life and I need to be needed, sometimes. Because of the painting. Because you inspired a bit of pity for a poor girl. Who could have been me. Because I feel responsible for the painting being stolen. And because I have a theory, and I want to see if it's a possible theory before I explain it.'

He stopped.

'You know who she was?'

She shook her head. 'No, not yet. Only a theory, built on pathways between places. I'm here because I want to know what she felt like.'

'Share the pain?' he asked ironically.

'Somebody must,' she said, lightly. 'If she's to find her way.'

They soon reached the point where Richard had sat. John pointed out the precipitous path, winding below the overhang.

'That's where he went. God knows how. This white clay mud's as slippy as ice. Come back, Sarah, come back . . .'

She was gone, sure-footed as a goat, slipping away out of sight. He waited, heart in mouth, utterly unable to follow. He was wrong about those townie boots. She did not falter. He sat down weakly and waited.

Then she was back, wiping her hands on her cords, leaving streaks of clay.

228

'I can see what tempted him,' she said. 'It feels like being inside the cliff. You can see the whole world.'

'He didn't know it was there,' John said. 'He has vertigo. He'd only have gone there to hide. Why aren't you afraid of the height?'

She squatted next to him.

'John, I've had two or three episodes of quite exquisite pain in my life. They made me rather nerveless. I don't have fear. Not that kind, anyway.'

'There's a medical condition of not feeling pain, you know. It means the patient doesn't know when something's wrong. They can walk round with a nail in the foot. It's a dangerous condition, not feeling pain.'

'I didn't say pain, John. I said fear.'

He stared ahead at the sea.

'If you don't have fear, it means you don't care if you live or die, doesn't it?'

'Don't suppose I do, much of the time, although usually I have a preference. And I did once learn to climb, like my brother. We both believed we could fly. Why did you want me here, John?'

He took a deep breath.

'Because you're a psychic witch. A lovable stranger. Because you'll see things that I can't. And because I'm afraid.'

She seemed reluctant to move, looked back down the path they had traversed so far, lost in thought, nodding her head, slowly.

'I can see her running up here. It's marvellous, up here.'

He felt perversely proud of it.

'Running towards someone or running away. Running with a purpose. She might have thrown

229

off a coat, if it was warm like this. You could get high as a kite on a day like this. Want to yell. Feel you could fly. Want to plunge into the sea. Suicide could seem glorious on a day like this. Which is better? Jumping, or being pushed? It could have been a delirium of hope.'

'I wish so, but she left nothing behind, Sarah. Somebody tidied her away.'

She picked up the black and red rainproof and jumped to her feet.

'The ravens' nest. Next. Show me.'

'It's two miles to Cable Bay, then a climb, and we might meet Edwin.'

'I thought that was the whole idea.'

'I'm terrified of Edwin,' John said.

'Yes, I know you are, dear, but I'm not. He's just a man.'

'You're a very dear stranger,' he said. 'Why didn't Richard hold on to you instead of getting himself that brittle, skinny wife?'

'I never want to be held on to, not even by the ankles. I'm the in-between woman. The path to someone else.'

They drove to Cable Bay. It was deserted. Maybe he was wrong about the cliffs being such hiding places for people, because no one ever seemed to come here. No fresh tyre tracks. The notices about the danger of crumbling clay, the threat of more movement, repelled the cautious, but it would not have repelled everyone, even with Edwin as guardian. Not everyone kept to the paths. Children would not keep to the paths; they never did. John could see his own daughter, skipping away from him, unconscious of danger, but even the intrepid did not bring tiny, uninhibited children more than

230

once, just as he had never again brought a dog. Here the path made an obvious deviation, and the sign directing it had all the authority of an order. Sarah did not glance at it.

'How do I see the nest?'

He hesitated.

'Another overhang. I crawled to it. I can't do it again. I never actually saw it. I saw *them*, feeding on the second body. The dog. Then I was sick. You'd have to hang over to see, and I can't do that. Do you have to?'

She looked small enough to break, with a backbone of flexible steel.

'A nest is a home, isn't it? I've always been curious about homes. Show me. I shan't fall.'

He led her up the slope, looking all the time for Edwin. Directed her, feeling feeble and foolish. You go right to the edge, you lean over, and even then you might not see it. While he showed her the way, he went on talking, realising he was less than coherent. He was using her, and it felt wrong, even though he did not know what it was he was using her for. He was babbling.

'The nests can be large and bulky. The parents build them in stages, starting with large twigs or small branches. They interline with smaller twigs, other stuff, earth sometimes, and line them with wool. There must have been a source of wool, to bring them here. They like to use the same nest again next year, although if they have the chance they alternate, to keep the bugs out. The nests get bigger with time, but this one's new. God alone knows what's in it. Old nests have treasures from other years. Stuff they brought back and hoarded. Not always useful.'

'Bits of wool coat, or dress material, perhaps.'

'Perhaps.'

She walked up to the edge as if she was crossing a clear road. Dropped on her knees only for the last yard. Shuffled forward on her elbows in the damp windbeaten grass, while he sat shivering. He could see nothing but her feet while he waited, twenty yards back. Waited for a long time, thinking, in a minute I'll grab her by the legs. I'll be able to do it, I shall, I shall. *I don't want to be held on to, not even by the ankles.* Then, to his relief, she reappeared, sat, facing inland, carelessly, then rolled herself into a ball, head between legs, and rolled towards him in a series of small, roly-poly somersaults until, breathless, she was at his feet, laughing and soaking wet. He felt as if his smile would crack his face.

She sat, reaching into the rainproof pocket for a cigarette. A crushed packet emerged. He shook his head at the offer and lit hers.

'Haven't done that in a while,' she said.

She puffed. He watched. Cigarettes somehow belonged indoors.

'I could see it. Just. You're right, Doc. It would be bloody difficult to see from land, well guarded, but your man Edwin misses the point. He's been guarding it on the land side, but you could always see it from the sea. And if it gets built over time, then someone would have seen. A boy, a fisherman, someone. The birds would be black against white: they'd be clear as daylight from the sea. I wonder if Edwin thought of that. No one could guard them from the sea.'

Then, as an afterthought, she added, 'I think this was where they came in. Down there, you could get a boat in, down there.'

232

She ground out the cigarette, making him wince. No litter on cliffs, please.

Close by the other landmark, he had pointed out the small fishing boats, bobbing optimistically, minnows against the ferry and its wake, like a plume of feathers cutting a white swathe across the water, a flotilla of birds surrounding it. It was she who had observed how awful to be on a fishing boat, constantly bombarded by hungry seagulls, desperate for the catch. She saw what he had never noticed.

Then came the sound of the hovercraft, a droning, mysterious echo, cutting in and cutting out, invisible, mysterious, forlorn. It died away, leaving a strange, maddening vibration.

'She wanted to go home,' Sarah said. 'Imagine it, being here, looking for a way home. Listening to that sound. Knowing your way home began *here*. You've nothing and no one, except some stranger you've found, or thought you'd found. A little help: not enough. And you hear that noise. Homecoming noise. Homegoing noise. You want to go home. You see someone you've seen before. Someone who brought you *in*. And can take you *out*. And with that noise in your ears, you run towards him.'

John could not follow what she was talking about, although he listened.

'Did you see the ravens?'

She roused herself and shivered.

'I saw the nest. But it's no home. It's empty. They're dead or flown. And your man, Edwin, is down on the rocks. Doesn't look dangerous to me. Go and look.'

'I can't.'

'Yes, you can. You must.'

233

He crawled towards the overhang; she held his feet. Go on, go on. Looked over further than he had before. Saw an empty nest, and down on the plateau where he had seen the ravens feed, Edwin, half naked, still with the scarf round his neck. Without the sound of the sea, his howls of despair could have reached the moon.

'Come on,' Sarah said. 'We'd better go. There's a man who needs company. He might not want it, but he needs it.'

Looking back, it seemed to have taken breath-filled hours to reach him.

John would never understood how Sarah found the way, as if she knew it all the time. As if she had an instinct for the path.

*       *       *

The tide was low, exposing dark grey rocks, constantly damp with water. Shapeless boulders, not yet worn smooth, the untidy detritus of the fallen cliff, the furthest away of them interspersed with pools. Edwin sat among the grey, looking to John as if he might be waiting for the tide to come back and carry him off. Sarah was scrambling around the jagged clumps adroitly, while he foolishly tried to climb over, until he followed her example, marvelling how easy it was. The view from above was deceptive. Then, as they drew closer, John saw Edwin stand, and, in a gentle but powerful underhand throw, lob a black bundle far over the spreadeagled rocks, into the sea. The black bundle sailed serenely, with a brief spreading of wings, as if it was flying, then landed in the distant water, silently.

234

Edwin's bare torso was streaked with brown mud, water and white clay. He wiped his arm across his face. The arm was raw with grazes and covered in bird faeces: John could imagine the smell of him. Then Edwin leant back against the rock, where his shirt hung, surprisingly tidily, as if to dry, while the rest of him was soaked. He scratched at the grazes on his arms, making them bleed. The sun gave pale warmth: John thought of hypothermia and shock. Sarah reached him first.

So much for wanting company. He seemed impervious to the presence of anyone else, unsurprised, careless, sobbing steadily. A dead raven chick with open beak and soaked feathers lay at his feet, enmeshed in a piece of net.

Sarah stood back, gazing at the scarf round Edwin's neck, balancing her dancer's feet on a rock, so she stood higher than they.

John was right, Edwin smelled like a sewer. He had slumped, raised his pale blue eyes to John's face, registered his presence, stared vacantly and then looked away, wiping mucus from his nose. John waited for him to speak.

'Fucking eejit,' he murmured to himself. 'Fucking, fucking eejit. Never thought they'd come in by the sea. Should've known, me more than anybody. You can land here. Robbers, with a fucking net. Climb like monkeys.' His voice broke. 'They've gone, Doc, they've gone. Two dead, they got caught in the net, and the others will die. The chicks'll *die* . . . they needed a few more days, that's all. Even a day. Was it you, Doc, was it you?'

John shook his head.

'Course it wasn't you. You never do nothing, you. Sad bastard you.'

'I didn't tell anyone, Edwin. When did it happen?'

'Dunno. Last night, this morning. Came here at midday, brought food. Looked for hours, waded out. Found the net, and the parents. Choked in the net. Stupid. All dead and gone. They'll never come back.'

He was shivering uncontrollably. Sarah's voice came clear from behind them.

'You *should* have known, shouldn't you? That someone might come by sea. You lead them in, don't you?'

He looked at her with complete indifference. She simply did not matter. A voice, not a presence, puzzling him with irrelevancies.

'Yes I did, but it wasn't them. Who cares about a boatload of fucking foreigners if they give you money? Easy to get in here, if you're careful. But I signalled them to stop. What would they want with ravens?'

'You're getting cold, Edwin,' John said as gently as he could. He was not feeling kind, felt cold and determined and revolted. He could have been in the prison cells, facing a man who had murdered and eaten the body, someone who stared at him with these livid pale eyes, full of self-inflicted damage, murderous sinner. *I think this is where they came in. What had she said?*

Hypothermia. Edwin had been out in the rock pools, looking for the corpses he had found, no doubt. Stripped to the waist and soaked to the buttocks, for hours, covered in bruises. The water was freezing. Peed in his trousers. In a bad way, but John could not feel pity.

'You had something for me, Edwin. Something

236

you promised you'd give me. Remember?'

Edwin fished in the pocket of his trousers, wet against his thighs and tight to his shivering skin. His fingers seemed numb. Then both hands went uncertainly to the scarf round his neck. He fumbled to untie it. The twist of the thing was elaborate, but he managed, with his fumbling fingers. Got out a small chain with a small medallion from deep within the wet cloth, handed it across. John took it, and clasped it in his palm. It was warm and wet, felt like a talisman.

'They took it off her,' Edwin said. 'The ravens took it. Dropped it down here. Found it. Must've wanted it for the nest.'

Then he began to sob again, racked with weeping, his thin, tensile body bent against it, his eyes on the dead chick, his callused fingers with their long nails scratching at his face.

John clutched warm, wet metal. He did not give a shit about Edwin. The smell in his nostrils was foul; he could see Edwin's long fingers, playing with the scarf. Ligature, hiding place, ornament, rope. He hated Edwin with every ounce of his own bone marrow, wanted to leave him to be reached by the tide. Washed away, obliterated, cleaned of the ordure from the dead birds he had cradled, cleansed of the burden of identity he had worn round his neck. Something he had found, and kept, the bastard.

Sarah had climbed down off her rock. John clasped his talisman, watched her pick up Edwin's shirt, take the phone out of the pocket, look at it, stick in her own back pocket and fold up the shirt, as if she was at home doing laundry. Her auburn hair had come free of the band that tied it back and frizzed round her head like an angry halo. Edwin's sobbing went back to howling. His feet were immersed in cold, cold water. The tide was coming back. He looked immovable and deathly pale.

John loathed him at that moment. A violent hatred that made him want to strike, mixed with a terrible, physical repugnance that made him want to vomit.

*You stinking bastard. You knew. You had her necklace, the one in the picture, all the time. You had it, they had it. Stuff for the nest.*

He opened his palm and looked at the medallion held on the cheap chain. *15 Cram Mans W1 0207* . . . On the back, the letter M was scratched. He felt a great gulp of disappointment. He had wanted a name. Like there had been on his dog when it went over the cliff. Wanted, wanted, something more, looked again. Salt spray hit his face: breeze was beginning, propelled by the tide. Conditions changed rapidly here. He read the inscription on the medallion again, feeling his own blood run cold. Richard's address, pressed into his palm on a card; Sarah's also, again delivered on a card. They had both given him cards, with that address. *15 Cram Mans W1*. Home.

An abbreviated address, but one he had learnt by heart. He stood completely still, swayed by a torrent of anger. The girl *lived* with them, was theirs. They would have known all along who she was: Richard, Sarah, too. That was why Richard had befriended him. That was why Sarah took him in. That was why she was here. To hide what they both knew.

He felt sick, turned towards Edwin. Sarah was beside him, ignoring the smell and the sobs and the slime of him. She was pressed against him, arms round his neck, his arms round her waist, hooked into the belt of her perfect, soaked, discoloured trousers, and she was embracing him, warming him, like a lover. C'mon, Edwin, she was crooning. Get warm. Come with me, and he was clutching to her, pulling her hair, almost dragging her down if she had not been, subtly, stronger. This way, Ed, this way, this way. They'll come back. Big boy Edwin. Fuck the bastards, come with me. He clutched like a limpet and let her lead, back over the rocks, stumbling and crying. She managed him like a puppeteer, carrying his shirt, and the dead chick raven wrapped inside. She was as filthy as he was, by now.

John found himself stumbling after. Full of overpowering disgust. How could she? If Edwin had wanted to kiss her, she would have let him. He slobbered; they were half carrying one another, lightweight, she was, until they were beyond the tide and facing the valley above. Stumbling on behind, John choked on disgust.

'Help me,' Sarah said. 'He's ill.'

He shook his head.

The sun had declined and the wind grew as they got to the top of the cliff. The sweet nothings of the sea resumed and nothing else could be heard, except her crooning voice. Edwin and she, joined at their slim hips, entwined, he trailing behind. Edwin needed warmth and she supplied it.

She had lost that fancy rainproof, but her feet stood firm. She found the car first. Stood, with him clasped like a limpet, holding on, locked into her body, like a corpse in rigor mortis. John caught up. The fresh breeze made his thick hair stand on end.

He was so angry, speech seemed impossible. Angrier, because she was probably right. There might have been no other way to move him. She had done what he could not, in common humanity, but she had lied.

'You bitch!'

The body locked into hers shivered less, the skin clammy, where he touched to feel for the pulse.

'You knew all the time who she was. Did she belong to you? Or Richard? Did you come here to hide what he'd done? She was yours. She came from your house. Did you send her away? Was she Richard's?'

She tried to shake her head, but Edwin's fist was somehow locked in her hair. She did not seem to mind. It did not seem to limit her capacity for calm speech, and made him despise her even more.

'You've got some of that wrong, Doc, you really have. Start the car, and get some heat. Otherwise he'll die. He's only a man and he's sick. And we need him alive, Doc, we really do.'

Her eyes were colder than ice. He had never noticed the colour, remembered warmth. Ice chips.

He started the car and got a blanket from the back.

Watched them in the rear-view mirror as he drove back to town. She still held Edwin, calming him. Reacting only to grief.

He wondered at her. She would have done that for any man. Whoever he was; whatever he had done.

\*　　　\*　　　\*

It was a strange sensation, to be holding a man, like

240

a lover. Steven could not remember ever having done it before. The fierce huggings of boys on a playing field had never been for him. He was always the loner, the one with the funny hand who climbed instead, never one for touching. And now he was seeing himself in the mirror, embracing a man who might have been his father, with feeling. There was such a contrast between this and his last embrace, it made him blush.

First, embrace the naked wife, and then the fully clothed husband, but this was not an amorous embrace. Steven had been following her in to say goodbye, when he had seen Richard, clinging to the desk with his legs buckling beneath him, caught him beneath the armpits, lowered him to the ground and knelt behind him, pressing the man's head between his knees. Lilian was kneeling, patting her husband's hand and begging him to respond. Fritz stood above them, wringing his hands.

'I think it might be stroke, Mr Steven. He had one before. Why did they hit him? Not hit hard.'

Richard stirred, making small protesting sounds.

'I don't know why anyone should hit him. Can you call an ambulance and the police?'

Richard was mumbling, trying to move, a strong man, fighting demons and unconsciousness.

'Police?' Fritz repeated.

'Yes.' Steven saw Mrs Fritz, hovering near Fritz, and the girl, both in coats as if newly returned. Mrs Fritz was shaking her head. Steven was somehow in charge and did not know what to do. Tried to think what Sarah would have done, and do that. Hold on, tight.

'Look, hide the girl downstairs, if you like . . . but

241

we must call the police.'

'I want to get Richard home,' Lilian said. 'That's what he would want. Not an ambulance. Get him home, where I can look after him, then call the police.'

What would Sarah do? Get the man home, call ambulance and police, in that order.

Fritz and Steven carried Richard into the lift. They made a seat for him by plaiting their hands and he hung between them with his arms round their shoulders. He was heavy and cooperative, and Fritz was surprisingly strong, saying thank God the lift works today. On the third floor the door to the Beaumont flat was open and the worst part of the journey was down the long corridor, where the flower pictures hung askew and the ornaments had been knocked to the floor. Lilian stopped by the phone. He could hear her voice, calmly asking for the doctor. Passing the kitchen, he could see doors hanging open, things strewn on the floor, as if it had been ransacked in a hasty search. The bedroom at the end was littered with clothes torn out of the wardrobe. They lowered Richard on to the bed. His colour returned. He opened his eyes and attempted to smile, looking straight into Steven's eyes.

'Only a rabbit punch,' he said. 'And things are only things. Are the women all right?'

Fritz was panting hard, looking round, less concerned with the casualty than with the mess. 'What mess. Those bastards, they look everywhere for *her*. They call her *it*. They keep saying to me, where is *it*? I say, she no here. Bastards.'

Richard had a mesmerising smile. Steven found himself smiling back, taking hold of his hand. Then Richard spoke.

'Bet . . . better go,' he said. 'Thanks.'

'Yes, better go, Steven,' Fritz echoed. 'Before police come.'

'Yes,' Lilian said. 'Better go.'

He was redundant. He did not want to go and, no, he did not want to wait and greet the police.

'Can you get Sarah?' Lilian was asking Fritz, quietly. 'Please.'

'She no here,' Fritz said. 'We manage, don't worry.'

Steven went. Out of the door, pausing to look at the mess of the living room, which could have been worse. Then ran downstairs to Sarah's flat. Again, the door stood open. The wonderful picture of the looming cow had been slashed with the swipe of a blade. Quickly he looked round the rest of the place, trying to imprint it on his memory, since he might not be back for a while. Mess, here, but not serious damage: they had been searching for *it*, the aim had not been to destroy; the damage and mess was the result of haste and anger. Even the cow could be mended, a clean cut with something sharp, no problem, but the shaky bit was when he thought where else the blade could have gone. Into flesh. Sarah's flesh, if she had been here, but she had not. Lilian's flesh, if she had come home sooner. He was ashamed as much as angry, to be thinking of himself. Needs must. Had he remembered, yesterday morning, to take away the climbing gear? Yes, he had: there had been a lot to carry and stash in the office, he remembered that. Check: Sarah's bedroom, no, nothing of his there, except shirts. She was good to him, his sister. Now, where had she hidden that painting? Richard Beaumont's painting, was it

243

here? The mess was superficial, but nasty. The shame came back but there was no time to examine it. They had been looking for an *it*, instead of looking for her. There was no time to look. He did not want to be part of it, did not want to be questioned by the police, and nor did anyone else want it for him. Because he *knew* what they had been looking for. And it was not *she*, it was IT.

Steven felt treacherous as he escaped from his sister's home, slipped downstairs and out. She should, after all, have known never to ask him to do anything. She would cope; she always did.

Out in the air, with the sunlight of a spring evening, after he had walked fast and was two blocks away, he stopped abruptly, veered left into a pub and got a drink. Whisky, treble, which he took to the window that looked on to the street corner, and sipped, looking out. He was recalling the cunning, friendly eyes of Lilian's husband, and tried to eradicate the impression that they already knew one another. Richard's face was superimposed on Lilian's face, backed by the strange impression that his sweet smile was the smile of one thief to another. The man would be all right, oh God, he hoped so. Such eyes, full of *zing*.

On the third sip of whisky, the rest of the day came back and his skin tingled. He straightened his spine and caught his own reflection in the window, smiling. A long, long day, an even longer twenty-four hours, and there he was, with his pale face flushed with happiness.

He cradled the whisky in his damaged hand. Made no difference in love, Lilian said, and Lilian knew. Love's love. He looked at his odd hand and

244

loved it. It made him what he was, this teeny-weeny disability, because that was what had set him apart, made him determined to excel, to climb. Made him demented, made him strive. Made Lilian pity him enough to make love to him, although it had not been pity, not in the end. God bless that missing finger.

He drained the glass, and wanted another. Wanted everything, ravenously hungry. There was absolutely nothing wrong with him in any department, except, perhaps, a few skewed morals. Otherwise, he was simply an overachiever. He had it all. And so much to do.

All he needed now was a home.

# CHAPTER TWELVE

*Please take your litter home with you*

Mess. Mess was the most constant factor of life. There was always a mess. You could hide and avoid it for so long, but it was always there. It was best to revel in it. Reflected in the mirror of the foyer, Sarah felt like a piece of litter.

'Where you been, Fortune?'

'Looking for Minty, Fritz.'

'You been away all night, Sarah, and all morning. We had trouble here, big trouble, yesterday.' He looked at his watch, examining the evidence that it was the middle of the day after. 'Chinese go berserk. They are rampaging. Policemen up top. Your apartment, a mess. Looking for *her* but they don't find. Rampage, kept saying where is *it*.'

He leant forward, confidentially, gleefully. 'But they've gone, Sarah, yes, gone for good. Take everything, leave mess.'

'I heard. I phoned. Everyone phoned me. Even my brother. You told me, remember.'

Fritz seemed triumphant, a man who had acquitted himself nobly; surprisingly nonchalant, as if disaster suited him and the only thing on which he could concentrate today was the fact that something good had come out of something bad. A good day for Fritz was simply a day that was better in some material aspect than the day before. It made her wonder what things Fritz had witnessed in his other life to make him as sanguine as this, so that whatever happened he went back to mournful cheerfulness as soon as one day declared itself an improvement on the last.

'Mr Beaumont still in bed,' Fritz continued, as if she knew all about that as well. 'He was very good and very brave, and so was I.' She rather wished he would go back to repeating everything from the very beginning, the way he usually did. 'He wants to see you. Everybody wants to see you,' he added with a touch of jealousy, indicating that she would never be forgiven for not being *there*.

'I went looking for Minty, and Minty's dead, Fritz.'

He nodded, unemotionally, although with tears in his eyes. The tears of resignation, life would go on. It was as if he had anticipated it, or had already absorbed it and moved on to deal with the consequences. Again, she wondered about his other life and the pragmatic fatalism it had created, and then she thought that perhaps they were similar and his approach was not so far from her own. They would deal with the present, and the past, however recent, would assume its proportion of life. It was why one buried the dead: to finalise and move on. There was always someone left behind who had greater need.

'Yes, I think so, too. Mr Beaumont think so, too. Her sister think so. She already knows, in her heart. You come down later. We gotta talk about her. Can't lose both of them, OK?'

She turned away, turned back.

'What exactly have we agreed to tell the police, Fritz? What's the story?' He shrugged.

'What story? Keep it simple. Chinese have servant who escapes. They go mad, looking for her, we dunno why they panic. Maybe think she go to police. We don't know nothing. I don't know nothing. Maybe they are thieves. Police very happy, anyway. You go up. They tell you.'

'Does the lift work today?'

'Oh, yes.'

Sarah went straight up to the top floor. Height lifted sadness, and she was bone-achingly tired. The spare room in the doctor's house had not been conducive to sleep, and nor had Edwin's story, told as she held his hand, and later repeated. That part of the story was finished. This was merely the subplot, the other, final chapters, in which she was playing her usual walk-on, walk-off part.

On the top floor, an open door led into a huge room, in a mess. Brilliant sunlight hit her eyes from a bank of tall windows and the air was alive with dancing motes of dust. It was a splendid room, suitable for a grand champagne reception or an exhibition, but instead it contained empty packing cases, rolled-up carpet, heaps of wrapping, old files and papers, a defunct computer screen and two women police officers sifting through mess. It was a room in which people had squatted, planned, recycled, packed and unpacked, using only the floor and the packing cases for furniture. A room which demanded the presence of an admiring crowd, but used as a makeshift warehouse. There were ugly marks where things had been shoved against walls; the dust was as thick as mist. It was irrelevant to think of the best room in the building being wasted in such a way, when a featureless cellar would have served the same purpose, but Sarah did think it, admiring the proportions of the place and the light. It had its own magnificence, should have been a happy room, never hidden; instead it was a room for transit and impermanence, currently occupied by the two women, cheerfully sifting and cataloguing what looked like mess. Clearing the stable after the horse had bolted, but happy enough.

'It's always us women left with the mess,' Sarah said, introducing herself.

'At least it's interesting mess,' one of them said. 'We've got quite a haul here.'

She wiped dusty hands on her trousers, looking critically at Sarah's crumpled, grubby clothes.

'You're the lawyer from downstairs, right? Heard about you.'

Sarah looked around the room. Her innocence and amazement were unfeigned. The woman was chatty. Nothing to hide, here; not any more.

'They were never very friendly, these people,' Sarah said, carefully. 'We never really knew who they were, or what they did, but why did they go so suddenly?'

'Search me. The girl hopped it and upset them. We reckon they were getting near the end of the scam, anyway. Left dozens of passports and stuff to show what it was, maps, plans, the lot. This girl does a runner down a drainpipe and they panic in case she might blow the whistle, I guess. They were importing illegals from four or five points down the south coast. There's big money in that and that was one part of the operation. Smuggling people and drugs. Get the people lousy jobs, make 'em pay and then launder the money. This was the laundry end. That's what it looks like. Turning it into legit art works and porcelain to flog in China and Europe. Good stuff, too. A factory for turning bad money into good assets. Respectable address, nice, quiet people. Who would think it? Clever.'

'I suppose it was several thousand per immigrant.'

'Yup. Something like that. Bastards.'

'Will you catch them?'

'We might.'

The woman looked at her shrewdly, after remembering to be suspicious, and reassured by the scruffy clothes relaxed again. Sarah did look so very ordinary, like someone who had been for a walk with a dog.

'Er, you weren't here. We've been hoping you'd come back. Why was it they searched *your* place, do you think? Yours and the Beaumonts', no one else?'

Sarah shrugged her shoulders and pulled a face.

'I don't know. Because we're the ones with balconies out the back in a straight line with theirs? The two flats where the girl might have got in,

249

instead of going all the way down? Because they thought we had something to steal?' She shook her head. 'I think it might be because Mr Beaumont and me, well, we're more friendly than most, which isn't saying much by the way. I probably mean nosy. We talk to people. Maybe they thought one of us had hidden the girl.'

'*Did* you know the girl who got out?'

'*Two* girls,' Sarah corrected. 'No, I didn't know the second. She'd only been here five minutes. Mr Fritz heard her, but thought he was mistaken. We were only just wondering if there was anything we should do. Was she a girl? Could have been a boy.'

'Pity about that. A girl, yeah, she left stuff. Cos *she* could be very helpful. We might be able to do her a good deal, if she was helpful. Might know other parts of the scam. We could see her right. And we were wondering what she took.'

'Took?'

'She must've *taken* something. Maybe cash, maybe something else. Else why did they go mad, looking for her? She might blow the whistle, but they were leaving anyway, and who would listen? Maybe they were just angry. Maybe she knew where they were going.'

She smiled at Sarah. 'You mind your own business in a place like this, don't you? Very quiet, very nice. Posh. Except today. I tell you, every single person in the block has been up here today to see this flat. We'll be charging admission next. There's been one lady practically taking measurements.'

'Well, everyone was curious about the penthouse, I suppose,' Sarah said with a lame lack of conviction. 'It's the biggest, lightest flat, everyone

250

would want it. A penthouse is supposed to inspire envy, isn't it? I expect we'll go back to minding our own business far too much.'

'I wish we knew where the girl was,' the woman said. 'She was a helluva climber.'

'Probably miles away by now,' Sarah said. The basement was, effectively, a million miles from here. They would have no entitlement to search down there. It was safe for now.

There was something appalling about an empty room. All that lovely light and elegant space. It was odd to be angry about the waste of that rather than anything else, such as cruelty and greed, but anger had to take the form in which it could be contained and put to use. She thought it might be the effect of her last view of the sea that suddenly made everything else, even this room, seem comparatively small and enclosed. The sound of traffic from the open window could be made to sound like the wind and the sea and she wondered if she would ever again want to live here.

She went downstairs, towards home, minding her own business.

Inside, she looked at the mess, analytically, deciding there were worse kinds of mess. Most of this mess involved nothing but work to restore order, put back torn-down curtains, pick stuff off kitchen floor: all that was only work and nothing desperate. What she mourned was the wanton damage to the painting of the cow, because it was spiteful and the malice of the knife wound was like a bad smell in the room. It was an envious, pointless message. But paintings often attracted malice and she could only think that, unlike the effect of fire or damp, a clean slash to a canvas was not fatal and this would mend as good as new after surgery and convalescence. She heaved it off the wall and laid it flat, touching it gently with promises of repair, telling herself to keep self-pity at bay because she had, in her way, asked for this. This was the price of involvement in other lives. Her own would be touched and potentially destroyed, but so what, a home is never quite permanent and no more indestructible than a nest on a cliff, subject to predators and storms. She was alive and lucky; she knew you never really owned a home, but she did feel a guilty responsibility for the painting.

Sarah opened the window and imagined the sound of the sea, and tried to focus her thoughts on the present.

Mess. There were tasks that preceded the dealing with the mess by a long way. Tasks far more difficult since they involved thought beforehand, which the simpler clearing of mess did not. So they had to be done first. Such as, what to say to Minty's sister. Truth would be unpalatable, in whatever translation it was given by Mrs Fritz, and unless Minty's sister agreed to assist the police, stand up and be counted and maybe get asylum, the girl could hardly come forward and claim her sister's body. How terrible not to be able to do that: they would have to find the in-between way. Sarah was counting on her fingers again. So, either Minty's sister could be persuaded to do just that, or Dr Armstrong and Miss Fortune would pay for a funeral or a cremation, whatever she wanted, or more aptly, get Minty taken *home*, or whatever. That was stage two. Stage one was how to rationalise the death with the minimum of bitterness. Stage three was the future of the surviving sister: she was already planning that.

Sarah shut her eyes and thought of the sea, used the sound of it to make a rhythm of Edwin's halting explanations in the waiting queue at a distant hospital. He might have said anything to get warm. She could feel the imprint of Minty's mobile phone in her hip pocket. She had taken it from him and given it to the police.

*Yes. I lead them in, four or five times, fifteen each. Got them out and over the rocks in Cable Bay, good money. Before the ravens came. Never saw any of them again, until that girl came back. I wasn't sorry for them, they paid good money, so they had to have money. I remembered some of the faces: I'm good with faces I see in the dark. That girl was one, fucking gypsy. I don't remember her at first, but she remembers me. She pointed at my scarf; she was tugging at that bright thing round her neck they all wore.*

*She followed the artist up the hill that day. I thought she was after him. I thought, he's picked up a tart last night, plenty of those, and now he doesn't want to know her. Then she saw me, coming from the other way, and she changed tack. Ran up to me, screaming Take me home, take me home, you can take me home. I knew she was one of them; there weren't many gypsies. She was tearing off her clothes, she said she'd fuck me if I took her to where the boat came in . . . She kept screaming she wanted to go back to where the boat came in, as if it came in every night, wait for it, to take her back. Take her home. She'd have shagged anyone for that. Disgusting.*

What exactly did she say?

*She said Take me, take me; she was mad as a*

253

*snake. And I thought, if I don't, she'll tell. She'll go to Cable Bay, and she'll frighten the baby ravens with her screaming, and she'll bring the whole world with her. She beat me with her fists, saying Take me, take me, take me. Dropped her bag, unbuttoned her dress ... she was hungry, only small. I backed off towards the ledge, thinking she'll never follow me, and she did. Take me or I tell, she kept saying. Take me there, to that boat, or I tell. Tell? How did she know about the ravens? I pushed her away and she kept coming back, and I thought of them, picked her up and threw her over.*

Did you think she would go to the police and tell them about the scam?

*I thought of the chicks. I thought of the babies and how they might die if they were scared. That's what I thought of. And I took all her stuff away. She'd a wool coat. They always need wool for the nest. They died, anyway. Never thought of someone coming from the sea.*

He had cried, this Edwin, but it was too late for crying. How would she ever explain to anyone else the reason for this death? Better to say Minty had tried to go home, and fell. No. Counting her fingers for the fifth time, Sarah shook her head. It was always better to tell the truth and let who would make what they would of it. Confusion was a hazard of truth, but lies and evasions were worse. Minty had died because of homesickness, and the death of dreams, and ultimately because of a nest of rare birds, who had been killed, too.

\*     \*     \*

Sarah unpacked her bag and took out the

254

Beaumont painting. Task number two, return *it*. Tell the artist, in case he wondered, that he hadn't killed the girl he had hidden from on the cliff. Her/*it*. Tell him it wasn't so bad to hide from someone who was in the way when you didn't have the faintest idea of what might happen next. Didn't make you a bad man, merely a frail one. Unless he had lured her there, which made him wicked.

It was easier to deal with the physical mess, since there was something therapeutic about that. Housework was irritating, an exercise in dust and hygiene control which never solved the root causes and was always done in the knowledge that the effect was temporary, and each resentful swipe of a cloth or flourishing of a hoover was going to be repeated, sooner rather than later. It never cured anything but a mood. But the clearing of this mess would at least have a dramatic effect for the better, instead of the usual, faint improvement. Looking at her sitting room with its wall bare of the painting, leaving a large rectangle of unfaded paint, Sarah felt the temptation to throw everything away and begin again with nothing, but that was a promise often made and broken, and she had done it once too often. It was usually better to carry on as before.

She checked the phone messages. Six, from the lovers, none from Steven. She could have done with him now. Her brother was indeed a great creator of mess, but he was equally good at clearing it up and was far more domesticated than his older sibling. He would have whisked through this, and she missed him, even in the wry acknowledgement that he was only rarely there when he was needed. In that respect, a brother was similar to most other men, and what a woman needed was a wife. At least he had phoned to warn her.

She pushed the window wider open to receive more spring sun, propped the Beaumont painting on the sofa to remind herself of the next tasks, took off her sweater and used it, absent-mindedly, to dust the mantelpiece. The framed photograph of her parents' wedding was on the floor with the glass smashed. She picked it up, glanced at the still intact faces and put it back. Did you fall or were you pushed? The Beaumont painting somehow drew attention. It was, she realised, with a purely objective eye, quite vividly good. Seen out of the context of the knowledge of the story, seen as artist, subject, paint and impact, it had quality.

She would never have seen in it what John Armstrong had seen. Would never have detected that chain round the throat of the broken corpse as anything more than light and shade. She pictured Edwin untwisting the scarf from round his neck with his shaking hands, extracting from the depths of its folds the yellow gold chain, complete with the tag. She could feel it in her hand, a poor, useless inedible trophy for a raven. Why on earth had the Chinese traders supplied their slaves with such incriminating identification? Not to identify themselves as the importers, surely, but as an arrogant badge of ownership, arrogantly supplied. Something that would rattle and glitter in the dark, marking the wearer as one of a new tribe, enable them to identify one another, supplying a name and address to be used only in emergencies. An address they confidently supposed would never be revealed. The insolent confidence was breathtaking. As if they never believed any of their immigrants would dream of telling, would go to their graves with this round their necks. Then why . . .

There was movement in the doorway, a waft of perfume, cutting through the mess.

'I should chuck it all out and start again, if I were you,' Lilian said.

She strode into the room and stood with her hands on her curving hips, turned full circle, inspecting the curtains that had been pulled to the floor.

'Never did like those, anyway. I've got some spares if you want them. Why on earth did they tear them down? Did they think that girl, whoever she was, was hiding behind them?'

Turning back to Sarah, Lilian's gaze fell upon the painting. Light flared in those brilliant blue depths and then faded.

'How did that get there?' she asked, flatly.

'I expect my brother found it,' Sarah said. Lilian looked at her, unblinkingly, until her expression assumed a dreamy softness.

'Your brother. He told me he was your brother. I'd never have guessed. He's so good-looking. The darling . . . he got it back, the darling. He said he would, oh the darling.' Tears swam in her eyes, making them glitter like reflective pools. Lilian suited unshed tears. Inconsequentially, Sarah thought of ravens and bright eyes: how they would peck at the eyes of lambs. They had taken the girl's eyes, and her identity.

'Tell him . . . tell him, please come back, but not yet.'

'I can never tell my brother to do anything,' Sarah said, 'unless he wants to be told and wants to do

257

it anyway.'

Lilian nodded, vigorously, the gorgeous golden curls around her head in full movement, creating a draught and an extra waft of scent. She looked tired but magnificent in uncharacteristic clothes. Denim shirt and jeans, nipped in at the waist with a narrow belt, tight over the hips and fitting perfectly. The shirt was open, showing a hint of cleavage, so the whole ensemble was a parody of working clothes. Again she looked at the painting, this time indifferently.

'I'm not sure Richard wants it back, after all. I'll have to see. We might have to say Fritz found it by the dustbins, or something. Unless you can think of something better. Perhaps it should stay lost.'

Sarah resented the use of the word 'we', but stayed silent until she asked,

'How *is* Richard?'

'A little vague, weak, but restless. He'll recover. Listen, the first thing he does when he could was phone some man friend and the kids. Doesn't need me just now. Anyway, enough of that,' Lilian went on, suddenly brisk. 'I came to help, really. Shall I start in the kitchen? Why did they pull things out of cupboards? She couldn't have been hiding in there, either, could she? What was she? A midget?' She shivered. 'Fancy living below a bunch of money-laundering slave traders. The idea! We could have been murdered in our beds, but oh, Sarah, have you seen that flat? It's quite magnificent. I've been on to the agents. Anyway, I'll get on with the kitchen. You look shagged out. Don't be upset about your painting, will you? Steven'll mend it. Oh I do hate mess, don't you?'

Sarah sat for a while and listened to Lilian

whistling in the kitchen, banging and crashing in a battle with the mess. Then she heaved herself off the sofa and went to stand in the corridor, leaning against the door jamb, enjoying the pleasure of watching Lilian work. As far as Sarah was concerned, the kitchen was the least interesting room in the house and the one demanding the least attention. She had painted it scarlet and put colourful pots on top of the units at near ceiling height. These had been broken by someone sweeping them to the floor in search of *it*.

'I think they were venting spleen,' Lilian was saying as she swept up debris and shoved it into a bin liner which she knotted, aggressively. 'They weren't looking for *her*, not really, by the time they got here. They were just cross. I suppose it's a natural reaction when someone's taken something from you. Someone, something, same difference. I'd be furious. And they were cross because someone had got the better of them. But they'd no right to be so cross. After all, no one owns anyone else, do they?'

She looked at Sarah, the last remark challenging a response.

'No, they don't. Just like I don't own my brother, and your husband doesn't own you. Or you him. Things have to be paid for, is all.'

Sarah doubted if this was the required response, but it seemed to satisfy. Having swept the floor, Lilian began to mop it with great efficiency. Amazing how she did not get dirty or wet. She was one of those women who seemed to repel dirt.

'Richard certainly doesn't own me,' Lilian said, mopping round Sarah's feet, and then undoing her own handiwork by treading back over the damp

259

floor to scour the sink. 'He won't even let me nurse him. What good's a wife if you won't let her look after you, I say to him, and he says, a wife has a different purpose entirely. Sex, I suppose. As if I was an *it*.'

'Is he very ill? Fritz told me he was hit.'

'He had a seizure of some sort, they don't know what, and he's supposed to stay in bed and have tests and stuff. Which is what he's doing, but already he says he can't stand it and wants to get out. Wants to go and stay with that doctor friend of his, near the sea, he says. I suppose he'd be better off with a doctor than anyone else. God save me from wailing women, he says. I did *not* wail. Not once. I bloody felt like wailing, though.'

She was crying now, working at the same time, replacing unbroken jars and condiments inside the cupboards.

'Because it's not *me* he wants. He wants his kids, they've all been, and his doctor friend. And I thought he was going to die. And he hates looking weak in front of me, and rambles on about not being able to paint any more. Just when I want him to do it, just when I see the bloody point . . .'

She brushed away tears, leaving unsullied make-up, and laughed.

'I tell you what, Sarah. We should do a swap. I'll have your brother and you can have Richard. More your age and you've probably got more of a knack for looking after men than me.'

She was tackling the hob of the cooker, which was already clean from disuse. 'Oh, and I forgot to say, can you go and see Richard? He's always liked you. I'll do your bedroom next, but if it's like ours was, it's not bad really. They were just throwing things about, looks worse than it is.'

'Are you sure, Lilian? You're being very kind.'

'No, I'm not being kind. I'm not a kind person like you. I know what I'm good at.'

Sarah stepped over the damp floor and hugged her. It took them both by surprise: Lilian hugged back, fiercely and then let go, embarrassed, giving Sarah a gruff pat on the back.

'You are kind, Lilian, believe me. Bloody men, they never know what they want . . .'

'Yes, they bloody do, they always do. I tell you what, Sarah, when Richard dies or leaves me, I'm not having another. I think I'll be a tart. I think I'd be good at that, don't you?'

'Tart with heart? Yes, I daresay you would.'

'Go and see my husband, will you? Where is it you keep your hoover?'

\*         \*         \*

The Beaumont flat seemed to have changed. Sarah remembered the fine living room and admired the long corridor with its artful lights, harmonious prints and ornaments, providing a vista of sterile good taste. No wonder Steven had thought he might find rich pickings here. There was an acre of pale cream walls, limpid pastels, interestingly neutral carpet, so that she could scarcely see where one surface met another. She remembered the subdued regency stripe of the receiving room, the off-white curtains folding on to the floor, the flower paintings carefully chosen to contribute to the pastel uniformity, offset here and there by a patch of vibrancy, like the glass display in the kitchen and the single bright ornament in the hall.

261

The pictures in the long corridor had been drawings, she remembered, architecturally exact prints of London, chosen for size and sepia tints and surrounded by slender, gilt frames, everything tailored to be restfully easy on the eye. In the living room, comfort was paramount. Deep seats arranged around a coffee table of pale, polished oak, where the putting down of a heavy glass of wine would not make a sound.

The corridor, leading towards the bedrooms she had never seen, showed the significant change. It was bare of all decoration and looked, with its predominant colour of cream, like a hospital corridor with no purpose other than to lead somewhere else. The reek of cleanliness added to the impression. Sarah liked it like that, free of tasteful clutter. She visualised the alignment of this flat to her own, thinking that the reasons she had given to the police officer as to why her flat and this should have been the only ones targeted by the fleeing Chinese had a convincing logic. They were unlikely to notice the chalk marks on the ironwork in the well.

Richard Beaumont had turned the matrimonial bed into a scene of carnage, which Sarah guessed Lilian would long to clear into the order that prevailed everywhere else. A satin coverlet had been thrown to the floor, a dismembered newspaper had been discarded sheet by sheet to the four corners of the room, looking as if he had chewed it first. The bedclothes erupted around him, the table by the bed was littered with small bottles of pills and three different unfinished glasses of fruit juice. His own presence was untidy and large among the delicacy of the lace-edged

262

pillows, hair sticking up on end, his pyjama jacket wrongly buttoned, giving him a sleepy but belligerent appearance. In Sarah's view, pyjamas were an abomination on a man. A vase of tulips drooped and twisted on the dressing table he faced. He looked like the proverbial bull in a china shop, with a large, swaying head, wondering what to smash next. He saw her out of the corner of his eye as his head was turned to the open window, as if seeking a route of escape. Then he smiled, faintly.

'Have you come to tick me off? Hello, Sarah.'

She sat on the crumpled duvet at the foot of the bed, regarding him from a distance.

'What I'd like is strong amber drink, like the sort the doctor keeps in his car. I want sea and cliffs and a view.'

He was aggressive and defensive in one.

'There's one thing I wanted to ask you,' she said, 'before I talk to you at all. Did you seduce Minty? What I mean is, did you lead her on? Only if you did, if you made her follow you and then ran away from her, I shall despise you for ever. If you *made* her follow you, and then abandoned her, that's despicable, to put it mildly. You don't have to answer but I do need to know.'

He had surprisingly stubby hands, toying with the duvet, clawing at it without desperation, the fingers agile, as if dying to do something else, expressing the energy that wanted to be somewhere else. He groaned.

'Do you think I haven't asked myself that? Again and again, since I manage to forget almost everything? No, sweet Sarah, I didn't. I looked at her, that's all. I watched her move, stared at her. Like I look at all women. I stared at her when she

263

sat downstairs. That's all. She was rather graceful. She was a body and a face.'

'And you might have encouraged her, by the looking.'

'Not as far as I knew. I looked at limbs and features, without desiring, or promising, I promise you. She had my limited sympathy, that's all. Oh no, I didn't encourage her. Believe me, Sarah, please, I didn't. What would she want from an old man?'

'An old, rich man.'

'An old man, with a mind going south, but the same old habits of fidelity. We do exist, you know. I look, never touch, unless very specifically invited by one woman at any time. Lord, you know that. I'm losing my marbles, but not my habits. Not my scene. Never done it. But I looked, I always look, I record it in my mind. Live models are hard to find. I love shapes and faces.' He paused.

'I've been working it out. Fritz told her where I went. I always told Fritz exactly where I was going, even described the places, in case I forgot. He might have thought I would help her more, at the right price. He might have encouraged her to follow. Fritz would never understand that a man goes off, really wanting to be alone. Not a man my age, anyway.'

Fritz had never quite been what he seemed. Sarah knew the man she faced fairly well. As well as you ever knew any man.

She made herself more comfortable. Difficult with hands crossed across bosom, perched on the very end of a vast bed.

'What's the matter with you?'

'They don't know. Could be the ghastly

264

breathlessness which precedes heart attack. Shock, blow to the head, more of a cuff, actually. Seeing Lilian come through the door with the light of everything behind her.'

He coughed, painfully.

'Maybe a cold. And because I'd been remembering earlier what I'd done and I was already ill with shame. I'd run away and hidden from that girl, because I knew she wanted something I couldn't give and it was a sunny day, when the light was perfect and there was so much else to see and do. And then I drew her. I didn't know who she was any more than I cared. She was a *form*. A model. She was *there*.'

'An *it*.'

'That's what's wrong with me. The ice chip.'

She counted her fingers, yet again. 'I found your painting of her. It's a good painting.'

'I'll never do a good painting. Never.'

'The difference between an amateur and a professional,' Sarah said in her official voice, 'is that either can produce a masterpiece, although one does it more consistently than the other. The learner can do it as well as the master, but not often. You did it.'

'Something with *zing*,' he murmured.

'And you do it at a cost,' she continued. 'To yourself and other people. You have to push people aside, I suppose. Why should they understand what you want to do? Perhaps all artists have to be shits, one way or another. By which I mean, full of selfish determination, not to miss the light, or the chance of a live model, even if she's dead.'

'Are you criticising, Sarah?'

'No, simply observing. In case you didn't realise

265

the cost. And what will really break your heart.'

His stubby hands had grown quiet. He reached for one of the fruit juice glasses.

'I do,' he said. 'And I shall have to go on paying and coping with my losses. And my mistakes. And living with my shame.'

She knew there was no worse punishment than that.

Lilian whistled down the hall.

'John sends his regards,' Sarah said, formally. 'He thought you might need male company, and says you're welcome. He wants to paint his house, and bury a body, with style.'

'Yes,' he said. 'Yes.'

# CHAPTER THIRTEEN

## *Guard against all risk of fire*

Spring had reached its zenith and faded out to make way for the less exotic pleasures of summer before the girl known as Minty was buried in accordance with her sister's wishes in a shady English churchyard, chosen for its similarity to something that was home.

A West End dentist named William found that he had hired an attractive young woman as a part-time receptionist, although he had not been aware that he needed one. She was a student the rest of the time, and although her command of English was not good, it was better than most of his patients' and improved rapidly with her studies. It was when she began to smile more, he noticed how useful she was. She kept the patients at bay. She would go far, he thought, and the bit of weight she had acquired since she began suited her.

Dr John Armstrong promised himself he would tend this grave and knew he would keep his promise. Look at you, he said to Minty: look at the lives you touched and changed. For the better, child: all for the better. Look at the hole you made.

He had asked his daughter if she would visit him and go to the funeral with him, and to his delight she readily agreed. You only needed to ask, she said. You shut me out: I thought you would never need me.

\*     \*     \*

A Chinese woman was arrested departing the country with a suitcase containing a valuable painting, ownership of which she could not explain, nor the cash in which it was wrapped. She was arrested as the result of anonymous information. Following that, forty Romanies, each with a yellow necklace, sought asylum in return for evidence. The deal was being considered. The process would take some time.

\*     \*     \*

Lilian Beaumont was busy, decorating the penthouse in an entirely different style to the flat below. She had plans for a lofty gallery, or something else, and had permission for either. She sang as she worked and complained about nothing.

\*     \*     \*

267

After a day too hot for the time of year, the cliffs were covered in a dense, kindly mist.

'Some might suggest,' John Armstrong said to Richard, 'that it is a waste of time sitting on a clifftop when there is absolutely nothing to see. It might clear in a minute.'

The early-morning, late-spring mist quarrelled with the threat of heat, swirled around them, eerie and thick, making them feel as if they hovered above ground themselves, weightless and invisible.

'I thought that was the whole purpose. To be content to see nothing. To have a new experience. I've never been out here when it's been as mysterious as this. Exhilarating in a way.'

'Now why would that be?' John asked, gently.

'You and your whys . . . is the word never off your tongue? All right, here goes. The mist saves me, because it blots everything out. I have to listen instead, and concentrate on what I can hear. That's good for me. It defines what I have to do: listen, concentrate, instead of trying to *capture*. I always hate that, when someone looks at a painting and says, he's really *caught* something, hasn't he? As if it was there to be tamed and reined in and put in a cage. Although that is what I was trying to do. Trying to capture what I could no longer remember. Train my memory; beat it into submission. It's easier just to listen.'

'Then you might get haunted by sound.'

'Yes, but I know I can't reproduce it. Whoever heard of a sound artist?'

'What else is a musician, or a composer? They might be similarly tormented.'

The hovercraft hummm filled the sky, throbbing

into a climax of echoing sound, then dying away. A requiem sound. A reminder of life in the mist. They sat peacefully, two no longer young men, happier on the bench than on the ground.

'Your memory is better than it was,' John said.

'Like the curate's egg, good in parts. Good when I'm with you, and I know not to be frightened by the blank patches. Better today, with this mist, because I know it's a real mist, not the one that seeps into my head so often. And I know it will clear. Sometimes I wish my brain was clear, although at other times, I wish it would remain as foggy as this.'

'You know you can stay as long as you like. And I know what you mean. Often better not to remember.'

'That's kind of you, John. You mean, perhaps, it's better not to remember the things which shame you.'

They stared into the mist from the new spot they had found by mutual consent, further away from the car park by the first overhang, still a long way from Cable Bay, a good spot, carefully chosen for the placement of the bench, donated by someone who had walked the cliffs and sat where they sat, countless times. It gave a sense of continuity. John was right. The mist was beginning to clear, form itself into mysterious threads, so that peering down and across they could begin to see the water. As the mist cleared, the sound of the sea rose from out of the blanket of fog, louder than before. The day promised well. Richard was good today, John thought, although he was still a man in mourning for a former self, the man he had been before the first stroke, and the second, equally mild one that followed the month before.

'I've been thief and charlatan, honest broker and faithful husband,' Richard said. 'Done nothing I've been ashamed of, much. Not the sort of shame which burns, anyhow. Until I hid beneath that cliff.'

'You didn't kill her, Richard. Edwin did that.'

In John's humble opinion, Richard did not suffer from Alzheimer's, or anything as inevitable. He suffered the physical effects of something else, as well as understated, formless grief, and if only Richard could believe it was capable of improvement it would improve. He needed faith in the vigour he still retained. He needed to know that he was not going mad. That he was not blind and could still *see*. Long enough to get out a sketchbook again.

'For which Edwin will suffer such punishment it beggars belief, and does not bring her back. Imagine, never to come here again. Bad enough for you or I, with our quieter needs, but for someone like him? That really is the wrath of God. Hell in life, worse than death. What would you wish if you were he? To be dead, I think.'

'What he did was wicked,' John said, rather primly to his own mind. He did not wish to dwell on it, because he felt a dark responsibility for Edwin. Friendship had been offered by Edwin: he knew that, now. He could have changed the course of Edwin's life, perhaps, if he had noticed or been curious. That was his burden. He could not share it. He handed Richard the hip flask, which was entirely contradictory to some other doctor's orders.

'Wicked? So is the punishment,' Richard said. Then he added with unexpected vehemence, 'She

270

was only a woman.'

John choked on his drink. 'Only a . . . ?'

'Only a woman who was in the bloody way. That's what Edwin would think, isn't it? Just another animal, of the lesser, female variety, a nuisance, a threat to something he held dearer. Moral values are movable feasts, John. He didn't like women much, did he?'

'He didn't have many good role models, poor sod. He didn't like anyone, much. He confessed to Sarah. Probably the only woman who ever hugged him.'

There was a note of bitterness in his voice. Since he was having a good day and all his senses were keen, Richard noticed.

'Sarah touches the untouchable, as well as the wholesome,' he said gently. 'There's nothing Sarah would not forgive. She will use what she has. Every bloke needs a Sarah, once in their lives. But she's Everyman's. Woman's, too.'

'Every man who pays.'

'Did you? Did Edwin? I did, in my time with Sarah, but then I had money to give, and preferred that kind of exchange. Don't misjudge her, John, it doesn't become you. She got your girl buried, and mourned. She finds the pathways, like a good witch. Like my wife will find hers. You can't stop a woman. You can't own one. Especially a tart.'

The mist continued to clear and the sun's reflection, ultra-visible on the water, struck with a wondrous light. It looked as if the light came from beneath in a series of secretive spotlights, pointed up from beneath the quiet waves, sending signals to the unseen, watching birds. And other animals.

'I'd hate to be a woman,' John murmured,

271

watching the sky.

'So would I,' Richard agreed, looking down at the sea. 'And we rely on them too much to prop us up. Which is why they have to let us down.'

He did not quite want the mist to clear. It was better it did not, so that he could listen, and accept the man he no longer was. After an interval of peaceful silence, he spoke again.

'I'll probably lose my wife, but most of all I hate losing my mind. And getting things wrong. Not only getting them wrong, but being sure I got them right. I got everything right in that bloody painting, didn't I? But you tell me, time and time again, that I didn't see a chough. I saw a raven, red in beak and claw. That was the end for me really. Having to doubt what I *knew* I saw. I could not bear what else I saw that day, although it became bearable. But I was so sure I'd seen that glorious creature, too. I saw *it*, I know I did. And like everything else, I was wrong. So sure I heard him, too. That voice, clatter clatter clatter. I'd known it once, though never well. That's despair, John, I tell you. That's when I knew I was going insane, and no further use for man or beast, or woman. No use to them, either. That made me cruel. The fact that I have to doubt not only about what I see, but what I hear. I knew then it was the last painting. The very last. That I was going blind as well as deaf, as well as unfeeling . . .'

'Listen.'

A chisel against chalk, tap, tap tap, clatter, clatter, clatter, sounding cross, like an old scold, oh, bugger, bugger, bugger, sod you. *Quork, quork*. The mist drifted, and the bird rose into sight. The wingspan black and vast, the body small, and the bird yelled, carrying its red feet like the half-

272

suspended claws of an aircraft, ready to land and still poised to claw. Emitting from the red beak a yak yak yak of protest and gossipy discontent. They stood in unison, mouths open, as the chough hovered over their heads, seemed to examine them as they examined it in return, wheeled and turned, before flying seaward, moving them from the bench to the very edge, so they could watch. The bird circled and dived, a silhouette of wings and fantail and curved, red beak, curious, first, pausing as if to look back, then plunging towards water and away. The Fire Raven, the Red-legged Crow, the Hermit Crow, *Pyrrhocorax pyrrhocorax* ... Richard could remember all the names for it, and then it was gone, gone gone. They were practically dancing with excitement.

'Oh, glory, glory be,' John whispered.

The mist cleared and the air was full of their shouted laughter. Louder than the sea.

*     *     *

Define spring, Steven asked himself. He liked defining things.

Spring is an interval in the equinox which falls between winter and summer, a period of growth and instability. It seemed inadequate to refer to a season of profound change as a mere interlude in which change occurred, whether one liked it or not. All that thrusting and thriving. The season developed, he could feel it in the pavements beneath his feet, and he had changed with it, significantly, in the last few weeks, had he not, although he had to admit to a useful consistency in most things. Such as making a mess and clearing it up. There were three criteria for a home, he had insisted throughout his brief, intense and ultimately productive quest. It must be light, must be high, must be secure; bugger the cost. Of course he should have done it months ago, but then there had never been the present imperative. He would never have been able to invite Lilian to any of his previous, cramped studios, however clean he had made them and whatever the quality of the fabrics, and he certainly could not invite her round to his sister's. Ah, Lilian, dressed in white, dressed in red, undressed in particular. She liked it here. Said it felt safe.

At the top of the house, small but sweet and not yet particularly comfortable, since it consisted of walls, chair, bed and a slightly irrelevant kitchen. From time to time he could hear trains from the station near by, giving him a sense of handy escape routes to other places and removing any feeling of claustrophobia. At a push, he could climb out, and in, although that was not an activity he wished to encourage in himself, or anyone else, now that he had responsibilities. He had checked the rear of the building assiduously. Oh, Lilian, so sweetly and only occasionally available, cleverly teasing him, her presence already celebrated by a photograph of her lovely self, sitting on the chair. Was she the catalyst to the new peace and the new home? Passion was fine but tiring. Energy was finite and far from inexhaustible. Passion also robbed him of something and he was not quite sure what. The ability to dream, for instance, and the desire to climb anything other than the glorious mountain of Lilian's thigh, for instance. She liked the roughness of his callused palms. It could not last. He felt immensely rich, but wary of his own contentment.

It was bad for a young man to have everything his heart desired. That could not last either, it was the death of fury and ambition. He rather missed his own bitterness, the badge of his exclusivity, his excuse for not loving and not being loved. It was only in this state of dangerous contentment that conscience could come creeping, like a sniggering voice in the background of some discreet, respectful gathering. Conscience was laughter in church, a shaft of light between ill-fitting curtains, which he did not like. It forced him to realise that he really had brought a great deal of mess into a couple of lives and it was particularly unfortunate that this should have involved his sister. Whom he loved and admired, to be frank. Still, it was a positive mess: her good painting was mended, no real harm done, and he had returned that sweet little nude he had pinched from her dentist friend—what more did she want? No, the conscience came from being less than frank about the whole business, and being *thanked* for the rescue of Minty's sister. As if *that* was the real result of climbing the wall and risking his neck.

He rose from his graceful recline on the bed, and left the room. As he did so, a series of images flashed through his mind, like old, cracked film. He was standing in that gallery, by that snooty girl, with the addresses on her screen, himself still fresh with *zing* and anger. Then he was in the biggest room of the penthouse, shushing the girl, telling her it was all for the best, come with me, I'm not here to hurt you. You, *it, she*, his jaw dropping as he spoke. Oh, my darling. There you are.

Steven left his new room, purely in order to come

back, slowly. There *she* was.

*Tiepolo, leading exponent of Italian Rococo. Style characterised by airy frivolity and playful effects.*

Look at it. Look at that triangular composition, the uncanny use of light and shade, the white, not pale, droolingly beautiful women at the very centre. Look at that bare shoulder and décolleté neckline. The way the ghostly white passages contrast so powerfully with the dark backs of the figures in the foreground. The gentle, summoning arm of Jesus, the preacher. Youth, beauty and age, all in thrall to the wise one. Found, easily wrapped, on the floor of the Chinese traders who dealt in art and slaves. Easily rolled up into nothing.

Utterly magnificent. A surge of ridiculous, jaw-dropping happiness. *Zing.*

He wondered if he would ever want more than the single, real masterpiece, supposed he might. Tiepolo was the reason for acquiring a home: *The Sermon on the Mount* deserved a home. In contemplation of his own deficiencies, Steven sighed.

Art was the real mistress.

\*        \*        \*

Sarah Fortune repositioned the painting of the cow on her living-room wall, where it fitted perfectly into its rectangle of faded paint. Then, dressed for the heat of the day in a black linen shift clinched in at the waist with a broad red belt and her red shoes, she went out to lunch with a lover.

She made him laugh, when he was sad.

That was the whole purpose of luck.

# CHIVERS
# LARGE
# PRINT
## *−direct−*

If you have enjoyed this Large Print book and would like to build up your own collection of Large Print books, please contact

## Chivers Large Print Direct

Chivers Large Print Direct offers you a full service:

• Prompt mail order service

• Easy-to-read type

• The very best authors

• Special low prices

For further details either call Customer Services on (01225) 336552 or write to us at Chivers Large Print Direct, **FREEPOST**, Bath BA1 3ZZ

Telephone Orders: **FREEPHONE** 08081 72 74 75